From the

# OUTHOUSE

to the

# PENTHOUSE

and Somewhere in Between


The Story of One Free Agent's Trip
Through the Ranks of Pro Football


By

**Bill Winters and JoAnne V. McGrath**

© 2002, 2003 by Bill Winters and JoAnne V. McGrath.
All rights reserved.

No part of this book may be reproduced, stored in a retrieval system, or transmitted by any means, electronic, mechanical, photocopying, recording, or otherwise, without written permission from the author.

ISBN: 1-4033-8617-X (E-book)
ISBN: 1-4033-8618-8 (Paperback)

This book is printed on acid free paper.

1stBooks - rev. 01/21/03

*From the Outhouse to the Penthouse
and Somewhere in Between*

## FOOTBALL? WHAT'S FOOTBALL?

"You gonna eat that sandwich, Joey?"

"Nah, it's gross. Why… do you want it?"

"Sure, toss it over. I'll trade you for two of my mom's oatmeal cookies." Parker Thomas reached into his brown lunchbag and grabbed the cookies. He slid them across the formica table top.

Their ritual was a familiar one. Every Wednesday Joey DeVito's mother packed an egg salad sandwich into her son's lunchbox, and before leaving home in the morning, Parker Thomas would grab two extra cookies on his way out the door.

"I'm gonna go get another milk. Do you want one?" asked Joey.

"Here's a dime. Get me two! Make 'em chocolate!"ordered Parker. Joey pushed back his wooden chair, stood up, and headed for the food service lines at Bailey Elementary School. Parker Thomas picked up the sandwich across the table, peeled back its waxed paper wrapping and shoved half of the egg salad sandwich into his mouth. Ten chews later, he gave a quick look to his left, then to his right. Burrrrpp! Parker Thomas let out the kind of belch any fourth-grader would be proud of. As he was getting ready to grab the rest of the sandwich, a hand whacked the back of his shoulder. His head snapped back, his torso lunged forward, and his right hand squished into egg salad. Parker clenched his fist and was about to jump up from his chair when he caught a shadow pass over his left side.

"Ha, ha, ha! Ho, ho!" A chorus of laughter broke out behind Parker Thomas. The sixth-grade hot-shots were on the prowl, and that day, Parker was their target. Ryan Corbett, the pack leader, smirked as he plopped down in the chair next to Parker.

"Hey, Parker, what's up?" querried Ryan Corbett.

"What did you do that for?" responded the irate, yet cautious fourth-grader.

"Me and the boys was just comin' over to talk to you. Guess my sneaker slipped or something. Musta been pudding on the floor!"

"What do you want with me?" quizzed Parker.

"Listen," said Ryan, as the smirk on his face became a more serious look, "There's this afternoon practice across town at New Shrewsbury. Me and the guys thought you might be interested in joining our team. We play for the Rhinos. You know, Football!"

"What makes you think I'd be any good at it? Parker asked, still unsure about the proposition before him.

"Hey, you're the biggest kid in the fourth grade, and you're the fastest kid at Bailey. Besides, our team just lost another game because Louie Selagoski's old man got transferred, and Louie was one of our best players."

"Well, suppose I'm interested," said Parker, "When and where do I have to show up?"

"We're having a practice tomorrow afternoon at the Cutler Street School at four o'clock. Just show up and look for the number seventeen jersey – that's me! I'll let the coach know you're gonna be there. What do ya say?"

"I'll give it a try," Parker answered.

"Cool, man!" smiled Ryan Corbett., "Don't let us down, now. Four o'clock tomorrow. Cutler Street. Let's shake on it!" Ryan put out his right hand, and Parker Thomas crossed his palm with a fist full of egg salad.

"I'll be there!" said Parker, slightly arching his eyebrows. Red faced, Ryan Corbett got up from the table, turned to the waiting pack, and ordered: "Let's go, guys. Time to hit the boys' room for a smoke!"

The boys and a chorus of chorttles followed Ryan Corbett down the tiled corridor of Bailey Elementary School.

The bang on the wooden screen door caught Alice Thomas by surprise. Normally her cue to get up from the couch was the Proctor and Gamble logo following her favorite soap. The moon and the stars always let her know that it was time for reality to once again overtake her afternoon. Somewhat startled, she blinked, pushed her arm into a firm gold cushion, and managed to shift her body into a sitting position. Her feet firmly planted on the carpet, she groped for the knitting needles and ball of grey yarn that lay in front of her on the coffee table.

"Hi, Ma! I'm home," called a voice from the front hall.

"Parker, is that you? returned the groggy female voice. "You're early today. Is everything all right at school?"

"Yeah, everything's fine. I got a 95 on my fractions test, and the teacher said I got the best grade in the class."

"That's nice, dear," responded the somewhat more coherent Alice.

"Hey Ma, are you busy tomorrow afternoon?"

"Honey, go put your books upstairs and we'll talk in the kitchen when you come back down."

"O.K. Ma!" responded Parker as he bounded up the front hall stairs two at a stride and headed for his bedroom on the second floor.

Alice returned the needle and yarn to their usual resting place on the coffee table, stood up, and steadied herself as she made her way out of the living room and down the hall. She walked over to the countertop, gripped the bottle of Old Grand Dad and placed it on the second shelf of one of the cabinets way behind the tea cups. As she closed the cabinet, Parker came into the kitchen.

"How about a snack?" the mother asked.

"Sure!" replied Parker as he headed toward the red cookie house that always served as a centerpiece on the kitchen table. Parker dropped down into one of the maple captains chairs, lifted the roof off the little house, and pulled out a fist full of oatmeal cookies.

"How about a glass of milk, Parker?"

"Sure, Ma," the boy replied, "Make it a big one." Alice took a tall tumbler from a shelf above the counter and walked over to the refrigerator. She took out a quart of milk and set down the bottle and glass in front of Parker. Then she sat down in the chair next to him and folded her hands.

"So, Parker, what's on your mind? What's going on tomorrow? Some kind of program at school?"

"I'm going to football practice," Parker announced as he jammed a cookie into his mouth.

"Football practice? What football practice?"

"Over on Cutler Street. Can you give me a ride over? I need to be there at four o'clock."

"But you have your music lesson tomorrow. What would Mr. Albertti say if you didn't show up for your piano lesson?"

"Ma, that's sissy stuff." replied the boy, "Besides, we're not stationed in Germany now. This is The United States! Nobody here cares if you're the next Beethoven or not!"

Alice Thomas knew from the tone in her son's voice that he was determined to have his way. She was aware that if she fought him, he would only fight back harder. She also knew that with his father out of the country on a flight mission for another month, she was left alone either to cope with her son's demands or to endure tantrums which she would have to give into eventually.

"How did you find out about this football practice?" Alice Thomas asked, her voice a little softer.

"From the guys as school. Ryan Corbett and the sixth graders all play, and they told me I'd be real good at it. How about it, Ma? Can you take me over to Cutler Street tomorrow?" pleaded Parker as he emptied the rest of the millk from the bottle into his glass. He reached for another fistful of cookies, waiting for the response that he already knew was going to be in his favor.

"All right, Parker, I'll drive you over there tomorrow after school." said Alice with a sigh, "Do you want any more milk?"

"Yeah, grab me another bottle, Ma!" commanded Parker as Alice got up from her chair and shuffled across the kitchen. When she returned to the table to set down the quart of milk, Parker stood up, put his arms around her and squeezed. His strength made her realize that her boy was at the age where she had to be very careful how she handled him. Life outside her home would begin to spin threads of influence around him. She was also insightful enough to realize that the best way to

*From the Outhouse to the Penthouse and Somewhere in Between*

win a war of wills with her son was to temporarily join the enemy camp.

After returning the hug, Alice stepped back and looked at her son's face. She no longer had to look down to meet his hazel-eyed insistence. His behavior was on-target with what she expected; she had read a good number of contemporary child psychology books in her spare time. But all the books she read hadn't prepared her for the uncanny growth spurt he had experienced in the past six months. Parker had already passed the five-foot mark his father had etched onto the kitchen door molding the last time he had been home on leave. And just two weeks ago, she had to go downtown to buy her son yet another pair of Bob Cousy high-top sneakers,white, of course, but this time size ten.

"Thanks, Mom. You're the greatest!" Parker affectionately exclaimed, "I've got homework, so I'm going up to my room now."

"I"ll call you for dinner, son. The meatloaf and baked potatoes should be ready in in about an hour or so."

Alice Thomas watched her boy walk out of the kitchen and disappear down the hall. She put the remaining half-empty quart of milk into the refrigerator, took out a square pan full of hamburger, breadcrumbs and onion, and placed it on the lower rack inside the oven. She had already washed the potatoes and had arranged them neatly on the top rack. After setting the temp control to 350 degrees, she turned the second control knob to bake position. From upstairs she could hear Parker's transistor radio play out a staticky Beatles' song, very unlike the piano sonata he had learned for his last lesson. She wished she had never bought him that radio before the start of school. Her eyes rolled and she let out a deep sigh. Three steps later she was in front of the tea cup cabinet. Her hand reached for the back of the second shelf.

*From the Outhouse to the Penthouse and Somewhere in Between*

## **YOUNG RHINOS**

Promptly at four o'clock the grey Ford Galaxie 500 rolled down Cutler Street. The two occupants had no conversation as they eyed the three-story tenement houses lined up like dominos. Women sat out on the front steps of porches and smoked cigarettes. Coveyed into the doorway of Mr. Zip's Corner Store were four or five men in leather jackets. The men eyed the sedan suspiciously, and though the driver wasn't familiar with this part of town, she had no desire to roll down the window to ask for directions.

Alice Thomas stopped for a red light. Half way up the next block she saw an open field surrounded by a cyclone fence. The red brick school, circa 1890, rested amid a huge concrete play area. Torn shades flapped inside the windows, most of which had broken panes.

"Ma! Ma! There it is!" blurted out Parker Thomas. "Just leave me here and come get me in two hours!" Alice steered the car past the school and rolled onto the driveway that led to the playing field in the back.

"No, Parker, I'll just wait for you. I brought my knitting along to keep me occupied," responded Alice. "I'll pull the car up a little more and wait there, off to the side." Before she could get the gear shift into neutral, Parker whipped open the passenger door and bolted toward the cluster of maroon shirts in the center of the field.

As Parker Thomas got closer to the semi-circle of bodies, he scanned the group and looked for Ryan Corbett. None of the shirts had names on them, and from the back, all the kids looked alike. Then he remembered Corbett's number, and after trotting a few paces to the right, saw the number 17 he was searching for.

The man in the middle of the group was a broad shouldered, nappy-haired giant.

He wore a blue Esso gas station shirt and a green khaki jacket. The name CHUMMY was embroidered over his left shirt pocket. As Parker moved next to Ryan Corbett and gave him a jab to the shoulder, the burly man began to speak: "O.K. That was good. But you guys have to stay lower! Tackling drill next! Go on over and see Mr. Stevens. He'll be on the dummy!"

The circle of maroon jerseys obediently turned around and trudged toward another part of the field.

"Hey, Ryan," said Parker as he grabbed the back of the number seventeen jersey.

"Parker, you're here. Good. Let's go over and meet the coach. Come on!" The boys approached Chummy Johnson. He peered through black-rimmed glasses at the two boys in front of him.

"Coach Johnson, this is Parker, the kid I was telling you about. He wants to join the team. He's the fastest kid in the school, faster than an Amtrack!" Chummy Johnson extended a mammoth right hand at Parker.

"Pleased to meet you, son. Your name's Parker, is that it?"

"Parker is my first name, sir. My last name is Thomas." said the boy as he returned the handshake. Parker had never before shaken a hand quite so large, so Chummy Johnson immediately commanded Parker's respect.

"So, you want to be a Rhino?" quizzed the amused coach. "You'll have to have your parents sign some papers and you'll need to suit up. I'll be right back with the forms."

"No problem, sir, my mom is right here. She can sign, can't she?"

"We really need to have both parents sign the papers. Where's your Daddy at? He here today?" The flush of excitement that had been on Parker's face suddenly drained.

"He's in Vietnam, Sir. He's a pilot. We really don't see him home much." Chummy Johnson knew that the football program would do the boy good. He had a handful of kids on the team who had fathers in the military. He was also aware that half the boys would next see their male role models shipped home in a coffin.

"No problem, Thomas. Your Ma can sign the papers. I'll go get them." said the coach. He turned and walked toward a blue Chrysler Imperial that was parked fifty feet away. He returned shortly and handed Parker a Pop Warner consent form.

"Have your momma sign right here." Chummy Johnson instructed as he pointed a big finger at the blank line on the bottom of the paper.

"Go get it signed and bring it on back."

Parker grabbed the sheet of paper from Coach Johnson's hand and whizzed off to the parked Ford. He got there in no time, and he flung the piece of paper in front of his mother's face.

"Ma, you need to sign this so I can get a uniform. Coach says you gotta do it before I can be on the team. Got a pen? Just sign this now!" insisted the boy.

"But Parker, I need to talk this over with your father, and you know he's on special assignment. I have no way to reach him. He won't be calling us until a week from tomorrow." replied the startled Mrs. Thomas.

"Ma, I can join the team today and get in on the practice if you sign now. The coach already went to get me a helmet!"

"Well, I suppose I could sign now. But if something happens to you, your father would be very upset. Promise me you won't get hurt, please, Parker?"

"No sweat, Ma. We're just gonna run around a little and throw the ball a couple of times." Grudgingly, Alice Thomas put her name on the blank line. Before she had the pen off the paper, Parker tore it out of the car and took off running towards Chummy Johnson.

"Here it is, Coach. Do I get a uniform, and what do you want me to do?" querried a winded Parker Thomas.

"I got a helmet here for you. Try it on." Parker snapped the chin strap loose from the bottom and pushed the helmet over the top of his head. He couldn't get the sides of the helmet over his ears. He tried pulling on the sides to expand it, but the fiberglass fought him. When Chummy Johnson saw the struggle, he smiled.

"I got one more left. It's the biggest one we have. It's a special size seven. I'll be right back." The coach returned and handed the helmet to Parker. He had an easier time with this one. It fit snug, like having his head wrapped in plastic.

"Ok, Thomas, and I'm gonna call you Thomas from now on," said the coach, "Get on over to where the other boys are after you suit up!" Parker loped toward the circle of maroon shirts, found Ryan Corbett again, and whacked him on the shoulder, a little harder this time than last time.

"Need a uniform. My Ma signed me up. What do I do? Where do I get one?" Before Ryan Corbett could answer his friend, a voice snapped: "Corbett!"

Ryan Corbett bolted, head down, toward a tackling dummy in the middle of the circle of players. He ran into it with all his speed. When he made contact, he fell back, lost his balance, and wound up on his ass. The other maroon shirts burst into laughter. The embarrassed boy got up, dusted off his pants, and limped back over to Parker.

"You got to get lower and lift up when you go for the dummy!" said the voice from behind the bag. "Take ten, team!" The maroon shirts again obediently turned and trotted toward the water buckets that lay on the side of the field. Parker and Ryan remained in place, and from behind the dummy emerged the Rhino's other coach, Rod Stevens.

"Well, who we got here, Corbett?" inquired the coach.

"This is our newest player, Coach. This is Parker Thomas. He just joined up. Got a jersey for him?"

"Back in a flash!" replied the coach, flashing a wide and winning smile in Parker's direction. He soon returned with a tattered maroon jersey. It had a ripped out armpit under the left sleeve seam and the number sixty-two sewn onto the back. He handed the shirt to Parker and gave him a pair of shoulder pads to put on. Parker put his arms through the holding straps, pulled the pads down around his shoulders and laced up the front. He struggled to pull the shirt down over his equipment.

"Take the helmet off before you put the shirt on, son," suggested Coach Stevens. Parker unsnapped the chin strap, took off his helmet, and stuck his head through the neck opening of the shirt. His arms flailed as he tried to pull the jersey down over the padding. After a few tugs, he managed to get his shirt down. He tucked it into his dungarees and put the helmet back on.

"I got thigh pads for you too, but you ain't gonna be able to stuff 'em into those jeans. I looked around for a pair of football pants for you, but I only found smalls and mediums. I'll have a pair for you by next practice, though." offered Rodney Stevens. "Now, let's see how you and the dummy get along."

The coach strolled back toward the team's only piece of sports equipment, a five foot high tackling dummy that had patches and stitches in it to prevent the padding from coming out. It had been used over and over again in the Pop Warner program and was in pretty good shape for all the bashing and slamming it had taken over the past eight years. It had the same tattered and torn look as the practice jerseys the boys had on that day at practice. Coach Stevens positioned himself behind the dummy, braced it with both his palms, and called to Parker: "OK, son, I want you to run at the dummy. Aim your helmet right at the middle!"

"Piece of cake, Coach!" returned Parker as he dug the sole of his right sneaker into the dirt and took off. After five quick steps, he made contact. His helmet slapped into the dummy and his shoulders rammed the bag.

"Not bad at all! Try it again, only this time don't put your head down. Run into it, put your face right in the middle of the bag, and wrap your arms around it." Parker dug in again, took six quick chops with his legs, and lunged into the waiting opponent. He wrapped his arms around the weighty mass.

"Good. Much better! Try it again. But this time, keep on running after you hit it," ordered the coach, who then pushed his knee against the dummy. Parker ran at the dummy, made instant and total contact, but was surprised that his opponent didn't budge this time. Despite the protective gear, Parker's body felt the impact. The blow that ripped through him reminded him of the first time he tried the high diving board at the community pool and hit the water belly first. Parker blocked out the pain and kept pumping his legs as he had been instructed. The dummy did not give way. The harder he tried to move it, the more it seemed to resist.

"Whoa, son, hold up! Hold up!" called Coach Stevens, "You're wearing me out!" Smiling, the coach stepped out from behind the dummy.

"Nice job, Thomas! Glad to have you on the team. Go on over to Coach Johnson now. He'll fit you into the scrimmage."

As Parker trotted toward the other Rhinos, he caught a strange sight out of the corner of his eye. Three boys were moving along the fence, and they looked like ducks waddling.

They were squatting down and walking at the same time. One of the boys called out to him.

"Hey Parker, how'd it go?" Parker recognized the voice; it was Ryan Corbett. He had been sent to the sidelines with two other boys because he hadn't paid attention to Coach Johnson and screwed up the same play over and over again.

"What are you doing over here, Ryan?" Parker Thomas querried.

"Coach gave us special muscle building exercises to do because we're his best players. It's a lot of fun. Called the duck walk." responded one of the other boys who was with Ryan.

"Hey Parker, wanna sit with us at lunch tomorrow at school?" chimed in Ryan Corbett.

"Yeah, sure. Hey, I gotta go see the coach. See you later!" called Parker over his shoulder as he continued to make his way to the other end of the field. By the time Parker got to where the other maroon shirts were, the boys were huddled around Coach Johnson, and the sun had already begun to set.

"That's it for today, men. See you at noon time Saturday." bellowed the coach.

"Oh, Thomas, you be there too!" he concluded. As the maroon shirts walked off in pairs and in different directions, Parker Thomas headed for the grey Ford parked off to the side. He opened the passenger side door and got in. He smiled at his mother as he scrunched his shoulder pads against the back of his seat.

"So, is this what you want, Parker?" quizzed a concerned Alice Thomas.

"Yeah, Ma, it is." answered Parker. "I'm gonna be a pro football player!"

"Let's head home for supper, dear. Don't forget, you have homework to do too," reminded Alice as she turned the key in the ignition and the motor began to hum.

The ride back was silent. Past the rows of tenement houses, over the winding main boulevard and right up to the tree-lined street the Thomas family lived on, both occupants were caught up with their own thoughts. Alice realized that her boy was now a child of the world, and took some comfort that there were people like the coaches out there, ready to adopt and nurture. Parker knew that he wasn't going to spend any more Wednesdays trading lunches with Joey DeVito, and that in order to find his place in life he would have to push harder and longer to be accepted. He felt an ache in his gut from his earlier batterings with the tackle dummy, and his mind shifted focus to his physical being. He thought that his biceps were kind of sore, and he felt a strange sensation tingling in his crotch.

"Hmmm," Parker Thomas thought to himself, "Didn't know that thing down there had a bone in it!"

*From the Outhouse to the Penthouse
and Somewhere in Between*

# FIRST LEG OF THE JOURNEY

The black Mustang zipped over the lower half of the New Jersey Turnpike in an hour and a half flat. With the radio cranking out Led Zepplin tunes, Parker Thomas sped past Wilmington, crossed the Delaware Bay Bridge and had made the Maryland state line before finishing the tape he had popped into the casette player at the last toll booth. He pulled into the first rest stop he saw when he noticed the fuel gauge warning light come on. After getting two cans of diet coke and a full tank of gas, he got back onto the interstate and headed south again. The night air blowing through the open window of the car had the sweet smell only a spring evening could – crisp, green and alive, just like the young man driving the car.

Only six hours earlier, Parker had dashed over to turn in his senior thesis to Professor McCoy, head of the history program at Ivy University. Now that his college years were a bona fide and documentable part of his life, Parker Thomas was ready to make his solo flight into the unsheltering real world. As the headlights of oncoming traffic appeared and disappeared, Parker flashed back to the uncertainty he had felt his entire last semester at Ivy. Most of the guys at the Tau Kappa Epsilon house had their lives mapped out for them before leaving for spring break their senior year. Mack Warren was headed for Georgetown Law. Mike Brennan had interviewed with and been hired by a secret government agency. Lenny Silverman had been recruited by I.B.M. and Lawton Biddle was heading for Harvard Med. Parker had spent his spring break in utter agony. After four years as Ivy's tight end and struggling to keep his grades above-average, Parker had sent out letters to all the NFL teams. His hope was that he would get a chance to try out for an NFL team, and get an invitation to training camp, and hopefully make the team. Half the teams didn't bother to answer his letters. The other half sent letters back stating that they offered no such camps. His only shot lay neatly folded and tucked away in the overnight bag on the front seat of the car. The Washington Redskins had responded with a form letter advising Parker that they would be holding free agent tryouts on May 23rd at a high school field. The letter additionally wished him success with his future and thanked him for his interest in their organization.

Armed with a letter, a pair of cleats, and sheer determination, Parker Thomas arrived at the Chantilly, Virginia Holiday Inn at midnight. He had six hours to go before he would know for sure what fate had in store for him.

Promptly at six, the bedside phone rang. Parker acknowledged the wake-up call, went into the bathroom and got into the lukewarm shower. He dried off, put on his sweats, and headed for the hotel lobby. He grabbed two cartons of orange juice and four bagels from the complimentary breakfast table, and shoved one of the bagels into his mouth as he walked across the parking lot to his car. Five minutes later he was at the field.

Parker got out of his Mustang, walked through the iron gates and headed for the table that had a cardboard 'T through Z' posted above it. He got to the back of the line and patiently moved up as did the fifty or so men who had lined up in front of him to register. Administrative assistants at the rear of the field all spewed the same information in different directions and in varying tones: "Get into the line that has the first letter of your last name! Keep up with the line! Move quickly!!" Parker eventually got to the head of the line.

"Name?" quizzed the redhead seated at the table.

"Thomas."

"Age?"

"Twenty-one."

"Height?"

"Six five."

"Weight?"

"270."

"School?"

"Ivy University."

"Did you graduate?"

"Later this month."

"Position?"

"Tight end and offensive line."

"Do you know your forty time?"

"Five. Flat."

"Sign here. This is a release form." She pointed to ten o'clock: "Report up to the field with your cleats!" she ordered.. "Next?"

Parker left the table and headed for the field. When he got there, more guys were barking orders: "Make sure you have signed in and signed the release form! If you haven't done it, go back and do it now! No one on the field unless they've signed in!"

Parker walked down to the corner of the end zone and began to stretch. Parker felt a bit lost. There were players everywhere. They were huddled in groups in the bleachers and out on the field. Some were laughing and joking. Guys were off by themselves practicing stance and starts. Others were paired up and tossing footballs. A few were wandering around and appeared to be out of their element. Their nervous energy transfused to every man on the field, that nervous tension often gut-felt just before the coin toss of each game. The dreams and aspirations of every player on the field that day would either be furthered with the hope of an invitation to camp or crushed forever by the realization that they didn't have what it takes to make it into the National Football League.

A blast from a bullhorn caught everyone's attention. A coach in a red jacket yelled toward the bleachers: "Everybody in the bleachers now! Everybody in the bleachers now!"

After a few minutes of milling and shuffling, the coach continued: "Everybody should be signed in. If you're not signed in, go over and see that man."

The coach pointed to his left. A squatty man in thick glasses raised his hand in acknowledgement. A half dozen men got up and walked over to him. The coach began his pitch: "Men, welcome to the Washington Redskins free agent tryout camp. This is your opportunity to show us what you can do. You will be timed in the forty, tested in the vertical jump, the bench press and the shuttle. You will be paired off by positions. And once we are done, some of you will be invited back for the afternoon session. Quarterbacks and receivers and d.b.'s, follow the gentleman in the blue shirt. Running backs and linebackers, follow that gentleman there, he has his hand up now. Offensive and defensive linemen, to the other end of the field under the goal post."

The crowd of men got up and went to their respective areas. A voice came from the bleachers: "What about the punters and kickers, coach?"

"Go with the quarterbacks and receivers!"

"Are we gonna be doing any kicking today?" called another voice.

The coach said: "Pick a position and go with that group for now! We will kick after we are done. It helps if you can play a position as well. This is the NFL! The more you can do!" Parker Thomas broke off with his group and ran toward the end zone. More than one hundred players milled about the man with the clipboard who was waiting in the end zone.

"O.K., men, listen up! We're gonna give you about five minutes to do some stretching and loosen up. Then we're gonna test you in the shuttle," said the man with the clipboard.

Parker Thomas looked over to the two sets of orange cones positioned in each corner of the end zone. They were set exactly ten yards apart. Parker bent over, touched his toes, and held the position for a few seconds. He then straddled his legs and touched his chin to his right knee, holding it for a few seconds. He then did the same thing with his chin on his left knee. The stretching helped ease some of the nervous energy that had been building up from the ride down. The undersized hotel bed had left him tight and stiff that morning. The man with the clipboard blew a whistle to get everyone's attention.

"Everybody up! Lester here is going to demonstrate the drill. Pay attention. You only get one shot at this, so make it good!"

Lester, at six foot three and two hundred seventy-five pounds, was obviously a lineman. He positioned himself in the middle of one of the sets of cones and nodded that he was ready. In a flash, he exploded out toward one of the cones, as if to get the jump on the stopwatch that had been clicked on his first movement. He touched the line by the cone and hauled ass toward the other cone. He again touched the line and raced back, lunging through his original starting position. The coach clicked off the watch.

"Way to go Big Les!" exclaimed the coach, "Here's a couple of pointers for the rest of you men: stay low, make sure you touch the line, and sprint as hard as you can. Stay on your feet. A good football player always stays on his feet. Don't ask what your time is. OK, men, half of you here, and half over there." He pointed to the other set of cones as he continued, "One by one come up and give your name. Nod that you're ready, then go!" Parker Thomas nervously watched as the men in front of him got put to the test one by one. Assistants with clipboards recorded their times. Finally, his turn came.

"Thomas." he called out as he positioned himself. His anxiety made him feel powerful and powerless at the same time.

Parker nodded and sprinted out of his stance. He almost slipped as his feet went out from underneath him when he wheeled around and raced toward the second cone. He made the second touch and bolted back through the middle.

"Two nine!" he heard the timekeeper say as he clicked off the watch.

Parker heaved a sigh of relief; he knew that his score was faster than most of the times earlier runners had done. He watched and listened as the last few players ran the drill. The coach called to them all: "OK, men, jog, don't walk, down to the other end of the field. Report to the weight room for your next test!"

When Parker and the others got there, they were greeted by six weight benches with two hundred twenty-five pounds on each bar.

"Men," yet another assistant with a clipboard called out, "Take off your cleats! Pair off in six even groups. State your name as your turn comes up. Bench press as many reps as you can. You will have spotters, so go until you can't go any more, and then some! When you're done, head over to the far wall."

Parker got into a group and fitted into the middle of a line. He watched his competition try to muster more strength with moans and groans as their muscles collapsed. When his turn came, he stated his name, lay down on the bench and positioned himself underneath the bar. He gripped the cold steel, adjusted his grasp, and began to pump. The first ten reps were a piece of cake. By the fourteenth rep, he felt like his arms were going to split open. He pushed through the seventeenth, and then gave in.

"Good job!" said the man with the clipboard. "We have a new record to beat. Which one of you is gonna do it?"

Parker's satisfaction with his effort gave him some hope for the first time that day. He shook out his arms a few times and headed over to the wall. He got into a line, and when he got up near the front, another man with a clipboard told him to put his fingertips into a pail of chalk. He barked: "Stand next to the wall, jump as high as you can, and touch the wall when you're up as high as you can get."

Parker looked at the wall and noticed it was measured out. A fifteen-foot measuring tape ran up the wall vertically. He approached a piece of tape that marked the starting point on the floor. He looked up at the wall, inhaled, exhaled, bent his knees and thrust himself up against the wall as high as he could jump. Slap! His hand hit the wall and he came down.

"Eight three. Twenty-two inch jump!" said the assistant that made notes. Parker's arms were just beginning to recover from the strain of the reps, as he watched the others in the line in back of him do the vertical jump. A voice in back of him shouted yet another set of instructions: "OK, men, when you're done with the wall, grab your cleats and head to the field. Get loose, because you're gonna be timed in the forty."

Parker's stomach knotted. The forty was next, and this was the tell-all test. The NFL put a premium on the forty time, and everybody knew it. It was the yardstick by which a player was rated. If a player was a free agent or an unknown, this could be his calling card; this was how to get their attention. Parker learned this fact from his friend Cris Keating, who had gotten drafted and played with Miami. Parker had met Cris during the summer following his sophomore year at Ivy. Cris came from New Shrewsbury and went to Boston College on a full ride. Parker had visited Cris at B.C. when he found out that Blesto, the scouting combine, would be in Boston. Cris ran a five flat. Parker ran a five two. Cris's words from that day were etched into Parker's mind: "This is it! This is the run for the money. How much they pay you and how high you get drafted depends a lot on your forty time. The difference between a couple tenths of a second can be a couple hundred grand. The faster you run, the more they pay you."

No one from Blesto paid any attention to Parker that day at Boston College. Cris got drafted in the fifth round that year, and he got a nice signing bonus.

From that day on, Parker worked on his forty time. He did countless stance and starts and stride drills. Today was the day he would find out if all his work would pay off.

Parker snatched up his size fourteen cleats from his gym bag, laced them up, and headed out onto the maincured field.

There, for the first time stood the coaching staff of the Washington Redskins. Coach Greg Arden and his assistants were assembled, and they were anxious to see if anyone in the group of hundreds there that day would run a world class time. Parker Thomas was in awe. He was actually face to face with the legend who had taken his team to the Superbowl the year before. Parker stood off to the side and watched the strain of the faces of the players at they crossed the finish line. He felt his throat tighten and his gut heave, so he stretched some more to ease the tension. As he was down on the ground, he heard a coaching staff member summon his group: "Offensive and defensive linemen, up next. Make sure you're all loose. We don't want any groin or hamstring pulls here today!"

After a few minutes, the coach continued: "All right, line up! Let's go!" Parker Thomas got into line.

When he got up near the front, he got further instruction: "Make sure your hand is behind the line! And make sure you run all the way through the finish. Don't slow up. When you're up, call out your name, make sure the timers are ready, and go like hell!"

Parker, as he was waiting for his turn, noticed that the staff was timing not only for the forty, but also for the twenty and the ten.

"Focus!" Parker said to himself, "Focus!" Parker's chance came. He stepped up, walked to the line, and called out: "Thomas."

One of the assistants yelled down the line to another who was waiting: "Thomas up." Parker Thomas knelt down over the line like a sprinter out of the blocks. He placed his right hand on the line and raised his left hand above his back. He gave a nod to the timekeeper, who nodded back, then focused on an imaginary target in front of him. He lunged out, staying as low as he could, and sprinted down the line. He pumped his arms as hard as he could. He kept his head straight and his jaw loose as he barreled down the course to the clicks of numerous stopwatches. To the click of the watch, he lunged his body over the finish line with every ounce of energy he could muster as the watch clicked off, and kept on going as he heard his time yelled out.

He turned around and ran back to the timekeeper at the end of the forty: "Five. Flat!" repeated the recorder. Parker was elated. He had run his fastest time, and he had done it in front of one of the finest coaching staffs in the NFL. For a brief moment, he felt as if he was on his way to the penthouse. His constant practice for the past two years had paid off.

One of the assistants approached Parker Thomas.

"After you've finished the forty, you're done for the morning. Go grab a light bite to eat and meet back at the bleachers at one o'clock." he nonchalantly uttered. Parker walked across the field, through the iron gates, and back to his car. The sun was high now, and the mist of the VIrginia morning had turned to sticky noontime haze. Parker opened the door of his black Mustang, collapsed into the front seat and took out one of the bagels he had stashed in his gymbag. He crammed it into his mouth and chewed. He searched for a carton of orange juice, opened it up, and took a big swig. The bagel and juice went down his throat in one big lump.

Parker took another bagel out of the bag, leaned over to the right, and popped open the glove compartment. He pulled out a cassette, slipped it into the player and turned the ignition key half way. "This will be the last time, this will be the last time…" Parker pumped his left ankle, keeping time with the Stones, and drummed his fingers on the console as he finished lunch. He checked the clock on the dash. Twelve fifty. Parker got out of the car, locked it, and headed for the bleachers.

He found a spot in the third row and sat down. The atmosphere was different than the noise and commotion of earlier that morning. Most of the players were quiet, self-absorbed. One of the coaches took a bullhorn and addressed the players: "First of all, the Redskins staff and I would like to thank you for all the effort you put out today. You all showed us what you could do. Now, I'm going to call out the names on the list we've put together. If I call out your name, stay! If your name isn't on the list, again, thank you for coming out today."

The coach put on a pair of glasses that dangled off the end of his nose. He started reading down the list: "Alsworth... Cheryziniski... Fullgarden..." It was obvious to the players that the coach was calling out the list in alphabetical order. It was also clear that since he had only a one page list handed to him, a quarter of the men who had come out had already been eliminated.

The coach continued: "Grecco... Mansini... Norton... O'Neal... Parrish... Petersen... Riker... Robilard... Sanford... Stankle..." Parker clenched his teeth and felt more tension than he ever had before. His jaw ached with anxiety.

"Staumbaugh... Tarser... Teasley... Thomas..." Parker wanted to jump up and shout, but he kept his emotions as contained as he could under the circumstances. The coach finished his list, waited a minute or two for the bleachers to empty themselves of the players who hadn't made it through the first cut, and then again raised the bullhorn: "Those of you whose names I called, go out to the fifty yard line and meet up with Coach Springer. He's gonna stretch you out and get you warmed up for the rest of the day."

Parker and the hundred or so others went to the center of the field. They were told to get into lines, ten men per row, each row approximately five yards apart. Coach Springer put them

*From the Outhouse to the Penthouse
and Somewhere in Between*

through a set of stretches and then gave them instructions about where to report. Parker Thomas and a group of twenty-five offensive linemen went to the twenty yard line as they had been instructed.

"Men, I am coach Weldon, the offensive line coach here. Line up on the twenty, here. Give yourself plenty of room. You're gonna do some stance and starts."

"All right, you guys, get down and show me your stance. Spread out! Give yourselves some room!" Weldon walked down the line and stopped in front of one of the players: "What's your name, son?" the coach asked.

"Mansini, sir." the player answered.

"What the hell kind of stance is that?" Weldon yelled, "Get your right foot back more. Now move it out a little. That's better!" The coach continued down the line and stopped in front of another player.

"Get your head up more! That's it!" Weldon looked down the rest of the line. He called out: "OK, now we're gonna do some stance and starts. I'm gonna say Set, Hut! I want you to go on the first Hut. Sprint out of your stance as hard as you can. Stay low for ten yards. Turn around and sprint back on the cadence. Got it? OK! Let's go!" A couple of the players dropped into their stance.

"No! No! Don't get down until I call 'SET'! Try it again. Set… HUT!" The linemen shot to the thirty.

"Let's try it again. Set... HUT!" The linemen sprinted back to the twenty.

"Good. Now we're gonna see how smart you are. I'm gonna change the snap count. This time, go on the second Hut! The call is Set... HUT... HUT. Got it? Set! HUT! HUT!" Parker Thomas and the rest of the line bolted to the thirty. A couple of players had gone off on the first 'hut'. The coach called out again as they waited on the thirty.

"Set! HUT! HUT!" The players headed for the twenty. Parker Thomas was one of the first across the line.

The rest of the afternoon consisted of drill after drill. The players did the monkey roll, practiced pulling to the right and to the left, and practiced run blocking and pass blocking footwork. By two thirty, the players had been put through their paces. The coach called them into a circle around him.

"All right, gentlemen, thank you for your efforts. If I call your name, stay! If not, take it on in." snapped Weldon. He flipped over a piece of paper and secured it with a snap of his clipboard. The coach called out six names. Parker Thomas was one of them.

"Gentlemen, we're gonna team up in a few minutes. We will work a little against the defense. Take five!"

Parker headed over to the water tanks on the side lines. He gave the handle a few pumps, picked up the hose, and doused his head. The temperature was nearing the eighty-five degree mark, unusually high for that time of year. After wiping his face with the bottom of his t-shirt, Parker opened his mouth, aimed the hose at it, and gave the handle a few more pumps. The water sluiced down his throat, and he just couldn't seem to get enough of it. Weldon blew a whistle, and Parker ran back over to him.

"All right, men, you're gonna work against the D-line. We don't have helmets, so I want you to go three-quarter speed and stay on your feet. Pair off! Defensive linemen opposite offensive linemen. Spread out!" Parker faced a golliath player who had intense determination in his eyes. Weldon gave further instructions: "Offensive line, get down in your stance. On the first 'hut' I want the D-line to come across the line of scrimmage for a couple of steps at three-quarter speed. Offensive linemen, set up in your pass set and keep them off the line of scrimmage. Get your hands on the D-linemen and stay in front of them with a good base! Set!... HUT!"

The mammoth player headed for Parker Thomas. Parker fired out his hands into the oncoming chest, trying to stay low and battled to stay in front of him, as well as keep his feet underneath him. The whistle blew.

"OK, good!" shouted Weldon. "Again! Set! HUT!" This time the bulky lineman charged even harder at Parker. As Parker shot his hands out towards the other player's chest, the D-lineman ripped his huge right arm in a pendulum motion under

Parker's extended arms. He knocked Parker off balance, left him with no surface to block, and blew right by him. Sauntering back to the line of scrimmage, the defensive lineman sneered at Parker: "Got you with the rip move!" the lineman gloated. Coach Weldon marched up to Parker Thomas.

"Stay in front! Stay in front next time! What's your name?"

"Thomas."

"Stay in front, Thomas!" said the coach and then turned to the other players: "Again! Set! HUT!" The lineman charged at Parker again. Anticipating what the other player would do, Parker went at him. This time, the other lineman slammed his left arm into Parker's shoulder and swam his right arm over the top of Parker's extended body. Parker looked up from the ground as the other player made a beeline past him.

"Come on, Thomas, stay on your feet!" yelled Weldon. "You can't protect a quarterback when you're on the ground!"

"Takin' you to school, Homeboy!" grinned the defensive lineman as the other players laughed along.

"OK, last time! Then the D-line gets some work!" ordered Weldon. "Set! HUT!" The lineman rushed at Parker. Parker fiercely thrust out his hands, trying to keep his body from getting over-extended. He fought to keep the lineman in front of him. The lineman did a three-sixty spin, but Parker was back on his heels and kept the behemouth in front of him. He didn't give the lineman any ground, and kept him jammed on the line of scrimmage.

"That's better, Thomas!" shouted Weldon. "Offensive linemen, remember to keep your head out of the block. You don't have any helmets on! And D-line, go only three-quarter speed. If you're really good at pass blocking, you don't even need a helmet! All right! Let's work the D-line. Offensive linemen, come across a couple of steps into the D-line and let them work on their technique. Parker paired off with the same lineman, and for the next fifteen minutes, either fired out as if to run block or held firm on the line of scrimmage as if to pass block. Weldon blew the whistle.

"OK, bring it up. OK, men, thank you for today. It was a great effort! Some of you, we'd like you to stay. If your name is called, stay here. To you others, once again, thanks for your cooperation." Again Weldon pulled a piece of paper from under the top of the clipboard. He called off ten names. Parker Thomas was among them.

"We would like you gentlemen to report to Redskin Park at seven tomorrow morning. If you have some turf shoes, bring them with you. Make sure you rest up and get yourselves a good meal tonight. If you have any questions, see Mr. Taylor over there."

Parker Thomas got into his black Mustang and drove back to the Holiday Inn. He was sky high. Out of the thousand or so who had been at the camp, ten were left, and he was one of them.

*From the Outhouse to the Penthouse
and Somewhere in Between*

## THE SKINS

At six forty-five, Parker hit the right turn signal in the Mustang and headed up Redskin Drive. The sodded field, the astroturf field, the executive office building, and the players' locker room building were all state of the art. It was the most awesome facility he had ever seen. He parked in one of the spaces that was marked off for visitors, and walked toward a red and gold building with a six-foot circular Washington Redskins logo on one of its sides. This is what the big time looked like, and Parker Thomas was once again overwhelmed.

Parker went into the second building and found the equipment room. He was greeted by one of the staff assistants.

"Can I help you?"

"My name is Parker Thomas. I was told to report here by the coach at the free agent camp yesterday." The equipment man scanned the list posted on the side of the door.

"OK, your name's on the list. Go up to the cage, get a mesh bag, a helmet and some turf shoes. You can get taped up in the trainers' room. Be on the field and ready to go at eight." At the cage, Parker was greeted by a man with the name 'Stitch' embroidered above his left pocket. Another older man was behind the rows of helmets, shoulder pads, and cleats that lay on shelves in the middle of the room.

"I'm Parker Thomas. They told me to come up here and get some gear."

"What size? Large or extra-large?" asked Stitch.

"Extra-large." Parker answered.

"What size shoe?"

"Fourteen."

"Here, try these. See if they fit. What's your helmet size?"

"Seven and three-quarters." Stitch handed Parker a helmet off the top shelf and Parker tried it on.

"Seems a little loose." Stitch put his fingers between Parker's ear and the inside of the helmet.

"No, that's fine." said Stitch. He took a small hand pump, inserted a needle into a hole opening to a bladder on the top of the helmet and squeezed the pump a few times. He inserted the needle into both sides of the helmet and repeated the action. Parker could feel the helmet mold to his head.

"There you go!" said Stitch to Parker, "You're all set!" Pulling two pieces of white athletic tape off a roll that was in front of him, Stitch wrote 'Thomas' on both with a black marking pen. He plastered one of the pieces of tape across the top of Parker's helmet in front.

*From the Outhouse to the Penthouse and Somewhere in Between*

"Put this other one across one of the lockers that are over there." Stitch said to Parker as he handed him the other piece of tape with his name on it.

As Parker walked over to an empty locker, he noticed that the other lockers had names engraved in plastic and permanently affixed to them. They were names of NFL icons, some of them the most recognizable and famous in the league. Parker stuck the tape across the top of a locker, took off his shoes, and put them in the locker. He put his keys and gymbag on the top shelf. As Parker walked into the training room, he recognized a few faces from the previous day's camp. One of the trainers called to him, had him sit down, and taped up his ankles. Parker went back to his locker, put on his turf shoes, and walked out onto the astroturf practice field. He jogged a bit to loosen up, as a handful of other players were already doing.

At eight o'clock, a coach poked his head out the door.

"All right, you guys, bring it up!" The players went over to him.

"We're gonna break into groups. Offensive linemen, go with Coach Weldon. Defensive linemen, go with Coach Clausen." Parker and two other players jogged down to where Weldon was waiting on the field.

"How you guys doing today?" The three players gave him a silent nod.

"Are any of you guys sore from yesterday?" the coach asked. Nobody responded, even though all three were stiff and sore from the day before.

"Today, we're gonna do the same drills as we did yesterday. We are also going to teach you some basic plays. And then we're going to run a few periods of team against our defense."

"You mean we're gonna work against the Redskins players?" asked one player.

"Some are still here from mini camp." snapped Weldon. He did not like to be asked questions or interrupted.

A tremendous excitement and extreme nervousness coursed through Parker Thomas. In all the games he had played, he never felt those emotions quite as intensely before. The hour of drills passed quickly. Parker was caught up in the reality of the moment: very shortly he would be putting himself to the test against the best. The air horn gave a loud blast from center field where a coach yelled: "All right, everybody up!" All the players gathered around him. Weldon called out: "Jackson, go to left guard. Thomas, you go to right guard when they call for the third team. Brown, you go to left tackle when they call for the third team."

"All right, we're gonna run team. First unit," Coach Arden barked, "Huddle up! The rest of you guys get back, listen, and pay attention to the play!" Parker and the other two players from his group stood back from the huddle.

*From the Outhouse to the Penthouse and Somewhere in Between*

"Red eighty. Red eighty. Set! HUT! HUT!" called the quarterback. The ball was snapped and the play was run.

"Holy shit!" said Parker to himself. "These guys are bigger and faster than I ever had imagined!" Parker watched as the team ran fifteen plays with the first and second units. He knew he would soon get a couple of reps.

All right, three's up! Three's up!" barked Coach Arden. Parker Thomas joined the huddle. The quarterback gave the play: "Red right. Thirty-two. Trap. On two! Ready? Break!" The players snapped out of the huddle and Parker Thomas was at the line of scrimmage.

"Red eighty! Red eighty! Set! HUT! HUT!" called the quarterback. Parker shot out of his stance and pretended to block an imaginary defensive lineman over his nose. Parker would never forget this moment.

"Brown! Jackson! Thomas! Take the next three reps!" called out Weldon. Parker went back and got into the huddle again.

"Blue left. Thirty-one. Trap. On one!" the quarterback barked, "Ready? Break!" Parker bounded up to the offensive line. They were calling his number. He was to pull to the left and pretend to trap an onrushing defensive lineman and make a hole for the back to run through.

"Red sixty. Red Sixty. Set! HUT!" Parker ran his course.

"Get up the field on that trap course, Thomas!" coach Weldon yelled, "And get into the line of scrimmage! This ain't the Ivy League!" As Parker went back into the huddle, the air horn went off to signal the last and final period. The defense was coming up, and Parker would be running against live men, not just air. He started to sweat from the nervous tension.

Parker stood back and gaped at the defensive line coming out of the huddle. They were huge! He recognized one or two of the players. They were All-Pros at their position, the very best. Who wouldn't know who they were? Parker was shaken by how big Doug Butts was. Butts was the defensive tackle that Parker was supposed to block. He was an All-Pro veteran in the prime of his career, and the heart of the Redskins' defense. In games, he was often double-teamed, even triple-teamed. He was six feet four, three hundred pounds, and looked like a refrigerator with a breadbox head. Parker's whole body went limp: his energy drained for a brief and scary moment. As play after play was run, Parker became imtimidated by the size and speed of the lineman.

"Third team, get ready! You're up next!" called out Coach Arden.

Parker stepped into the huddle, and before the quarterback could give the play, he heard one of the coaches call to all the players on the field: "All right, let's pick up the tempo! I know this is slap and tickle, but play hard to the whistle. You offensive linemen, fire out and stay on your blocks!"

"Red right. Thirty-two man. On two. Ready? Break!" The players went to the line of scrimmage. Parker was shitting bricks as he heard the quarterback bark 'set'. As he got down in his stance, Parker saw Butts stare at him. It seemed to Parker that Butts was staring right through him!

"What's up, Rook?" quizzed the Refrigerator with a big wide grin. Parker Thomas trembled in absolute fear.

"HUT! HUT!" called the quarterback. Parker exploded off the ball with all the strength he could summon. He tried to burrow his head into Doug Butts' chest. Parker knew it was slap and tickle, but he was going balls out. Parker dove into Butts, and Butts beat him off the ball. The impact stuffed Parker into the hole, causing the back to ram into Parker, who was quickly discarded like a rag doll. Butts arrogantly tagged the running back to signal that if this were a real game, he would have made the tackle.

As Parker Thomas walked back to the huddle, he heard a comment from the coach: "Who's in there at guard? Shit! We need better movement up the middle than that!"

In the huddle, the quarterback threw Parker a look and arrogantly chanted: "Red right. Thirty-two. Play pass. X hook. Y drag. Z post. On one. Ready? Break!" Not over the humiliation of the last play, Parker desperately tried to remember what his assignment was. He had been whipped and humiliated, and for a brief moment, his mind had blown a fuse. As Parker got to the line of scrimmage, he had completely forgotten the call and the snap count, but recalled the word 'pass' at the last second. Parker Thomas knew what he had to do: he knew he had to slam into Butts and sell the run, then gather himself to stay in front of him to pass block while the quarterback faked thirty-two run, stuck the ball on his hip, and rolled out looking for an open receiver.

"Set! Blue seventy. Blue seventy. HUT!" Parker fired out. Unlike the previous time, he was under control. Parker jammed his hands into Butts' chest like two meat hooks on a big slab of beef. He battled to stay in front of the oncoming mammoth. The quarterback faked the ball, and the back came flying up to the hole. Butts was off of Parker and on a course to the quarterback in a heartbeat. Parker recovered and flew at Butts. Parker's helmet crashed into Butts' chest just as he was reaching for the quarterback.

"Take it easy, Rook!" the Refrigerator yelled in Parker's face. Parker's heart was pounding through his chest. The quarterback threw the ball and hit the open receiver just as he got two feet in bounds.

"Nice pass, Billy!" called out Arden to the quarterback. On the way back to the huddle, the quarterback looked at Parker: "I don't care what you do. Keep that big guy off me! Good job!"

As Parker Thomas got into the huddle, his motor was going all out. His pulse was racing faster than he thought it ever could.

"Blue left. Motion. Thirty-one. Trap. On three. Ready? Break!" Parker bounded to the line of scrimmage. He could tell Butts was taking him a bit more seriously now because he could see the fire in the golliath's eyes.

"HUT! HUT! HUT!" barked the quarterback. Parker ran his trap course, thankful that he did not have to fire out at Butts. He pulled and sprinted down the line to trap the defensive tackle opposite Butts. Just as Parker went to pull, the middle linebacker screamed,"Watch the trap! Moony! The trap!" Parker had tipped his stance that he was pulling to trap. Moony Sasquach, the other defensive tackle and another genetic freak, just like Butts, stepped into the hole and closed off the trap. Parker wheeled around and slammed into the huge lineman with everything he had. There was no hole as the D-lineman easily tagged the running back.

"Don't tip your stance, Thomas!" called Arden. "Come on, you're an Ivy Leaguer!"

"Oh, we've got an intellectual among us, gentlemen!" jived Butts.

"Gee, shouldn't you be out running daddy's company?" called Moony.

"He didn't go to the University of Mars like you, Sasquach!" Butts called back. Both sides laughed at the hazing that Parker Thomas was the target of.

"All right, first unit, get back in there!" Arden snapped. Parker went to the sides and watched the first team play until the final whistle.

"All right, guys. Pack it in for the day. Go and turn in your gear. Thomas, you report to Mr. Palumbo in the executive offices after you hit the showers." Coach Arden said. Parker Thomas walked to the locker room with the rest of the players. He stripped and let steamy water pour over him for a few minutes. He toweled off, got dressed, and returned his Redskins greys to the equipment room. Then he walked across the courtyard to the executive offices.

Tim Palumbo, the team general manager, took the stogie out of his right hand as he held out his hand to Parker.

"Glad to meet you. Have a seat." motioned Palumbo as he pointed toward a black leather wing chair across the desk from him. Palumbo continued: "You graduating in a couple of weeks?"

"Yes, sir." responded Parker.

"Well, the coaches like your size and they think you have some potential. They've authorized me to make you an offer. We would like to sign you to a three-year contract with an option. Twenty-five, Twenty-seven-five, and Thirty."

Parker glanced around the room and saw pictures of players, action shots from big games, and trophies. Everything that caught his eye was a reminder of the glory that went along with the sport. The Redskins had a storied past, and a great tradition. Their philosophy was to trade high round draft choices for All-Pro proven veterans, then fill the rest of the roster with free agents and low round draft choices. Their philosophy was contrary to that of the other teams, which built their squads with unproven high round college draft choices. Parker Thomas knew how fortunate he was to be sitting across from Palumbo that afternoon.

"Well?" said Palumbo as Parker snapped back into the scene before him.

"Yes, sir. Thank you, sir." responded Parker Thomas.

"Just sign the contract in front of you." stated Palumbo. "It's a standard NFL player's contract." Parker Thomas blinked a few times as he reached for a ball point pen. His swollen hands clumsily grasped it as he put the point to the paper. Parker Thomas wrote his name on the dotted line. He was in the penthouse, and the lease was signed.

*Bill Winters and*
*JoAnne V. McGrath*

# HOLD THAT, TIGER!

Five orange and black tassles swung to the rhythm of the bodies walking down the front steps of the Tau Kappa Epsilon frat house. Black graduation gowns flapped crisply as the men wearing them walked toward Ivy University Common for the school's two hundred tenth commencement exercises.

"Looks like the friendships made at Tau Kap are for life, right, Lenny?" stated Parker Thomas.

"You bet! Just think, in a few years you'll need one of my IBM computers to keep track of all the big dollars you'll be hauling in!"

"Yeah, and I can help keep track of all those contracts and endorsements that will come your way!" added Mack Warren.

"Don't forget to hand out my business cards in the locker room." added Lawton Biddle, "You never know when one of your teammates will get his brains bashed out and need a top-notch surgeon to sew them back into his head!" The group laughed as they exchanged quips and walked on to the ceremony. Parker Thomas looked over at Mike Brennan.

"Hey, Brennan," Parker said with a suspicious look on his face, "What's your role in the plan?"

"That's easy," countered Brennan, "I'm gonna be the one who sends out the court orders, confiscates your property, and scrutinizes the books. Of course, that's after I've been named director of the FBI, CIA, or IRS!"

The five continued down the sidewalk and soon saw the neatly aligned rows of seats filled wih classmates, parents, family, and friends. Parker Thomas was now ready to take his place among his graduating class and feel the same pride that the others had. He had hope for his future too. And he knew it wasn't a fluke that the way others on campus spoke to him or treated him was based on the fact that word about his contract with the Washington Redskins had spread rapidly throughout the campus. Debra Metzenbaum, who sat next to him in history class, never gave him a second look when he was a mere college jock with little direction. As Parker passed the last row of students already seated, she arched her back, stuck her chest out as far as she could, and blew a kiss at him through firey red lips to attract his attention. Earlier in the day in the library, Parker ran into Professor McCoy. McCoy not only called Parker by his correct name, but told him that if he ever needed a recommendation, to let him know. Parker wasn't sure if the stodgy old duck really enjoyed writing letters, or if he was fishing for the promise of front row seats for a future Redskins home game. Even Tony Couture had called Parker and invited him to interview on the campus radio station. And Parker's college coaches had called him to tell him how proud they were of him and signed off telling him to go down and kick some ass. People were treating Parker Thomas differently, and he relished the special feeling he got when he encountered others who were aware of his signing with the 'Skins. Ironically, Parker was also uncomfortable with all the attention. He knew, as most of the others did not, that if he did not survive training camp and make the cut, his contract would not be worth the paper it was printed on. That thought haunted his every step and grasped at his every waking breath. To make it as a free agent in the National Football League was a one in a million shot. And Parker knew he was the longest of long-shots. The only way that he could comfortably accept congratulatory handshakes and pats on the back from his friends and other well-wishers was to beat the odds and make the ballclub.

Parker and the other Tau Kaps found their seats and tolerated the ceremony that followed. They arose on cue, lined up, got their sheepskins, returned to their seats and listened with little interest as Ivy's band struck up for one more song.

Parker's four years in college had given him a degree and an academic education second to none. The National Football League would teach him street smarts and pure moxie. It would be harsh, cold reality. There would be no class to teach him how to hit and play with pain. There would be no tutor to push him through the dog days when he was so sore he couldn't get out of bed, but would have to anyway.

When the band stopped, the Chancellor of the University stepped up to the podium and tapped on the microphone.

"This year's final award is to a most deserving student. It is my pleasure to present The Horace Greeley Medal for Self Reliance to a young man who not only contributed to this institution with his athletic ability, but also uplifted the public image of Ivy to the rest of the world when his success was so well publicized in the national press last week. It is my pleasure to congratulate Parker Thomas. Parker, please come up here and receive your award.

Everyone in attendance applauded loudly and cheered as Parker walked to the podium. The chancellor continued: "Mr. Thomas has just signed a contract to play football for the defending NFC Champion Washington Redskins." Parker arrived at the poduim and shook hands with the Chancellor.

"We wish you the best in your career, young man!" Parker nodded acknowledgement, took the medal, and left the stage. As he was returning to his seat, calls came from out of the crowd.

"Way to go, Parker!"

"Kick some butt!"

"Go for it! Make us proud!" Even the staunchiest of academic communities contained rabid football fans.

"Thank you, ladies and gentlemen, for attending our commencement." the Chancellor said, closing the ceremonies. The Band broke out with a chorus or the university's alma mater, and students tossed their mortar boards with orange and black tassles into the air and hugged each other. Parker Thomas walked into the bustle of the crowd, found his mother, picked her up in his two mighty arms and gave her a big kiss.

"Oh Parker, your father would have been so proud of you!" sobbed a beaming Alice Thomas as she tried to hold back her tears. "If only he had lived long enough to be here with you!"

*From the Outhouse to the Penthouse
and Somewhere in Between*

## HUMAN CANNON FODDER

The Rhinegold truck rolled down South Street and pulled up in front of Nick's Bar and Grille. The driver glanced at his order sheet, got out of the vehicle, and went into the restaurant. Behind the bar, Nick Ward was rinsing glasses and putting them upside down on rubber mats.

"Sure you want only three kegs today?" called the driver.

"Better make it four," Nick said, "Game tonight. The crowd will be coming in!" The driver walked back to the truck and snapped down the latch on one of the panels. He gripped the handle on the bottom of one of the roll-up doors, and with the snap of his wrist, the metal shield flipped up. The driver thought about using the dolly, but quickly dismissed the option. He wrapped his arms around one of the silver kegs, squatted slightly, and inhaled. He tightened his muscles around the two hundred pound silver container, locked his fingers between each other and hefted the mass. He turned around, walked into the front door of Nick's Bar and Grille, and across the main dining area.

"Usual spot?" the driver asked.

"Yeah, in the cooler out back!" answered Nick Ward.

The driver carried the keg down past the bathrooms and into the walk-in cooler. He set the keg on the floor and went back to the truck for the other three. When the last keg was in the cooler, the driver went over to the owner so that he could sign the invoice.

"Need to sign this." the driver said as he put a sheet of paper on the bar.

Nick Ward scribbled his name on the paper and handed it to the driver.

"Hey, I know you from somewhere!" said Nick Ward. "I've seen your picture somewhere, in the paper maybe? Yeah, you're that Thomas kid aren't you?"

"Yeah." responded the driver.

"You were with the 'Skins for a while, weren't you?" pressed the owner.

"Yeah," responded Parker.

"I remember reading about you. Things didn't work out for you, did they? Geez, that's too bad."

"Gotta make the rounds." said Parker as he headed back out the door and climbed back up into the cab of the truck.

Parker made five more deliveries that morning before maneuvering the truck up a tight alley and parking it at the back door of Riley's on Canal Street. He opened the emerald green door with the shamrock painted on it and went in.

"Six today, right?" shot Parker to the man in the cardigan sweater who was posed behind the bar.

"Better drop seven. The Giants are playing Dallas tonight." answered Mike Shea. Parker finished the delivery and brought the lading slip to the bar. He put it down in front of Shea.

"Sign." said Parker.

"No problem," answered Shea, "Hey, you want a sandwich or something? The corned beef's real good. Come on, it's on the house."

"Make it on rye, not on the house." Parker answered. Parker took a seat on one of the plastic covered stools that lined the front of the bar, and a minute later Mike Shea emerged from the kitchenette behind the mirrrored wall. He put a plate down in front of Parker.

"Beer?" Shea asked.

"Can't. Driving. How about a coke?

"Sure thing." responded Shea. He grabbed a bottle out of the small stainless steel refrigerator that rested on the floor behind the bar. He set the bottle in front of Parker. Parker picked up the sandwich and took a big bite.

"Good. Nice and lean. Thanks."said Parker.

"Don't use the two-wheeler like the other guys that used to deliver here,huh?"

"Nope." A man two stools away from Parker took a look at him and exclaimed: "Holy Mother of God, but you're a big strapping lad ain't ye?" Parker chewed on his sandwich and ignored the comment.

"My, but your dear mother must have had to milk a lot of cows to get you to such a size as that!" again called the man who was already in his cups.

"Mind your manners now, Buzzie!" said Mike Shea.

"Glory be to God, but isn't this the land of the free?" again injected the barfly. "Can't a man even sit at a local pub and enjoy a pint or two?"

"Better take it easy or you won't make it 'til two o'clock!" admonished Shea. From the end of the bar another voice called out: "Tone it down, Buzzie!"

"What's the problem, can't keep your books unless it's quiet in here?"

"Stuff it, Harp!" half mumbled Jimmy Cooper.

"Hey Jimmy, what's the line on the Giants game tonight?" injected Mike Shea.

"Dallas favored by fourteen and a half. The Giants don't have any running game, and they're gonna fire their head coach. The Doomsday Defense will kick their asses! Do you want in?"

"Give me Dallas five times." Shea answered. The front door opened, and in walked Herb Hanson.

"Afternoon, Mike!" said Hanson.

"Glorious weather for football tonight!"

"How are the supplies, What do you need besides the usual?"

"Give me another box of stirrers and four gross of coasters."

"Got 'em out in the trunk. Be right back." Herb Hanson brought in the additional supplies, laid them on the bar and sat down on the stool between Parker and Buzzie. Mike Shea gave a pull on the tap and set a mug of Guiness down in front of Herb Hanson.

"Thanks, Mike." said Hanson.

"Nothing like a cold one!" said Shea. Hanson lifted the mug, tipped it at the bartender and took a long drink from it.

"Gonna get busy later." Hanson stated. "Monday night football!"

"For sure, and I'm short on help tonight. Need a hand at the door."

"Why don't you ask Golliath there to help you out?" injected Buzzie. "He carries those kegs in. He'd be able to toss the rowdy ones out four at a throw!" Mike Shea and Herb Hanson both looked at Parker.

"Doing anything after work?" Shea shot at Parker.

"Nope." Parker answered.

"You could pick up a couple of extra bucks. Cash money. Better than the three-fifty an hour you make driving that truck." proposed Shea.

"Let me think about it." Parker uncommittingly stated. Herb Hanson was studying Parker.

"Haven't seen you too much. How long you been driving for Rhinegold?"

"About a month."

"You local?"

"Yeah." Parker blankly answered. Hanson looked at the size of Parker's arms.

"Big kid like you, think you'd be playing football or something."

"I did." Shea got in on the conversation.

"What's your name?"

"Parker Thomas."

"Doesn't ring a bell. Who'd you play with?"

"Signed with the 'Skins." answered Parker.

"Hey, I know him," called the bookie at the end of the bar, "He was a one hit wonder!" A silence filled the room. No one was sure what to say next.

"Yeah," Cooper the bookie continued as he directed his next comment straight to Parker, "A real Ivy League candy ass!" Herb Hanson felt Parker's tension as he sat next to him. He watched Parker form a fist and decided to jump in before any real trouble started.

"No shit! You played for the 'Skins?" Herb asked trying to divert Parker's anger, "What happened? How come you're not playing now?"

"I got released."

"Yeah, that's because Butts and Sasquach kicked his ass in camp." added the bookie, "He was human cannon fodder!" Parker didn't respond to the taunt thrown his way. He stared at himself in the mirror behind the bar, relaxed his fist, then turned to Herb Hanson.

"I gave a pretty decent account of myself, but I didn't get much of a chance to play. They had an All-Pro at my spot, and they had veterans and veteran back-ups that they were gonna go with. No rookies made that team."

"Yeah, I know," said Herb, "Washington always goes with the proven veterans. No rookies make their roster, do they?"

"Yeah, one did, but he played in the World Football League with the Birmingham Americans for a couple of years. I played special teams, some center and guard, and I snapped for punts and field goals. I did pretty good. I hung in."

"How does a big guy like you play special teams? I thought that was for fast guys." Herb Hanson asked as he became more interested in Parker's story.

"I snapped for punts and field goals, and I got pretty good at it. When the coach cut me, my offensive line coach told me I should hang it up. Go to law school or something with my Ivy degree. But the head coach, as I was going out, told me that I needed to get a little bigger and stronger and work on my footwork in order to play in the league. The fact that I could snap for punts and field goals would give me an outside chance of making the league next year. The coach told me that a lineman who could snap and play more than one position on the offensive line was a valuable asset to a team. I played some center, too, and I think that's my best position. Played it when I was a kid. The coach said to me, 'the more you can do keeps you around'."

"You kind of remind me of my best friend in college," said Hanson, "He got drafted in the fourth round by San Diego. Leo Fanucci. He was an All-American quarterback and he had all the tools. He got released because Fouts was 'the man', and they had a former number one backing him up. The third string quarterback, he could punt, play wide receiver and play special teams, so they kept him and released Leo. The coach wasn't bullshitting when he said, 'the more you can do'. You know what my advice is to you, kid? Give it another try. Leo never did, and he's regretted it even to this day, even though he's done pretty well for himself in the insurance business. You have the rest of your life to drive a beer truck, if that's what you want to do, but you only have one shot at being young and in good shape. You should take it."

Hanson's words hit Parker in the gut. For the past two months he had been living at home and just going through the motions. He was just beginning to get back to life and to shed the numbness he felt for over a month.

"Where are you staying right now?" Hanson asked Parker and snapped him back into the real world.

"With my mom." replied Parker.

"Sounds like real fun!" said Herb sarcastically.

"She's cool. I've just been in kind of a funk since I was released, and she was concerned because I was pretty beat up when I came home. She's a little disappointed that I took this job and that I'm not on Wall Street working as a banker, or something, but she knows I'll eventually get my act together and get on with my life."

"Well, listen, here's my card." said Herb as he slid an engraved Crown Distributors business card across to Parker, "I got a room in my basement that a guy's moving out of later this month. He's a rep for a sporting goods company and got transferred. I live just behind the high school practice field. If you're interested, it's twenty-five bucks a week, cash. And you'd be close to where you could work out if you wanted to. They got a gym down the street so you can build yourself up and get bigger and stronger. Did you lift a lot in college?"

"A little, but all they had was a universal, and it was always being used…" Before Parker could say any more, the sound of breaking glass came from Herb Hanson's other side. Buzzie O'Keefe had fallen off his barstool and landed ass down on the wooden floor in front of the bar.

"Whoa! Buzzie! What's going on? Are you all right?" asked Mike Shea, "What are you making such a commotion for?!" A stunned but unhurt Buzzie O"Keefe pulled himself up and steadied himself on the bar.

"Don't know what in the hell they're putting into that Rhinegold these days, but whatever it is, it sure packs a hell of wallop with me after a few pints!"

Buzzie O'Keefe took a few steps, swayed, and then staggered out the front door.

"Knew he wouldn't make it until two o'clock!" bragged Jimmy Cooper from the end of the bar. "Pay up, Shea, you owe me ten bucks!" Mike Shea pulled a ten spot out of the register and laid it on the bar in front of Cooper.

"Thanks for the advice and for the card, Mr. Hanson." Parker said as he got up, put out his hand, and got ready to return to the truck.

"Give me a call!" said Hanson as he returned Parker's handshake.

Parker walked back out into the alley and closed the green shamrocked door. Back in the bar, the conversation continued. Cooper the bookie shot a comment at Herb Hanson: "What are you giving that kid delusions of grandeur for? He's gonna be nothing but human cannon fodder!"

"You never know," Herb mused, "You just never know." Herb Hanson had seen the fire in Parker Thomas' eyes before he left the bar.

*Bill Winters and
JoAnne V. McGrath*

## **STUCK IN THE OUTHOUSE**

Parker Thomas hit the button on the top of the alarm clock when it rang at six thirty in the morning. He got out of bed, went downstairs, slugged down a quick glass of orange juice and the headed off to work. The chill in the air that late October morning was a direct reflection of the cold atmosphere in the house. Despite his mother's well-intentioned attempts to network interviews for Parker and spur him into the white collar world, Parker stuck to his routine of driving the Rhinegold truck. Day after day he carried keg after keg with every delivery he made. The routine carried him through the days, and somehow the days had become months. Most of these days blurred into others, but Parker was a little more upbeat this Tuesday because it was the last one in the month and he knew that Herb Hanson would be at Riley's on Canal Street during the lunch hour.

Parker made his morning deliveries and once again rolled the beer truck into the back alley and next to the emerald green door. After confirming the order with Mike Shea, Parker went back out to the alley and snapped open the roll-up door on the side of the truck. Just as he had locked his hands around a silver keg and was ready to lift it, he felt the butt of a gun in the middle of his back.

"Stick 'em up, mister! Stick 'em up!" Don't turn around or I'll shoot!"

"There's more than one of us, so don't try anything funny!" said a second voice. Parker had to think fast. Before the hold up men could say another word, Parker, with all his might, whirled around and slammed the keg to the ground. The metal hitting the pavement made a thunderous clang, and the pressure of the impact caused the beer to spew out of the top of the keg. Caught off guard by Parker's quick response and the cascades of beer in the air, the would-be stick-up men took off. They bolted around the corner and down the street before Parker could wipe the beer out of his eyes and give chase. The only evidence that remained to let Parker know that the event had really happened was the black plastic Luger that lay on the pavement next to the rear wheel of the truck.

"Son of bitch!" thought Parker to himself, "Glad it was just punks and that nothing happened." Parker bent over and picked up the gun. The commotion in the alley had attracted the attention of the bar patrons, and Mike Shea and Jimmy Cooper came rushing out the back door.

"What the hell's going on?!?" querried a breathless Shea.

"Just the Canal Street gang." said Parker, playing down the incident.

"Is that a gun in your hand?" asked JImmy Cooper.

"No, it's a four leaf clover!" quipped back Parker, trying to appear collected.

"Glad you're all right." said Shea, "Come on in and get some lunch!" The three men went back into Riley's Pub and took their usual spots at the bar. Just as Parker and Cooper sat down, Herb Hanson walked in the front door.

"What happened to you?" he said to Parker when he noticed that Parker's hair was soaking wet. "Shea put in a double order or something?"

"Canal Street gang is at it again, Herb." volunteered Cooper from the end of the bar. "They tucked it to your friend here in the back alley with a toy squirt gun! Better check the back of his pants. Might need to change him!" Two other patrons in a booth laughed, and Parker ignored the barb that came from the bookie.

"Is that right?" asked Herb as he sat next to Parker.

"No big deal." said Parker, "But they did have me going there for a second."

"Well, that would make an interesting headline: EX-FOOTBALL PLAYER ROBBED BY KIDS IN BACK ALLEY FOR A KEG OF BEER. Is that what they're going to put on your tombstone, Parker?" joked Herb.

Although Parker knew the comment was made as an attempt at humor, Herb Hanson's words again hit home with him.

Parker didn't spend a lot of time socializing, and quickly finished his lunch.

"Thanks for the sandwich, Mike." said Parker as he got up to leave. "Running behind in the rounds today. Gotta go." Parker grabbed the black plastic Luger that rested in front of him on the bar and walked out the back door. He got back into the truck, and made the rest of his deliveries. Then he went home for dinner.

"Got any more milk, Ma?" asked Parker as he stuffed a chicken leg into his mouth. Alice Thomas got up, went to the refrigerator and returned to the table with a half gallon of milk. She sat down in her usual spot and looked across the table at her son. Parker knew what was coming, so he ate as fast as he could, hoping to escape to the solace of his bedroom as quickly as possible following the meal. Alice Thomas cleared her throat with a little cough and began: "I got a call today from Mrs. Fairbanks, you remember her, don't you, she and I were on the booster club committee when you and Donny, her boy, played on the Rhinos together. Anyway, she told me that Donny was working for this cosmetics company and that he needed another assistant on his sales staff. He's the Vice President of Sales now for Pearl Stick Lipstick Company. I told her that you were looking around, and that with your credentials from Ivy, you might like to look into it. I think that would be a good job for you, Parker, out in the world in a suit and tie, talking to people and doing something nice. You might even meet a nice girl when you make your sales calls. What do you think? I told her you'd give Donny a call tomorrow."

Parker downed the rest of the milk in his glass and stood up.

"Yeah, Ma, I'll think about it. I'm going upstairs now. Good night." Parker Thomas walked down the hall and trudged up to the second floor. He flipped on the light switch, threw himself down onto his bed, and mashed his head into a pillow. After letting out a deep sigh, Parker reached over to the nightstand beside the bed and switched on his stereo. Jimi Hendrix deep voice came from the speakers "ALL ALONG THE WATCHTOWER, LIFE IS NOTHING BUT A JOKE. TWO MEN WERE APPROACHING…" The irony of the day rushed back at Parker Thomas as he picked up the squirt gun and shot a stream of water across the room at the Redskins poster on the wall.

He got up off the bed, pulled a card from his wallet, and walked down the stairs. He went to the small table on the side of the front hall, picked up the phone, and dialed.

"Herb, this is Parker. Is that room still available? Yeah? Yes. Tonight." Parker Thomas went back upstairs, packed as much as he could into a duffle bag, and walked out of the front door.

Bill Winters and
JoAnne V. McGrath

## IT HAS TO BE ALL OR NOTHING

A mattress on a wooden platform. One bureau. An unshaded lightbulb dangling from a chain in the middle of the ceiling. The spartan room in the basement of Herb Hanson's house served as a constant reminder to Parker Thomas that without football, his life would be empty. He would no longer allow himself to be cradled in a comfort zone. There was no time to delay his dream.

"Hey Parker," Herb called out, "Are you going to be doing any running today?"

"Yeah, I'm gonna run a couple of miles around the cross country course at the high school."

"Hey, I'll go with you. Give me about ten minutes to change and put on some running shoes."

As Parker Thomas and Herb Hanson bounded over the cross country course together, Herb motioned to Parker. He pointed off to his left.

"Hey, Parker, look at that! I betcha that thing would really get you bigger, stronger, and faster, and give you that foot work the Redskins said you needed. Parker's eyes went right over to a rusted one man blocking sled that lay of to the side.

"Yeah, that thing's a bitch! It always separates the pretenders from the contenders. Screw this twelve-minute run thing. Call me when it's fourth and one!"

"Maybe you need to use that sled in your drills." Herb suggested.

"Well, it doesn't have a pad on it."

"Screw it! We can always get a pad."

"Well, I'd need somebody to bark out the cadence and stay on me when I'm on that thing." Parker said. "If I'm gonna make that piece of equipment work for me, I've got to have a trainer. Somebody out there that will push me when I'm sucking it up. I also gotta find somebody to snag a hundred punts and field goal snaps a day. Someone to record my snap time and my forty time. I can't find anybody to do that either." Herb and Parker ran on for a few more yards.

"Well, I'd be willing to work with you a few afternoons a week."

"Nah, Herb. No disrespect intended, but I've got to find someone who's willing to work with me every day, twice a day. Time me in my sprints, crack the whip on me when I'm on the sled. Catch the ball when I snap. Push me hard in conditioning drills. I was gonna run an ad in the paper and offer a hundred bucks a week and a percentage of my signing bonus as incentive."

"What percentage?" Herb asked.

"I don't know, depends on the size of the bonus."

"Let me go you one better. I'll represent you and take five percent of whatever you sign for. We'll train in the morning and again after I get home from work."

"You got a deal!" Parker blurted out. "I don't need an agent, just someone to take the calls from the ball clubs. There's no negotiating. They tell you what they're gonna pay you. Unless you're a top first or second round pick, you don't need an agent. Now, Herb, I'll go you one better! This is gonna be four months of two-a-days, six days a week until those free agent try-outs in April. You're gonna earn your five percent. I have to give it everything I have. I don't want to be some old man sitting back on a park bench feeding birds and wondering 'what if…'! I have to prepare like a heavyweight boxer getting ready for his title shot! It HAS to be ALL or NOTHING!! The only time I feel alive is when I'm playing football, and I don't want to be dead! Are you in or out?!? Everything I've ever done in my life, the years at Ivy, all those hours of practice and training, I've GOT to make them pay off!"

"You gotta be fuckin' kidding me!" said Herb. "You're insane!"

"Listen, this is my last time around! I've got to shit or get off the pot! I've got to get out of the damned outhouse!!"

## STAYING ALIVE

"First down!" the ref called, "First and goal."

"Huddle up!" Parker Thomas yelled at the team gathered around him. On one knee, the quarterback leaned into the huddle.

"Red right. Thirty base. On two. Ready? Break!"

Parker snapped the ball, fired out and slammed into the huge defensive tackle over him, knocking the tackle back as the back skirted through the huge hole opened up by Parker at the point of attack. The back ran virtually untouched for a few yards before being slammed to the ground by a huge pile of defensive players just short of the goal line.

"Way to go up front!" yelled Thompson, the quarterback. "Double tight. Double tight. Red right. Motion. Thirty base. On one. Ready? Break!"

"Red eighty. Red eighty. Set! HUT!"

Parker snapped the ball and fired out low, as the submarining defensive lineman tried to take away the territory. The back half-leapt into the air and landed on his feet. He scored standing up and virtually untouched.

"Touchdown!" signalled and called the ref.

*Bill Winters and
JoAnne V. McGrath*

The Giants had just taken a ten to seven lead over the Jets with about twenty seconds to go. It was the last exhibition game before the start of the regular season, and Parker had gone all the way at center. Even though it was an exhibition game, the intra-city rivalry had the stadium packed. Both teams were playing balls out because the regular season would begin in a week. This game was the final tune-up.

"Extra point. Extra point. On the hand signal." barked the back-up quarterback as Parker broke from the huddle and positioned himself to make the snap. The ball pumped right through the middle of the uprights. As Parker Thomas ran toward the sidelines, he could hear the shouts of the Giants players: "Way to go, offensive line, way to go!" The Giants had just taken the ball eighty-seven yards in fifteen plays to score the go-ahead touchdown and leave the Jets with almost no time left on the clock.

As Parker headed toward the bench, he was bombarded by players who were yelling out and high-fiving one another.

"Way to go, O-line! Way to kick some ass!" Parker made his way through the crowd of congratulatory and celebrating bodies, and took his position on the bench where the offensive linemen always sat. Coach Patten, the line coach, knelt down in front of the men who had just come off the field and said: "That's a great job, offensive line!" Before he could say anything else, the head coach leaned his face into the players and yelled: "Good job! Offensive line, Good job! That's the way to go up front!" The pure emotion and elation that had come with the victory let Parker know that this was what it was all about. As the Giants' kickoff team squibbed the ball down the field in an effort to prevent a return, Parker knew he had come all the way. His mind flashed back to the countless conditioning drills and sled work he had done that had gotten him to this point. He had beaten the odds: he had been a free agent walk-on and had come virtually out of nowhere to become the starting center. He had secured a spot in the NFL only after putting his body through almost unendurable workouts; he was now the bigger, stronger, faster football player with the footwork he needed. Herb had even tied a three and a half foot rope around Parker's ankles when he worked on the sled in order to teach Parker the footwork and balance he needed. There had been nothing pretty about the four months of training. It had been a test of will.

Three. Two. One. The gun went off. As Parker bounded across the field to congratulate the opposing team, he was overwhelmed by a wave of emotion he had never felt before. Rocky Balboa didn't have anything on him that day! The Giants went into the locker room. The team discarded their pads and helmets, and formed around Coach McEllroy to listen to his post-game speech.

"That was a great job out there today, men! If we take one game at a time and play like we did today, we can make the playoffs." Jim McEllroy was a medium-sized, square-jawed man. He was a rookie head coach in the NFL, and he had just taken a Giants team with a handful of veterans, selected free agents from the defunct World Football League, a couple of high round draft picks, and one free agent walk-on, and had gotten them off to a three and one start in the pre-season. Everybody knew that the pre-season didn't mean shit, but for a team that had a dismal record the year before, it was an auspicious beginning with new players. Coach McEllroy had come from the defunct Memphis franchise in the World Football League, where the team had had a seventeen and two record and had won the league's title the year before.

Parker and Herb Hanson had gone to the Giants' free agent camp in late April, and Parker had blown the Giants' coaching staff away. Parker had run a blazing 4.9 forty, weighed in at 295, and was one of the strongest guys on the team, having bench pressed 225 pounds 26 times. He had bench pressed 405 pounds. The coach, after having witnessed Parker's performance at that camp and having watched Parker snap back frozen ropes on punts and fieldgoals, had pulled Parker aside at the camp and said to him: "You're gonna be my starting center." Parker Thomas had defied the odds and was delivering both for himself and for the head coach and the team. There had been nothing pretty about how he had gotten there. He had survived six weeks of two-a-days, four exhibition games, countless inter-squad scrimmages and inside drills, and four months of his own personal camp with Herb Hanson to rise up in this gruelling war of attrition. He had become a starter in the National Football League. He was in the penthouse, and the feeling that rushed through his body was one of unbelievable elation and joy. It was more intense than anything he had ever experienced or anticipated feeling. Parker started to cry with joy.

"Men, relax tonight, take it easy. Be back here tomorrow at nine sharp for some light running and stretching before we go to watch the film." finished Coach McEllroy as he dismissed the players. Parker headed for the showers. He dried off and shaved, and planned to meet Herb Hanson after the game.

"Hey, what's going on?" called one of the players.

"There's a party at The Fireside, around the corner from the hotel." answered another player.

"See you all there!" the first returned. Parker walked through the players' exit and was met by Herb Hanson and his girlfriend Jennifer, Cooper, Buzzie, Mike Shea, and another girl.

"Let's go to The Fireside! They have a buffet there for the players and their guests. We'll sit down and eat, and just relax." Parker said to the crew.

"To hell with the roast beef and chicken, have they got Guiness on tap?" querried Buzzie.

"I wanna meet some of them dames that hang around the players!" chimed in Cooper. Herb Hanson turned to Parker and said, "Parker, this is Tracey, a friend of Jennifer's."

"Nice to meet you, Tracey." said Parker.

"That was a great game today, Parker." beamed Tracey, "This is the first Giants' game I've ever been to. It was awesome! You were awesome!"

"Thanks." said Parker. He smiled back at Tracey and looked into her excited eyes.

"Let's go!" chimed in Mike Shea. "I want to check out the downtown competition!"

The group walked down the street and up to the front door of The Fireside. There was a long line waiting to get in, and an area was roped off to keep back the crowd. When Parker Thomas and his guests approached, one of the team assistants nodded, and the maitre d' snapped the clip on the end of the rope.

"Great game today! Have a good time!" the maitre d' said as Parker and his friends walked into the main banquet room. Crystal chandeliers hung from the ceiling, and the walls were done in Mediterranean Rococo. Gilded sconces lined the walls, and the plush red carpet was so thick it felt as if it were sinking with every step made on it. The room was jammed with players, coaches and staff, guests, and a few select members of the press. Girls, lots of them, dressed in Giants' fan regalia filled out the backdrop.

Cooper elbowed Mike Shea: "Do you believe this? Not exactly like the bar on Canal Street, is it?"

"I guess not!" said Shea back to his wide-eyed friend.

"And Mike, look at all those broads! I've never seen so many good looking women in one place before, not even in the Miss America contest on TV! Look at the knockers on that one in the blue and white dress!" drooled Cooper.

"Ain't got a bad pair of pins, either!" quipped back Mike Shea.

"There's our table, number five," said Parker to his guests. "Let's go!"

As the party of close friends enjoyed their meal, the thrust of the conversation focused on the day's game. Often their words were interrupted by a fan or two who approached the table either to congratulate Parker on the game or by someone who wanted an autograph. Despite all the activity, from time to time Parker Thomas would lean back in his chair, glancing out at the almost surrealistic scene in front of him. He would be getting his last pre-season paycheck the next day, and he revelled in the fact that he was going to be paid a lot more money in the future than the three hundred dollars a week he made during training camp. He couldn't wait to get his own place and put himself in some surroundings that would make him feel better than the basement apartment.

"How lucky could a guy be?" Parker mused to himself, "Playing for the hometown team, being here with old friends who had watched him make it this far, and with new friends on the team."

The Giants would announce their roster the following day, and although Parker knew he had made the team, he wondered who the last five players that would be cut that night would be. The final cut was always a brutal twenty-four hours. A few players were on the bubble; they were good enough to play in the league, but would be cut anyway because the ball club had to carry forty-three guys on the roster. The cuts could become extremely political as coaches fought among themselves to keep their players from getting the axe. Factors such as a player's versatility to play more than one position, where they had been drafted, how much money they were making, their age, and what kind of camp they had had, as well as their performance on the field, all entered into the equation. Sometimes it was blatently obvious who would be cut; other times it was a complete surprise. No one ever really knew for sure, and it would be a nervous and tension-packed twenty-four hours after the game. Often, a player could be released, picked back up within twenty-four hours and resigned, many times to a lower contract, or put on a two-man taxi squad. Or a player could be traded to another ball club, be hidden out on injured reserve, or just flat out released. No one really ever knew what the coaches were thinking, as the coaches made roster moves to try to put a better product out on the field. There was no security in the National Football League unless a player was a top draft choice with money invested in him. And even then, the league only gave that player a year or two to produce and measure up to justify their investment. If a player was a free agent, his skills had to show quickly to get attention.

So Parker Thomas took an even greater appreciation for his position that day, knowing that he had made the ball club. He had started all the pre-season games, beating out a veteran who had been traded to another team. Parker could start at center, back-up or start at guard or tackle, snap for punts and field goals, and even play tight end on short yardage and goal line if need be. Because of his versatility, he felt secure in a roster spot. The Giants might keep eight linemen, as opposed to nine, which would allow them to keep an extra player in another position. It probably would be a 'skilled player', one that could score points.

As Parker Thomas lay in bed later that night, he thought of the pocket full of phone numbers some of the women, including Tracey, had handed to him during the banquet, and he drifted off to sleep. He revelled in the fact that he would be the starter in the Giants' first regular season game. He had worked extremely hard physically, and even had negotiated his own contract and secured the signing bonus that he and Herb had trained so hard for.

"Ironic," thought Parker. "Even though they were hot to sign me and had called me several times at Herb's and even had tried to get to me through my mother, we still had to hold out for a month to get the signing bonus that Herb and I had asked for! Management hadn't relented until the day before mini camp late in May, when the coaches put pressure on management to get me in so that coaches would have adequate time for me to learn the offense and their new system."

Parker had been smart enough not to use an agent, remembering what Mr. Palumbo had told him the year before: "You have no bargaining power – sign the contract and be glad to get what you're getting!"

Parker knew that no matter how good a player was, that unless he was in a position with leverage, a club would sign him for as little as they could. The four weeks of training camp with the 'Skins, and all the gruelling workouts had drummed the college 'rah rah' right out of him and reduced Parker to feeling like he was a play-for-pay independent contractor hitting-machine working for a business that was called a team. Parker knew it would be tough business to stay in the penthouse. It was very difficult for a player to maneuver himself into a position to get what he deserved. With the injury factor, the fact that a career lasted only three years on average, the politics of the draft and money, and the time it took a player to establish himself as an important part of a team, the odds were always stacked in management's favor.

*Bill Winters and
JoAnne V. McGrath*

# ALIVE AND WELL

"Now introducing the starting offensive line-up for the New York Giants!" blurted out the announcer on the public address system. Parker Thomas stood in the tunnel waiting for his name to be called. His vision blurred as he choked back tears of incredible joy. When he heard his name and he ran out onto the field in front of seventy-five thousand cheering and screaming fans, he was overcome with complete and thorough ecstasy. Adrenalin pumped through his every muscle. The game was being played for real, and would count in the standings.

The Cardinals kicked off, and Moore, the Giants' return man, brought the ball to the Giants' twenty. As Parker Thomas ran out onto the field, he felt a tremendous wrenching and nausea in the pit of his stomach, but it quickly subsided as the quarterback spoke: "Red right. Sixteen. Wham. G. O. On two. Ready? Break!" Parker set himself up on the line of scrimmage. The Cardinal defensive lineman was not as big as guys Parker had worked against with the Giants in pre-season and with the 'Skins. The quarterback barked out the cadence. Parker glanced at the defensive tackle that he was to fold down and block while the backside guard pulled. Parker snapped the ball and fired out, and made a good hit and block on the defensive tackle. The back took the hand-off and ran around the right end for a nice eight yard gain. Parker's one hit got rid of the butterflies and calmed him down.

Late in the fourth quarter, with a minute and a half to go in the game, the Cardinals fumbled the ball on their own forty. The game was tied. Thompson, the quarterback, on the second play from scrimmage, had thrown the ball downfield and completed the ball to the thirty-five yard line. The Giants were within field goal range, and had a shot at winning the game. The Cardinals had no time-outs left, so the Giants ran three meaningless running plays in order to wind down the clock. Parker nervously waited with anticipation, as he would be the one snapping the ball for the winning field goal. As the coaches wound the clock down, head coach McEllroy finally signalled a time-out; there were three seconds left on the clock.

"Field goal team. Field goal team." he called. The field goal team bounded out onto the field and took their position in the huddle. This was what it was all about and what made Parker love the game. "The films didn't lie – If you beat your opponent, it was there for everyone to see. You would either kick the ball through the uprights and be heroes, or shank the kick and be a goat. In no other venue of life was there such instant gratification or instant misery. The only thing that could compare to that was sex," thought Parker, whose thoughts then turned to Tracey, whom he had a date with that night.

As the ball sailed through the uprights and time expired, all the players came running onto the field in celebration. What a win, and what a way to start the season. The Giants had played shabbily in the first half, and even though their ground game was strong, they killed themselves with penalties: a game that should have been more one-sided had become a close contest decided by a field goal.

As the snapper for punts and field goals, and even though he had snapped hundreds of times in practice, nothing would have prepared him for snapping in a real game in front of seventy-five thousand cheering onlookers, with the game on the line and the Cardinals coming hell-bent for leather. The intensity of the rush and the flailing of out-stretched and out-laid bodies, as well as the violent collisions, made the task of snapping the ball a thousand times more difficult than in practice. As the referee, with his out-stretched hands, signalled that the field goal was good, Parker Thomas heaved a huge sigh of relief. A bolt of confidence flew through him. He had executed a good snap with the game on the line, and had had several running plays run over him during the course of the game. Parker had delivered. He looked forward to his date with Tracey after the game. He was once again alive, and well.

*From the Outhouse to the Penthouse
and Somewhere in Between*

\* \* \* \* \* \* \*

Looking across the candle lit table at Parker, Tracey dabbed the sides of her mouth with a pink linen napkin and and set it down next to her plate. She took another sip from her chianti and smiled. She ran the tip of her tongue across her top lip and set her glass back on the table.

"My, that lasagna was wonderful!" Tracey beamed.

"I'm glad you enjoyed it so much!" said Parker.

"And this is such a lovely place to eat, too." commented Tracey as she looked across the room at the strolling violinist. The virtuoso caught Tracey's eye, and walked over to the table where Parker and Tracey were sitting. He played a few bars of Santa Lucia, looking for Parker's approval to continue and hinting at the tip that would be forthcoming. Parker nodded back at the gypsy-like fiddler, and his melodic vibratto filled the air where the young couple sat. When the song ended, Parker pulled out his wallet. He did a quick count – "forty-five dollars left," he thought to himself, as he pressed a five spot into the musician's palm.

"This place is so romantic! It reminds me of the time my mom took me to The Metropolitan Opera to see 'Carmen'. Have you ever been to the opera, Parker?" Tracey blinked her eyes and waved long dark lashes at Parker Thomas.

"I went once, in college, but couldn't really get into it." Parker responded.

"Maybe we could go sometime, together," hinted Tracey. "The costumes are so beautiful, and the scenery is fantastic. You feel like you're in a fairy tale when you're there. Everyone looks so awesome! I just love their lavish clothes!" Before Parker could say anything, a waiter came to their table and scooped up Tracey's silver casserole dish and the plate underneath it.

"Dessert, Madame?" the waiter inquired.

"I'll have the spumoni." Tracey answered.

"And for you, sir?"

"No thanks." said Parker, "Just another glass of water."

In a few minutes the waiter returned with the ice cream and set it on the table in front of Tracey.

"Don't you think this is just the prettiest dessert?" asked Tracey as she swirled her fork into the pink, green, and white treat in front of her.

"It's nice." said Parker dryly, and then he took another gulp from his water glass.

"Are you sure you're not hungry, Parker? After using up all that energy in the game today, all you ate was a salad. How can you play that hard and not be as hungry as a bear?"

"I suppose I'm just used to the training regimen I was on for so long. Can't really eat a lot until the next day." gulped Parker as he grabbed the glass and threw more water down his throat. The waiter returned to the table and placed a silver dish next to Parker.

"I'll bring that up for you sir, whenever you're ready." the waiter said.

"Will you excuse me, please, for a minute?" Tracey asked. "I'm going to the powder room." Tracey slid out of the booth and winked at Parker as she got up.

"Be right back!" Parker swallowed hard and turned over the bill. Thirty-one seventy-nine. 'Gratuity not included' was printed in bold type at the bottom.

"Got it made," Parker thought to himself, as he remembered the valet parking claim check in his pocket. Parker took thirty-five dollars out of his wallet and put it on the little silver tray. The waiter came over, scooped up the tray and money, and brought it up to the front of the restaurant to the cashier.

"You should see the mirrors in the bathrooms, they go floor to ceiling!" Tracey said as she slid back into the booth across from Parker. "And the faucets on the marble sinks are gold, and only have one handle!"

"They probably don't have mirrors like that in the men's room!" Parker quipped as he noticed that Tracey had put on new lipstick, and the scent of her newly freshened Estee Lauder wafted across the table at him.

The light of the candles reflected in Tracey's earrings, and made them sparkle with each movement of her head. They were dainty flowers of clustered rhinestones set with a single blue stone in the middle. The blue was the exact same color as her eyes.

"Flowers, sir?" asked a young lady standing at the side of the table and carrying a wicker basket filled wih long-stemmed red roses.

"Oh Parker, they smell so nice!" said Tracey. Parker plucked a single red rose out of the basket and presented it to Tracey. He dug out his wallet and pressed a five spot into the flower vendor's hand.

The waiter returned to the table with the change and stood there. Obviously the three dollars and twenty-one cents that lay on the little silver tray was deemed insufficient by the man in the black cumberbund. Parker took his last five-dollar bill from his wallet and put it on the tray.

"Thank you so very much, sir. Have a pleasant evening, sir," said the waiter who disappeared before Parker could scoop up the three dollars and twenty-one cents from the tray.

"How the hell will I get the car from the valet now?" Parker thought to himself, "and what about the coat?" Parker remembered he had given Tracey's coat to the check room attendant.

"I think I'll go to the men's room, Tracey." said Parker. "Why don't you take this coat check, get your jacket, and I'll pull the car up front for you," said a desperate Parker Thomas as he remembered the pile of change he had squirreled away in his ashtray in the Mustang. Parker was thankful that he had never taken up cigarette smoking.

"See you out front, Tracey!" he said as he shot up from the table and headed for the swinging door that had a top hat on it. When he saw Tracey look down at the booth seat to find her clutch purse, Parker did a quick about face and, valet ticket in hand, headed out the front door. The valet brought the car around, and Parker jumped in, pulled the ashtray from its holding clips and dumped all the change into the waiting attendant's hand.

"Thank you, sir!" the valet said with an amused look on his face. Tracey emerged from the front door and Parker held open the passenger side door for her.

"Care for some tunes?" Parker said as he drove, "Lady's choice! Check the tapes in the glove box and pick out the one you like." Tracey picked a few casettes out of the glove box, very quickly dismissed Parker's favorites, and handed Parker a Roy Orbison tape.

"I like this one," Tracey said as she handed Parker the tape.

"Pretty Woman it shall be!" said Parker as he popped the casette into the dashboard player and hit the play button.

Tracey flipped her blonde hair over her shoulder and snuggled into her seat in anticipation of the romantic ride.

Parker turned up the volume on the player, but no sound came out. He took the tape out, looked at it, and put it back in the player. He hit the button again, and still no music came from the player.

"Darned thing!" said Parker. He pulled the casette out of the player and strands of crinkled audio tape spewed out.

"We don't need any music, anyway." said Tracey, trying to help and adjusting her short skirt on her thighs.

"I'll get the tape player fixed next week." said Parker, attempting to make the best of the situation.

"Why not just get another car with those quad speakers, Parker? You're a professional football player! You can afford to treat yourself now."

Tracey had no idea of the reality of Parker's money situation. Even though Parker had been living at home and in Herb Hanson's basement, and had worked driving truck, he hadn't been able to save any money. He was making modest car payments on a used vehicle, and the money he had left, he had invested in his training. Between the vitamins, protein power shakes, huge quantities of food, and equipment he needed to get himself into shape, there wasn't any money left to tuck away. The offer of the room from Herb had been a God send, in a way, because he had felt guilty about the fact that his mother had to get by on a widow's pension and he had dutifully given her fifty dollars a week, even after he had moved out, to help her out. Sure, he was a professional football player, but he wasn't a player with a hundred thousand dollar signing bonus in the bank. The five thousand dollar bonus he had received had been a disappointment. A third came off the top and went to Uncle Sam. As promised, Parker cut a check for five hundred dollars to Herb Hanson, even though Herb tried to decline the check. The rest went to student loan payments, back bills incurred while training and day to day expenses. Parker couldn't wait to pick up his first game check the next day so that he could really feel like a pro. He couldn't help but feel the irony that he had played a large part in the day's win, yet his checking account was nearing zero balance. Here he was, in the penthouse, and he didn't have the money to pay for the utilities, let alone the maid service. He also knew that while the checks would roll in during the season, he had to be cautious because the league offered no guarantee against catastrophe, and the checks only came in for sixteen weeks. He still had to think of the off-season and the money he would need to make it through. There was no room for 'fluff' in Parker Thomas' budget. There was hardly even a budget to begin with. Parker realized that there was a class system in pro football. "You had the one or two players coming every year who were proven college players and had been given large signing bonuses in order to start feeling right away what it was like to be a professional football player. They came in the front door to the penthouse. Then there were the others, the players, who had to fight, kick, scratch and claw to get in through the back door. Both doors led to the the same place, but the back door was definitely the harder to open and kept players in fear. That fear would hopefully go away with the next fifteen weeks of the season."

Parker dismissed the negative notion, like all good football players do by minimizing the negative or minimizing an injury. He was just happy to be alive in the moment. Parker's dream was coming true, and the realities and ironies of pro football would not chip away at his positive outlook for the rest of the season.

A voice called from the bedroom: "Parker, can you come in here for a minute?" called Tracey. Parker Thomas walked into the bedroom and found Tracey naked and prone on the bed.

"Let me rub you down and make you feel better, Parker. You've had a hard day."

Parker Thomas dropped his clothes and joined Tracey on the bed.

"How about if I start at your shoulders and work my way down?" Tracey asked, "Just tell me when to stop." Parker Thomas didn't say another word all that night.

## MASH 737

As the film projector rolled, showing the Giants' win over Philadelphia the day before, the entire mood in the film room was upbeat. The Giants were four and one, and a game out of the division lead. They were the turn around team of the league, and no one was taking them lightly. Dallas sat at the top of the division at 5 and 0, and if the Giants could go down and beat Dallas, they would have a share of the division lead. The mood was strong that the Giants were coming together and playing some solid football on both sides of the ball. This was the first time the team had watched the film together. Normally they had broken into offensive and defensive rooms to watch the films. The coaches had brought them all together to watch the film as a team to reward them for their sterling effort against Philly and to further develop the concept of 'team' that this gutty ballclub had demonstrated the previous five weeks. The team watched as the defense intercepted the ball and ran it back eighty yards for the winning touchdown just as Philadelphia was going in for the touchdown that would have iced the game for them. As Parker watched the film and applauded the plays made by the defense, he looked down at his right hand and saw all the skin gouged out of his knuckles, and the purple nails on some of his fingers. He couldn't help but think how it looked like hamburger. On his left hand he saw the thin athletic tape wrapped around his pinkie and ring finger. Parker had come back from one of the running plays late in the ball game and looked down as his hand rested on his knee and saw his pinkie flapping loose from his knuckle. He silently chuckled when he thought about how he had flipped up the pinkie and quickly taped it back up to his other finger so that he could complete the game. He looked down at his shin and saw the one and a half inch deep hole where he had been kicked accidentally by a defensive lineman two weeks before. It would take six to seven months to heal. The big toe on his fight foot ached along with a huge black toenail that had festered. He had huge turf burns on his elbows, and a gash that wouldn't heal across the top of his right hand. The bridge of his nose had a deep gouge from all the helmet to helmet impacts during vicious inside running plays. Parker even remembered back to the game where he had pulled down the line to block for a quick screen and had peeled back to collide with a fanatical pursuing middle linebacker. The collision had left him feeling like his teeth had literally been powdered from the impact. He could taste little pieces of teeth in his mouthpiece.

But somehow, it had all been worth it. The Giants were going for the division lead, Parker was banking his money, and these injuries were nothing compared to the love of being with the team both on and off the field.

The coach turned on the lights, and then he paused for a few seconds. He began: "Men, we have Dallas this week." The words hit Parker Thomas like a piece of raw steak in front of a rabid and starving dog. Parker Thomas was alive and living his dream.

\* \* \* \* \* \* \*

The gun went off to end the first overtime. The Giants and Dallas were going into the second overtime tied seventeen and seventeen. The game had been a virtual standoff due to the oppressive 120 degree heat on the astro-turf that day. Players had been dropping like flies due to dehydration. As the Giants went into the second overtime, they had five healthy linemen left out of the eight they had brought with them on the travel team, and two of them were back-ups. One of the linemen had gone down with a knee, and the other two from heat prostration. Parker could not come out of the game, like the others had during the game; due to injuries up front, he was the only one left who could snap the ball.

Dallas took the opening kick off, ran the ball back to their own twenty-five yard line, and after a few plays, drove the ball to outside field goal range in Giant territory. Then Dallas called time out. What happened on the field that day was nothing more than the will to survive. It had been a football doubleheader, since an average football game was only about sixty-five plays long on offense. The Giants O was going into their one hundred eighteenth offensive play in the stifling Texas heat. Even a quarter of the stadium emptied out because the game was a long, drawn out affair due to fatigue from the heat and injuries.

During the time-out, the Cowboys decided to go ahead and kick the field goal in order to end this torturous affair. Dallas lined up for the field goal attempt and the ball was in the air. The ball hooked to the left and was no good. The Giants were hooting and hollering with every ounce of energy they could muster. They got the ball on the thirty yard line.

"Blue left. Seventeen. Sweep." the quarterback barked in the huddle, "On three. Ready? Break!"

The Giants lined up, and the quarterback leaned over to take the snap from center.

"Red forty-five. Red forty-five. Set! HUT… HUT… HUT!" The quarterback took the snap and handed off to the running back as he attempted to sweep around the left side. Referees blew their whistles and yellow flags flew into the air. Both teams were now so tired that they were making ridiculous fatigue penalties.

The Giants got back into the huddle, and the quarterback called the same play, but on two.

"Red eighty. Red eighty. Set. HUT! HUT!" The quarterback handed the ball off to the back as he attempted to sweep off to the left again. Yet again, flags flew and whistles went off, signalling another penalty. Guys from both teams were bitching at one another because the players were too tired to do anything else. Even the refs were getting tired of picking up the yellow flags. The quarterback screamed: "Get back in the fuckin' huddle! Fuck this shit! God damn it! Remember the snap count! I know you guys are dying, but stay with it! Now, Red right. Sixteen. Bob G O. On the FIRST sound. Ready? Break!" The quarterback hoped he'd get the play run this time without the penalty.

"Set." said the quarterback. Parker snapped the ball and fired out as both guards pulled right to lead the blocking for the back who was going to get the football and sweep around to the right end. As the entire Doomsday defense flowed to the right side and tackled the running back, Thompson, the quarterback had deftly faked the hand-off to the right halfback and stuck the ball in his hip. He sluggishly bootlegged the ball around the left side outside Dallas' contain man on the back side. Thompson lumbered for forty-five yards before getting knocked out of bounds on the Dallas twenty-nine yard line. The coach immediately sent the field goal team out to line up for the winning play so that they could put the game to bed. As Parker leaned over to snap the ball for the field goal attempt, the Dallas defense took on a defeated look.

Parker snapped the ball. The ball hit the holder perfectly in the hands, but he bobbled it, and, in his attempt to recover the ball from the on-rushing Dallas defense, fumbled it into the hands of Dallas' outside linebacker Monte Ruffin. The linebacker scooted seventy yards for the winning score. You could hear a pin drop and a collective sigh from the now-melted Dallas crowd, which was more happy that the game was over than anything else.

On the ride home, Parker sat in the back of the airplane with a can of coke in his hand and an ice pack on his forehead. He surveyed what looked like a flying M.A.S.H unit. Three stretchers lay in the aisle. Huge bodies with I.V.'s in their arms were on stretchers, and nursing aids roamed up and down the aisles attending the players. Buford Dupree, the Giants' star running back, had blown a knee and was sedated. He lay on the aisle floor with his leg in a clear blow-up cast. Two or three other players were on crutches. Every player had an ice pack on the back of his neck or pressed against his forehead. Trainers walked around the cabin handing out salt tablets and extra iced-down towels, and they urged the players to drink fluids. Hawkeye and Pierce would have had a hard time trying to handle the injuries from this battle.

Silence filled the cabin as the players, who were too tired to move, reflected on the freakish defeat and the way they had lost the game.

Parker Thomas leaned back and felt a sharp pain in his right side and a dull ache in the pit of his stomach. There was nothing pretty about playing in the N.F.L. That day had been flat-out dehumanizing to both teams, and served as a stark reminder to Parker Thomas about the viciousness of the game. Parker closed his eyes, but he could not shake the vision of the linebacker running all the way for the running score. It played over and over again in his mind.

*Bill Winters and
JoAnne V. McGrath*

# EVEN WHEN YOU'RE DOWN, YOU'RE UP!

When Parker Thomas opened his eyes, he learned that he was lying in a hospital bed. He tried to call for help, but the tube stuck in his throat prevented him from doing so. He could see an I.V. line that ran into his arm, and he had a brief flash about what had happened the night before. Too tired to drive home after the flight from Dallas, Parker and a number of players and staff had checked into a hotel near the stadium. After collapsing into bed, Parker woke up about three in the morning with severe stabbing pains in his abdomen. He knew something was radically wrong, so he picked up the phone and tried to call the front desk so they could summon someone from the team to help him. There was no one on duty, so no one answered the call. Parker pulled himself out of bed and walked out into the hall, hoping to find the room the trainers were in. One of the coaches found him on the floor, got him into the elevator, down to the lobby, and into a police car for transportation to the nearest hospital.

Parker's memory was beginning to clear a bit now. He recalled being stuffed into the front seat of the squad car with his legs scrunched and jammed up against the gun rack bolted to the floor. And he could remember the coach in the back seat behind the cage telling him to stay awake, while the pain got worse and worse. When Parker was taken into the hospital, a short man in a white medical coat looked at Parker, who was laid onto a gurney. Besides the red jewel in the turban that the man in the white coat wore, Parker remembered his words: "We've got to operate! Now!! Get him into the emergency room! It's Ruptured!!!" The door to Parker's room cracked open and a head wearing a scrub cap peeked in. Parker turned his head to the side, and a figure wearing hospital blues entered.

"Well, you're finally awake!" said the petite figure who walked to Parker's bedside.

"Hi. I'm Lori. I assisted Dr. Assad when he took out your appendix earlier this morning. You had quite a time in there!" Parker could not respond because the tube in his throat kept him from speaking. He nodded his head and smiled around the tube.

"You gave us all quite a scare, you know." continued Lori, as she took off her scrub cap and shook a long mane of chestnut hair down over her shoulders. Parker gave her a head to toe once-over and, and he felt a tingle in his crotch: "Glad that's still in gear!" he thought to himself.

"You know, the doctors said they had never cut open anyone quite like you before. Doctor Assad said you had the biggest appendix he'd ever removed. And the tightest abdominal muscles he'd ever put a scalpel to." Lori walked over to the chair opposite the bed and got comfy as she sat down.

"Mind if I stay here with you for a while? They called your mom and she should be here late this afternoon." said Lori as she took off her shoes and set them under the chair. She wiggled her feet and turned her ankles, rotating them again and again as she continued her monologue: "I just got off shift and was interested to see how you were coming along. Thought you'd like to know that Elvis died last night. Do you like Elvis Presley? He's my favorite. I just love that Hunka Hunka song." Parker looked at Lori's jade green eyes as they became wider and brighter with every sentence.

"It was really funny the way you tried to choke those two attendants who were trying to transfer you to the operating table. But then again, the way you were all twisted up and the pain you must have experienced was probably terrible! One of the nurses said she could hear your screams all the way to the third floor." Parker's eyes moved from right to left, then back. He had no memory of the event.

"But you probably don't remember too much of that, do you? I couldn't believe how much morphine they shot into you to sedate you. Probably would have killed a normal person. Mind if I take my socks off? I really ran around a lot in this place last night!" Parker nodded to let her know he didn't mind.

"Anyway, I wanted to tell you how impressed I was by you in the operating room. You must be one tough football player, because for the entire six hours you were in there, you kept getting erections just like clockwork." Parker's eyes widened and he watched Lori slip off her scrub pants. Her blue silk panties rested over firm, tanned thighs that any player would love to tackle. Lori crossed her left leg over her right and began moving it in a kicking motion, back and forth, back and forth.

"You know, you really turned me on. I was getting all wet myself after the fifth time you got hard."

Parker noticed that her chest rose and fell in cadence with the motion of her leg.

"Oh, I wonder who the flowers are from? Do you know?" Parker looked at the nightstand next to the bed and shook his head to the side.

"I'll read the card for you if you'd like." offered Lori as she got up from the chair and walked over next to Parker's bed. He wanted to reach out and stroke her butt, but his arms were in restraints.

"Hope you get well real soon. We need you. The Giants. Isn't that nice, the whole team chipped in to send you a little pick-me-up." said Lori as she sat on the side of Parker's bed and pulled the blue v-neck cotton scrub shirt up above her head. She stood up, turned around, and faced Parker. She unhooked the front of her blue silk bra. Then she dropped her panties to the floor.

"I'm in heaven!" Parker thought to himself. "I've died and gone to heaven!! Lori's nipples became erect as she pulled down the white sheet covering Parker and climbed on top of him.

"You know," continued Lori,"When I left that operating room, I had come three times. I hope you don't mind, but I just had to find out if the real thing would be as exciting." By now, Parker Thomas was fully erect and ready for her. Lori slipped down on top of him, guided him in and began to ride back and forth, back and forth. Lori rubbed Parker's chest and thrust her head forward and back as she gave the lineman the fuck of a lifetime.

As Parker climaxed, he flooded with events beyond the present moment. The snap going through the holder's hand and the Dallas linebacker running down the field. The incessant workouts in the school field and thousand of hits on the training sled. The agony of pain coursing through his legs as they moved like pistons pumping against the sled. The rush of adrenalin he felt the day he made his debut on the Giant's field. The day Coach McEllroy told him he would be a starting center. The loading of beer kegs and the butt of a gun in his back. The burial at Arlington and the twenty-one gun salute for his father. The evenings across the dinner table at home and his mother's insistence that he join the white collar world. The graduation ceremony at Ivy. The broken finger flapping in the breeze. The scraping of coins out of the ashtray. The image of Tracey naked on her bed. The snapping of footballs. Three, two, one...

"Aaagggghhhh!!!" Parker cried out despite the tube stuck down his throat. Lori slipped out of the bed, tidily put the sheet back over Parker, got dressed, and headed for the door.

"See you tomorrow, Giant!" she called as she closed the door behind her.

"How ya feeling?" asked Coach McEllroy as he sat in the chair in Parker Thomas' hospital room.

"I'm ok," responded the player.

"You played a hell of a game the other day, and I'm proud of you."

"Thanks," said Parker as the coach got up and paced a little.

"I wish I could have spelled you, but we didn't have anybody who could snap, so we had to go with the five men we had. Everybody else was hurt."

"Coach, I'll be out of this hospital in no time, and back in the line-up soon, I promise!"

"I hope so, Parker. We really need you."

"How's Buford?"

"Dupree is out for the year. He got operated on this morning. I'm gonna stop by and see him too."

"Tell him I said 'hey', will you?"

"We also might have lost Fitzie, possibly for the season."

"What happened to him?"

"He's got a concussion, and this is his third one. The team doctors are getting worried."

"Sounds serious."

"Well, listen, we have a short week because we leave for San Diego Friday. I've got to get to some meetings, so you take care, Parker. See you when you're up and about."

"Thanks, Coach." said Parker as McEllroy left the hospital room.

Parker Thomas grabbed the remote control for the television and flipped the 'on' button. He channel surfed, but not anything that appeared on the screen interested him. He dozed off for a nap, and was awakened by a booming voice: "HUT! HUT!" Parker snapped open his eyes.

"How's it going, buddy?" inquired Rodney 'Roadrunner' Roberts, the Giants' star tailback. He was a legend in the game, a perennial All-Pro, and one of the highest, if not the highest paid players in the league. He had played five years in the NFL, had done it all, including MVP of the Superbowl on a winning Superbowl team. Roberts had jumped the NFL and been with Coach McEllroy for two years in the World Football League, and now, had followed McEllroy to the Giants for even bigger money. Rumor had it that he was making ten thousand a week. Some guys thought it was ten thousand a day. Nobody knew for sure. He was a huge tailback, so big he could have been a middle linebacker. He was a virtual refrigerator on wheels, and those wheels could move.

"Roadrunner," said Parker as he tried to wake up, "Thanks for coming."

"Hey, what are teammates for! I thought I'd stop by with some girlie magazines for you, 'cause I know you ain't getting any in here." quipped Roadrunner.

"Don't be too sure," shot back Parker with a shit eating grin on his face.

"No shit?!"

"Yeah, I just got done getting some."

The door to the room opened and in came a short, rotund woman in her late fifties. She had grey, stringy hair, like a mop head. She was carrying a bed pan. She smiled coyly at both men, and shoved the bed pan under Parker Thomas' butt. Then she left the room.

"She's the one?" asked Roadrunner with an amused look on his face.

"She just takes care of the bottom, pal. I got me a real looker to do the top!" shot back Parker after he was sure their conversation was not overheard.

"Hey Parker, I gotta tell you something. I was outside the coaches' office, you know, down by the locker room, and I overheard them talking about you. I went down there to get me a coke to wash down some painkillers, and I heard them talking. They're really upset that you're hurt." said Roadrunner as he was sure that Parker was really listening to his message.

"You should have heard McEllroy bitching out Austin." Austin Green was Parker's line coach. He didn't know shit as a coach, but he had been with McEllroy since their college days and had been on every staff with him since then.

"Austin's tripping! Has he been here to see you?"

"Nah," said Parker, hoping that the player would continue his earlier thoughts.

"Probably doesn't know what to say to you. I guess I really shouldn't tell you this, but what the hell, the coaches are really hoping to get you back. McEllroy really bitched out Austin about how long you were left in that game. Listen, I've been on a championship Superbowl team built with free agent offensive linemen just like you. And you remind me of Langley. You're on your way to being as good as him. You know Langley, the All-Pro center? Well, listen man, hang in there. Don't let this get you down. Just try to get back as soon as you can, but make sure you're ready when you do. Listen, I gotta go. Meeting in a few minutes. Hope you enjoy the skin magazines. I'll put them under the mattress for you."

Roadruner stuck a big hand under the mattress, lifted half of it up off the support spring, and shoved the magazines underneath.

"Thanks for coming, Robby," said Parker as the player walked toward the door.

"Take it easy on that old one, Parker!" grinned Roberts as he slipped out into the hall. A few minutes later, the nurses' aid with the grey, stringy hair rushed back into the room and had to pause to catch her breath.

"How can I help you, Mr. Thomas? What can I do for you?" she asked and moved her hand to the side of her head to spiff up her hairdo. "The man who was just in here said that you WANTED me!"

"It's no big deal," said Parker Thomas. He felt like a speck of prey before a black widow spider. Parker knew what clowns the other players could be from listening to their locker room stories and from seeing them in action. Parker knew that Roberts had pushed the old bat's buttons and was trying to push his too.

"I don't need the pan, ma'am." said Parker as calmly as possible. "Earlier today the doctor said I could get up a little, I mean walk around, so I don't need the pan."

"No problem." said the woman as she reached under Parker's butt and pulled away the pan. He shifted his weight so she could remove it more easily, and faster. Parker wasn't sure whether the plastic had a nub in it, or if the aide goosed him when she pulled away the pan.

"Well, thanks for your help. Guess I won't need it again. Thanks." said Parker.

"Oh, call me, please, if you ever need a thing, anything!" said the woman as she walked out the door.

As Parker lay in bed flipping through the magazines later that afternoon, the door opened.

"Hey, Rook," called the husky voice, "How's it going? I just saw Roadrunner and he said you were pulling nurses. That one with the grey hair out there is kinda old for you, isn't she?" Parker smiled. Now he was sure why the woman had come rushing into his room earlier.

"Knock it off, Ruck!" said Parker as he greeted the oldest vereran on the Giants. He had come up the hard way through the ranks of pro football. Joey 'Ruck' Rucker, or "Big Joe" had played semi-pro and had joined the Giants as a free agent. Ruck was one of the few guys who had tenure. The Giants would have to retire his jersey before they'd ever release him, because the New York fans wouldn't tolerate anything else. The fans loved Rucker. Joe represented to New York what the city itself stood for. He had been a solid, go-to guy for over ten years with the Giants, and even during some dismal seasons had made the Pro Bowl a couple of times. He had survived three coaching staffs and was older than the tight end coach who coached him.

"I betcha you're gonna try to make it back for the next couple weeks of the season, aren't you?"

"Hell, yes!" said Parker, "I want my starting job back. I earned it. I don't want to be lost for the rest of the season."

"Kid, let me give you some advice. If I were you, I'd tell them that I'm done for the season so they'll put you on injured reserve. You'll get all your money and a year on your pension. And that's important. If they try to do anything else with you, tell them you want to go on injured reserve.

Parker didn't know quite what to say in response to the advice that had been laid in front of him. Didn't Rucker want him to come back and help the team win? He quickly dismissed that thought. Parker Thomas hadn't known Rucker for too long, but he knew he was a straight shooter. To Parker, Rucker served as a role model and a career ideal.

"You have to look out for yourself in this league, and after your own best interests. They make it that wayI I'm not telling you what to do, but if I were you, I'd tell them I want to go on injured reserve."

"No way in hell, Ruck." responded Parker. "I haven't busted my ass to get this far so some other guy can take my job. I gotta get back in the starting line-up. I promised the coach that I'd be back in a few weeks."

"Screw 'em! If I were you, I'd still tell 'em I want to go on injured reserve. Listen, kid, the wife's outside in the car, and I promised I'd spend some time with the family tonight. Maybe I said too much, but it's in your own best interest. Well, gotta go."

Rucker looked at the open page of the magazine lying next to Parker: "Hell of a beaudacious set of tata's on that one! I'd take the magazine with me if the wife and kids weren't in the car. See you later, Parker. Get yourself well."

"See you later, Ruck" said Parker as the tight end walked out the door. Parker leaned back into the pillow and thought about the day: "The head coach told me he really needed me back, and Roadrunner told me I could be All-Pro. Big Joe told me to cash it in for the dough, take a vacation. Think I'll call for a morphine shot and sleep on it!" Parker Thomas rang the nurse-pager button, and he ordered a shot to relieve his pain. The phone rang. Parker lifted the receiver to his ear.

"Hello Parker. This is Tracey… The shot took effect, and Parker Thomas drifted off.

*From the Outhouse to the Penthouse and Somewhere in Between*

## PLAY BY THE NUMBERS

"Frank Marshall, Daily News." said the man in the straw hat who sat in the reception room of the Giants' Executive Office suite. "You're Parker Thomas, aren't you?"

"Yes," said Parker courteously and cautiously. Parker laid his crutches between the reporter and himself.

"Can I have a word with you? Not waiting for an answer, the reporter continued, "Everyone wants to know what's going on with you. You're in limbo right now. Have they told you what they're gonna do with you?"

"No, they haven't, I'm going in to talk to Guthrie now." curtly responded Parker.

"Can I get an interview with you after you come out of your meeting?" pressed the reporter. Parker, still not equipped to deal with the press said, "I'd really rather not, if you don't mind."

Parker had received extensive publicity when he was named the starter for the Giants. He looked at the media as an apparatus that could shape public opinion in a big way. A lot of times, it was a writer's opinion, and not the truth, that would wind up on the printed page. Not fact, but opinion, was filtered to the public, and Parker's motto when dealing with the press was, 'the less said, the better'. One day, Ralph 'Comic' Kwasniewski, the team funny man, blurted out a nickname for Parker that he thought was funny: "Parker you look like the Pillsbury Dough Boy," said Kwasniewski, "You look just like the Pillsbury Dough Boy!" One time, Kwasniewski had even brought a chef's hat to a team luncheon so that he could jokingly put it on Parker's head in front of the rest of the team. Kwasniewski kept poking Parker in the side and saying, 'Tee Hee! Tee Hee!", the sound that the character made in the television commercials. Soon all the team members were calling Parker Thomas "PDB".

The media had already given Parker another nickname, "Pretty Boy Parker", and after the Pillsbury one caught on, the implications that Parker made an enormous salary took off. One irate "Sporting Times" reader had even sent in an editorial about Parker Thomas. It seems the 'Pillsbury' had somehow dropped off the nickname, so 'Dough Boy', the newer and shortened version caught on. Naturally, the people who heard this version thought that Parker had gotten the name bacause of some alleged fat-cat pay check he was taking home. Parker read about himself one day in the letters to the editor column, and the man who wrote about Parker's alleged pay checks was off the wall. His comments were totally off-target, and Parker and everyone who knew the facts felt that the newspaper was remiss in allowing the letter to be printed. Parker even got a call from a lawyer who, offering to take the case on contingency, suggested that Parker sue not only the writer of the letter but also the publisher of the newspaper.

Parker's current tenuous status with the team and his past experiences with the press made him skittish about volunteering his private business so that it could be flaunted in the face of the public. Parker looked back at the reporter when a secretary told Parker that he could go into the General Manager's office.

"Have a good afternoon, Mr. Marshall." Parker said as he hobbled into the inner office.

Craig Guthrie was a former Giants' defensive lineman who had been put in the office because during his playing days, he had been a favorite of the owner. He was a squatty fire-plug type of guy who was hell on the field in his day, but would have been bounced around like a pinball by current players, were Guthrie still in a Giants uniform.

Parker didn't know quite what to make of the Giants' front office. First he had been hit by Jim Bramble, who had gone down to negotiate Parker's contact. Bramble took Parker out to dinner so that they could talk. Bramble kept writing offers on bar napkins, and the more Bramble drank, the more money he wrote down. But Parker kept holding out for the bonus. He had seen better negotiations when he got his job with Rhinegold. Parker, having grown up a die-hard Giants' fan, had watched several poor seasons in which the Giants had won only a handful of games. He had been less impressed with the professionalism of their negotiations.

"Hey, Parker! Come on in." said Guthrie in a deep, throaty hoarse voice. "The doctors say that in about a month, you should be able to resume practice. Do you feel that way?"

"Hell, yes, Mr. Guthrie. I want to get back in the line-up and help us make the playoffs." The Giants had been routed by San Diego the week before, and, with a field goal, had just gotten by the Buccaneers in the last ten seconds of the previous game. In his hospital bed Parker had watched the New England Patriots give the Giants a 40 to 3 thrashing. Parker figured he'd be back for the last four or five games, and help keep the Giants' play-off hopes alive.

"Parker, we're going to put you on a non-football-related injury list." said Guthrie.

"What's that?" asked Parker.

"That's the list the players go on if they are injured by such events as car accidents, and slip and falls at home. If we put you on injured reserve, you're lost for the season, and the coaches and I would like to see you come back for the last five or six games, providing you're healthy enough, for the stretch run. If we put you on the non-football-related injury list, we can activate you at any time. Besides, we're only allowed a certain number of players on injured reserve; the list is almost full now, and we still have a lot more games to play. OK, Parker?" said Guthrie, who then added, "You are going to meetings, aren't you, and films?"

"Yes, yes I am." responded Parker.

"Well, try to start coming out and watch practice too, as soon as the doctors say you're up to it. You were going great guns, Parker. We're hoping you can get it back."

"Thanks, Mr. Guthrie." said Parker. "I won't let you down!"

"That's what I want to hear, Parker. Use this time wisely and watch a lot of film. It will help. Don't you guys have a meeting in twenty minutes? You'd better get going!" said Guthrie as he took Parker's crutches and handed them to him. Then Guthrie added, "By the way, Parker, we sent your last couple of game checks to your address in Shrewsbury. You're probably looking for them."

"Thanks, Mr. Guthrie." said Parker as the General Manager closed the door.

\* \* \* \* \* \* \*

Parker Thomas stood in the hallway of his home in Shrewsbury.

"Want some cookies and milk, dear?" asked Alice Thomas.

"No, Ma, gotta make a phone call. Parker dialed and waited four rings.

"Hello, Herb? This is Parker Is there any mail there for me from the Giants?"

"Yeah, Parker old boy, I've been saving it for you."

"Do me a favor, Herb. Open up the envelope and take a look at the amount on my check." Parker waited for the voice on the other end of the phone to give him the number.

"HOW much? $750?!?" The answer that came back was the same as the previous one.

"You all right, Parker?"

"Yeah, I'm fine. I'll drop by later tonight and we'll watch some t.v."

"See you later, Parker. Glad you're out of that hospital!" Parker would make it a point to see Guthrie the following day at practice.

Parker Thomas felt ill, like he was running a mild temperature, but dismissed the discomfort as just one of the few rough healing days the doctors had told him he would have following his surgery.

The next afternoon, as Parker watched the team run through a light workout the day before the Washington game, he saw Guthrie and an administrative assistant come out of the tunnel. Parker decided to approach Guthrie after practice, not during, so that Guthrie would know that Parker's focus was on the practice, not on his contract. It was the same subtle kind of psychological warfare that Parker had used ever since his days as a Rhino. Parker would show he was focused and that his head was in the game. Little things, like not asking for water until the water break. Not sitting on his helmet or on his butt, but staying in a ready-to-go position on one knee. Keeping his hair cut short. Not drinking at team social functions. Not taking off his helmet until the coach told him to. The tactics were nothing more than telling coaches and management that he was a 'company man', a true team player. Coaches loved disciplined players, and those were the nuances that let them know that players were following their doctrine.

One thing that Parker always loved about football was that the films didn't lie; the best players played, and their efforts were on game films for the coaches to see. The white collar suit-and-tie world of sucking up and kissing up for promotions and for getting ahead, which could take years, could be completely eliminated by kicking ass, taking names, and getting an instant promotion. The instant gratification and the chance for instant success and big dollars had been Parker's motivation. He would never have had such an opportunity by loading beer trucks, even if he was the best beer truck driver around.

In the bone-chilling November rain, Parker crutched over to Guthrie in the tunnel after listening to Coach McEllroy tell the team how badly they needed to win the next game if they wanted to make the play-offs.

"Parker, what can I do for you?" Guthrie asked.

"I noticed that my game checks were for only half of what I was getting before I got hurt. Was there a mistake or something?"

"No, Parker, that is what we decided to pay you. When you get healthy and get back in the starting line-up, we can talk about maybe giving you more of your salary. And that shouldn't be very long, should it? You'll be ready to go in a couple of weeks, right? Yeah, so don't worry about it, just get yourself ready to play."

"OK, Mr. Guthrie."

"Listen, Parker, in all frankness, we really don't have to pay you anything. Just be happy to get what you're getting!"

Guthrie's words cut through Parker's soul. Parker was disappointed, just like when he had gotten his signing bonus. After laying his ass out on the line during training camp and the first nine ball games, both pre-season and regular season, and playing for one of the richest franchises in the league, with games sold out for the next ten years and a five-year waiting list, and thousands of season ticket holders, the Giants were nickle and diming him for a lousy seven hundred fifty a week. "What the hell is this shit?" Parker thought.

His impulse was to see the team rep, and file a complaint with the players' union, but he caught himself. If he did that, he would be blackballed as a clubhouse lawyer and ruin any chances for getting his starting job back or even playing in the league at all. This was more like bottom-line business than sport. One thing a player didn't do was be a clubhouse lawyer. Becoming a player rep and voicing concerns to management was a ticket to catching a greyhound. Dan McCardle, the player rep earlier in the year, had gotten up during a closed-door meeting and had spoken to the team about the possibility of a strike. The teams were making thirty million dollars a year, and spending less than two million on players and coaches. If the books could be pried away from the accountants, the facts would be exposed. There was a rumor that the players had been written off as a depreciating asset like office furniture so that teams could show even less of a profit. In fact, some of the teams were crying poor mouth.

McCardle had gotten so incensed that his reward had been to be released. Nobody wanted to take the players' rep job, and the union was a toothless tiger. A player just kept his mouth shut and played the game, both on the field and in the busiess office.

Parker felt unwanted, and somewhat used, and upset that the Giants had thought so little of him. He felt like a piece of equipment that had worn out, and management was going to replace him with the next hitting part. Parker realized that 'NFL' really stood for 'No Fun League'. Maybe Rucker was right. Parker should have bitched at Guthrie the day before and demanded that he be put on injured reserve. "Fuck it!" Parker thought to himself. "I'll show these motherfuckers; I'll come back and win my starting job and help get this team in the play-offs and show them!" He would then hire an agent and let the agent deal with management in the off-season. Parker knew they owned him lock, stock, and barrel, and the only way he could get to the bargaining table was to perform. And he would perform.

Parker watched the game on television the next day as the Giants were humiliated by Washington. The Giant team looked totally out of synch. Butts and Sasquach were dominating the Giants up front. "Hell, I can do a much better job that that!" thought Parker. After watching the game, Parker was even more determined to make it back and make the Giants pay for their lack of respect.

"Parker, can you come into the bedroom for a minute?" called Lori.

## TO THE OUTHOUSE

Parker Thomas waited for his luggage to come around the baggage carousel at Montreal International Airport. A short, dark haired man approached Parker from the back and gave him a polite tap on the shoulder.

"You Parker Thomas, eh?" Parker nodded. His plane had just landed in the French occupied metropolis, and his escort was there to take him to his hotel. Parker followed the man and got into a car. He thought about what had happened to him the previous fall.

Parker had begun light jogging the week after the Washington game, and had been getting slight fevers on and off. He had felt generally lousy. The team doctor kept dismissing the symptoms as healing pains, but Parker had felt that there was a little more to the symptoms than the doctor had let on. But Parker couldn't be sure. He called Lori and asked her for a referral to a private doctor where he could get a second opinion. This was a big no-no, but what the team didn't know wouldn't hurt them. Parker started taking Ruck's advice and began to look out for himself.

"Do you know another doctor I can see to get a second opinion?"

"Sure," Lori had said, "My dad has a friend who's an internist. Maybe I can get him to take a look at you tomorrow night. Why don't you come over after practice and have dinner with us. I'll call Dr. Kline. He'll come over after he's done with his patients."

At the table that night, Parker had been so nauseated that he couldn't eat the light meal that was in front of him. Dr. Kline, who had been nice enough to stop by, had quickly diagnosed that Parker had peritonitis. Parker had been sewn up with some of the poison still in him. Parker could literally die if he didn't get back into the hospital and get the poison out. As Lori took Parker to the hospital, she asked, "What happened at practice today? What are they doing to you over there?" Parker was reoperated on the following morning after indeed being diagnosed correctly by Dr. Kline. Parker spent another two weeks in the hospital with tubes shoved down his throat to pump out the poison that literally flowed through his entire system. The Giants, now knowing that Parker was lost for the season, made a trade for Jamie Clarke to fill their needed center. As Parker lay in his hospital bed for the second time, he just wanted the whole nightmare to be over.

Everything had gone bad. The Giants had gone into the tank. The straw that broke the camel's back was their loss

*From the Outhouse to the Penthouse and Somewhere in Between*

against Philly. The Giants' quarterback, Thompson, had actually fumbled the center exchange from Clarke as they were running out the clock, and Philadelphia had scooped up the ball and ran it in for a touchdown to win the game with virtually no time left. The offensive coordinator had been fired right after the game. Injuries had dessimated the Giants, and the O-line was running with two starters that had been with the team only a week or two and who barely knew the system. When the team came out for its last home game, the fans booed the entire ballgame and wore paper bags over their heads. Parker had stood on the sidelines trying to fight back the tears.

Parker had been kept on the same list and had received only half of his money. And when Parker approached Guthrie to find out what the team would do, now that he was gone for the season, Guthrie told him they would talk about it when the season was over. The postponed conversation never took place.

The offensive line coach, Austin Green, had been fired at the end of the season, and the new line coach, Jerry Winston, had not let Parker go back to his starting center position during off-season workouts or the mini camp the following year, because the team had traded for Clarke. WInston was also looking at some veteran players that he had brought in from his former team. Although Parker gave a good account of himself in training camp, because of the devastation of the injury, he was not the same player that he had been the previous year. But he felt that with some playing time, he would round into starter. Further, the Giants had drafted as their first round pick a lineman, an offensive tackle, the very spot that the new line coach had been working Parker. Parker felt that he was better than Clarke, definitely better than the back-up, and just as good as the number one. When he approached Winston about whether or not he was going to get the opportunity to play center again, Parker had Winston tell him: "I've got you slated for tackle this year. I know what you can do at center, but we need help at tackle."

Getting very few reps during exhibition games and looking for a chance that never came, Parker felt the politics of pro football. The Giants had a number one pick from two years before, and he had been a bust. They had traded him to New England for Clarke, so he was their man. It would be tough to justify to the press how they could let their number one pick go for a back-up. They were going with Clarke, and the politics dictated that decision. Parker was released in the second exhibition game at the same time that the Giants' number one pick was released by New England.

Parker couldn't comprehend how the year before, he had been 'the man', and now he wasn't getting even an opportunity to show what he could do. Even if Parker had come in as a world beater, better than he was the year before, he would not have been able to overcome the politics of the situation. Big money, answering to the media, and the pressure to win right now on the coaching staff became more important than giving a previously proven player an opportunity to play. The Giants team that had welcomed him with open arms and was desperate for offensive linemen the year before was now shutting the door in his face. Parker saw the handwriting on the wall: "You could always tell when you were gonna get cut. The coaches would hardly talk to you in meetings and film sessions, and you would sit in rows that delineated a pecking order."

Where previously Parker had sat in the front row, he was relegated to the third row with a coach who barely acknowledged him. Parker was frustrated knowing that he could kick ass, and the mentality of 'just put me in there and let me show you what I can do, and let me prove myself and earn my spot' kept Parker's hopes alive and sustained him during training camp. Parker found those days tough hitting with little or no hope of making the club. But in football you kept battling everyday because you could never be sure of what could happen.

One never knew what the coaches were thinking. But as the team consistently made cuts, it became apparent that things were not going to change and that the axe would soon fall on Parker as well. Perhaps he would get released and picked up by another team and be given a chance to play. Parker had prayed for the nightmare to end. It was like slamming into a truck rolling down hill – he just wasn't going to win no matter what effort he made.

Now here he was in Montreal with a defending championship ball club that had captured The Grey Cup, the Superbowl of the Canadian Football League, just the year before. Perhaps Parker could get a fresh start.

"We're here, eh?." said the man driving the car. "Hampton Arms Tower, sir." The eighteen story building was plush and luxurious, and had suites that could be rented by the day, week, month or year. All the Canadiens hockey players who were Americans, most of the Expo players, and all the Americans that played for Parker's new team, the Montreal Alouettes of the Canadian Football League, stayed at Hampton Arms. The building was affectionately know as 'Animal House', after the movie that had been such a big hit the year before.

"We booked you into room 809. You'll be here for a week, maybe more, eh? Take Le Metro down to the stadium as soon as you can and report to Coach Beck, the offensive line coach."

"Le Metro, what's that? Is it a bus or something?" asked Parker.

"No, it's the subway!"

On the drive from the airport, Parker had noticed how there had been this crazy language on top of American words on signs and on city streets. He remembered seeing 'Le Metro' over the word 'subway' on one of these signs. Parker realized that he was in a foreign country, but outside of hearing conversations with the word 'eh' at the end of every sentence and of seeing the two languages, one on top of another, everywhere he looked, Montreal appeared to be pretty much like the States. In fact, it was nicer than the States in a lot of ways. The downtown was full of skyscrapers, highrises, and amazing shops. RIght around the corner, within walking distance of the Hampton, was Crescent Street, an avenue filled with bars and clubs and teeming with night life. Montreal had just come off the Olympics, and everything was new. Olympic Stadium now housed the National League expansion Expos baseball team, as well as Parker's new ball club, the Al's, as they were know. The staduim was large, and was always packed for every game. The city was major league in every way, and so far, Parker felt comfortable in his new environment. But he would have to wait until he banged up against some of the Canadian League players and see how he felt before he could become too comfortable.

"I'm here to see Coach Beck." said Parker, having enjoyed his first ride on 'Le Metro'.

"Your're the new player,eh?" asked the absolutely stunning receptionist. "I'll tell him you're here. Have a seat, eh?" Parker wanted to strike up a conversation with the woman, but felt that he should lay low, so he passed on the opportunity.

"Coach Beck is expecting you." said the receptionist as she returned to the room. "Third office down the hall. On the left." Parker smiled at her and politely thanked her. Then he bounded down the hall and turned into Beck's office. A tall, silver haired, retired-looking gentleman with a military bearing stuck out his right hand.

"Hey, I'm Coach Beck. Glad you got here." Parker Thomas returned the handshake.

"Was your trip o.k.?"

"Fine," answered Parker as he noticed the ashtray full of cigarette butts that lay next to a film projector in Beck's office. The projector was loaded and ready to go. Beck, at one time, had been a coach in the National Football League, and had also been in the college ranks.

"Parker, I want to look at you at right tackle. We've flown you up to take a look at you and to see if you can help us. I know you can play guard and center, but those positions go to Canadians. Most of the teams carry only one import American lineman."

"Import?" Parker said.

"Yeah, we only carry twelve Americans on a thirty-three man roster. The rest are Canadians. Most of the teams only carry one American at left tackle, but we carry two Americans at offensive tackle and run the ball a lot in a league that most of the time throws it. You're up here on a five-day trial. The day before the game, the day of the game, and the day after the game don't count toward those days. Since we're playing a game on Wednesday night and then again on Sunday afternoon, you'll be up here for a week or so and you'll be given a chance to show us what you can do. I'm gonna let you know now that after practice, I'm going to work you hard against the D-line. Don't get upset if you don't get many reps in practice for the next week. We 're going with the players we have right now, but if you are what I'm looking for, things could change. And we'll give you an opportunity to start. Here's some paperwork that you need to sign so that we can get you on the field. There's no sense talking contract at all until after this week is over. That's not my department anyway, so someone else will talk to you about it later. Now, let's watch some films of last week's game to give you some idea of what I expect from you."

Coach Beck flicked off the lights and the projector started to roll.

"This is us versus Winnipeg in a game we should have won, but we broke down and self-destructed up front, and I think you'll see what I mean as we watch the film."

As Parker Thomas watched the film, he noticed that there were twelve men on the offense instead of eleven, and that backs could go in motion towards the line of scrimmage before the snap of the ball, a move that would have been a penalty in the States. The field was wider and longer, and the defensive line had to line up a yard back from the football. As the Montreal offense ran play after play on the film, Parker started to see that the games were very fast and that many of the players were just as good as the NFL players and that some were not.

"Parker," said Coach Beck, "Kind of different, isn't it? There are some differences in the way the game is played, but not many. It's still football, and some of the players up here are better than guys I've coached in the NFL. The way they line up with that yard spacing between the ball and the D-line is all you need to concern yourself with. There will be some adjustment on your pass sets, but the run blocking is still the same. I want linemen that are tough and get after people up front. And right now, I got two rookie offensive linemen fresh out of college that aren't getting it done. They're sharing the spot right now, and neither one of them is doing the job for me. Don't worry about the rest of the stuff – the man in motion, the extra player, and the fact that the field's a lot larger. Hell, we even got this thing called the rouge. Don't worry, you'll get used to it. Just get after people up front. You'd better go on up to the locker room and get fitted for some gear. Make sure when you come out to practice that you're ready to go. We got a quick meeting at three o'clock before we go out onto the field. Red, the equipment man, will tell you where to go when he suits you up. OK, that's it, Parker. You got any questions?"

"No, coach, I just want to say thanks for giving me the opportunity."

"Make the most of it, Parker." said Beck as he lit up another cigarette.

Parker got on the elevator and headed for the bottom floor. The elevator took him past the floor of the mall that circled the stadium, past the floor that was the entrance to the Metro and had the ticket windows, past the floor that housed the Expos' offices and down to the level that held the Alouettes' locker room. He got off the elevator and walked around the corner. As he strode to the cage, an adolescent with red hair and freckles looked at him and said, "You that new player Parker Thomas, eh?"

"Yeah, I'm up here on a five day trial and the coach told me to get some gear for practice.

"Did you bring turf shoes?"

"Yeah, I did."

"Well then, I just need to set you up with a helmet and some shoulder pads. I'm glad you brought your turf shoes; I don't have a size fourteen. I'll have to get them from Adidas in the next day or two. That helmet fits, Parker, eh?"

"It's fine. You guys don't use air helmets, do you?"

"Yeah, some of the guys do, but this is the only helmet I got in your size. You'll have to make do. If it's too tight or loose, I can adjust it by changing the pads in it. Here, try on these shoulder pads. They feel good, eh?"

"A little too loose. You know, I snap for punts and field goals, so I need a different kind of shoulder pad, one that isn't so large and bulky."

"Well here, try this Rawlings."

"That's better."

"Well, let me lace you up and adjust the straps. I'll tape them up for you, eh? Then you'll be good to go. Where'd you play last?

"I just got released from the Giants."

"Well you're a big son of a bitch."

"Watch out, Red, or he'll kick your ass!" said a voice behind Parker. "Or we'll give you another tape job!"

"No fucking way!" Red said. "You know, I got a hand gun back here with dumb-dumb bullets, and I'm not afraid to use it."

"Yeah, well, the gun's only got six bullets and there's thirty of us! You won't stand a chance!" Red wrote Parker's name on a piece of tape and gave it to him.

"OK, Thomas, stick this on an empty locker. You've got a meeting in forty minutes."

As Parker turned and walked towards an empty locker, a tattooed, fireplug of a man stuck out his right hand and said, "Nice to have you here. I'm Wesley Rogers."

*From the Outhouse to the Penthouse
and Somewhere in Between*

"You're Wesley Rogers? Nice to meet you. Man, I saw you play in the greatest college game ever, Nebraska versus Oklahoma. Man, you had the greatest game of any running back I've ever seen."

"Thanks, man. The team ain't gettin' off up here, 'cause there ain't no holes on the right side to run. I hope you're gonna help us."

"I'm gonna do my best. I'll open ya up some holes!" said Parker.

"That's what I'm talking about, man!" said Wes Rogers.

"Nice talkin' to you. I gotta get ready for practice. Where are the meeting rooms at?"

"Just follow that bearded platypus looking body over there!" Rogers said as he pointed to a huge lineman pulling up his practice pads. A lit cigarette drooped out of the lineman's mouth.

"Who's that?" asked Parker.

"That's Patten, our left tackle. He's been on this team for ever. He'll dial you in."

"Thanks, Wesley." said Parker.

"No problem, man" said Wes Rogers as he walked away.

Parker knew who Patten was. Johnny Patten had been the number one pick of the Eagles about eight years back, and he had spurned the NFL's offer and had gone up to Montreal with a fat contract. Parker wondered where Patten had gone and why he hadn't read about him playing in the NFL.

As Parker Thomas neared the group of large men in the corner of the locker room, he couldn't help but notice how many of the players were smoking cigarettes and how loose the locker room atmosphere was. As Parker strode over, another hand was thrust in his direction.

"Hey, Johnny Patten. Nice to meet you. You're Thomas, right? They bring you up for a five day trial?"

"Yeah," Parker respoded.

"You GOTTA be better than them two guys we have now! Both of those guys are rookies and they keep making those rookie mistakes. This is a veteran ball club. The coaches don't give a damn what we do off the field as long as we take care of business on the field. The head coach, Scarpacci, was an Oakland Raiders' assistant coach, and he treats us like men. He's a strong candidate for a head coaching job in the NFL with either St. Louis or his old team, Oakland. He's getting real impatient with those two rookies, so I think he brought you up because he wants a veteran at that spot so we can control the ball and let Joe Burnes, who's the best quarterback in the league, get on track. We won it all last year, but until we get things straightened out up front, we ain't gonna win. I hope you are the answer."

"I am!" said Parker Thomas.

*From the Outhouse to the Penthouse
and Somewhere in Between*

Parker hurriedly dressed and followed Patten to the meeting room. In the meeting room, the chairs were arranged in rows. Parker sat down in the row behind the two offensive tackles one of those whose job he hoped to take. Parker leaned forward and put out his hand.

"Hey, Parker Thomas!" he said to the guy seated in front of him. The man barely acknowledged Parker and gave him a steely stare. The coach came in the room: "All right you guys, settle down." he said as he chalked up some plays. "Oh, by the way, before I get started, we got a new player here on a five day trial. Parker Thomas."

No one said a word. A few guys glanced in Parker's direction and nodded, as if to say hello. The tension in the room was a general reminder that no player's job was secure, no matter how loose a team was. Teams were always making personnel moves. The two guys in front of Parker were well aware that one, maybe both of them were going to be shipped out. It was something a player learned to minimize and cover up with jokes and a seemingly loose attitude. A player could only control what he could control. Rookies, a lot of times, would drive themselves nuts thinking about what they thought the coaches might do. Parker, having been through two camps, had come to the conclusion that it didn't matter to worry about things he couldn't control.

"Just control what you can," thought Parker to himself. "Come off the football and knock the snot out of them."

Even in the Canadian Football League, that intense fear that a player could lose his job any day or get hurt at any time rested in a player's subconscious.

As Parker watched the Ottawa film, the division-leading team Montreal was going to play Wednesday night, he suppressed every feeling that he had to prove himself all over again. He focused on the film, glad he had the opportunity for his five-day trial.

*From the Outhouse to the Penthouse
and Somewhere in Between*

# LE PENTHOUSE IN MONTREAL, EH?

Parker Thomas watched the Alouettes practice in the chilly September air. He started to get stiff and cold. He wished he had a warm-up jacket, as did the other players.

"Fuck! It was COLD!" Parker thought as his frosty breath streamed from his nostrils.

The first offensive team scrimmaged hard against the second team defense, as was always the case a couple of days before a game. It was a work day where there was heavy hitting, and players proved that they still deserved their spot in the pecking order by basically playing football at full speed. The only difference was, they didn't tackle the ball carrier. Parker, after several plays, started to notice that the American players were at strategic positions on the field. The tackles on offense, the ends on defense, tailback and middle linebacker and quarterback, and corners, free safetys and wide receivers were Americans. The outside linebackers, defensive tackles, center and guards, flankers and back-ups, and some D.B.'s were Canadians, as if to mask the fact that the Canadians weren't as good as the American players. It seemed the key positions on offense and defense were manned by Americans. The names on the backs of the players jerseys – Gregoire, Roberge, Boucher, DeLaVille, – let Parker know who the foreigners were, even though the Americans were the real foreigners. They were playing an American game, and it was obvious which country had weaned the better players. The Canadian league, the nine team CFL, had been around longer than the National Football League, and had a history and a tradition of its own.

Montreal had a rich tradition of being one of the better teams in the league, and the Canadian players just acted differently on the practice field, as if they weren't worried about being cut. The players just seemed to be looser and having a better time, but still playing football at an intense level.

Parker started to feel the cold chill into his bones, and tried to stay loose that first day and get ready for the coach to blow the whistle signalling the end of practice. He started to stretch to get ready for his try-out. The coach blew the whistle.

"Everybody up!" called the coach. The head coach quickly told the players that the next day, they would dress in shorts and helmets, go through a brief hour's practice, and then leave for Ottawa. He told them to get rested, and then the team broke to the locker room. As Parker stood waiting for Beck to signal that he was ready to give him the reps that were promised, Parker noticed a few defensive linemen staying out with Coach Beck.

"Thomas!" the coach barked, "Come on over. I'm gonna work you against the D., some one-on-one. Make sure you're loose, and let me know when you're ready." Parker could hear the muffled bitching of the defense line as they were asked to stay out after practice.

"You ready, Thomas?" called Beck. "All right, let's go! I want you to fire out and run block for the next couple of minutes. I'll signal the snap count." Parker set up and nodded to Coach Beck that he was ready to go.

"Set! Hut!" Parker fired off and slammed into the huge, onrushing Samoan lineman. The collision rocked Parker as the two men slammed into a virtual stalemate. An imaginary back carrying a football ran past him. Even though there was a stalemate, Parker had stayed on his man and wheeled his hips in order to keep the huge Samoan from touching the back. A whistle blew.

"OK, Parker, not bad. Again!" called Beck. As Parker got down in his stance, he couldn't help but think about how every Samoan player, though he had only slammed into a few of them during his playing days, always seemed to have a lot of lead in their pencils. Parker really hurt when he hit them! Parker didn't know what they fed those kids on the island, but they sure were strong. Parker knew he was in for an ugly fight for the next half hour.

"Set! HUT!" yelled Beck. Parker had fired out and a huge forearm came ripping up and blasted him under the chin as Parker tried to bury his head in the Samoan's chest and knock him out of there. Parker, at the last second, fired out his hands, and just as he was about to come off the block, was able to get a push on the big man, just making him miss the imaginary back who would have come skirting through the imaginary hole.

"Keep those feet moving and stay on the block, Parker! Again!" The D-line man's eyes had absolute fear in them, as if he was playing for his life. The handful of players who had stayed out after practice to watch this contest were starting to cheer, firing up both Parker and the Samoan.

"Come on, Manu, you dog, KICK HIS ASS!" they yelled Before Parker could get out of his stance, the defensive lineman came off the ball and slammed into him. He had anticipated the snap count.

"Come on, Fiatoa! Go on the snap count! That's a penalty!" called Beck to the Samoan.

Parker knew that in these kinds of drills, the defense usually had the advantage because in a real game they didn't know ahead of time whether a player would run or pass block them. In this drill they knew, so they could tee off. An offensive lineman had to be violent, but always thinking, and many times guessing what the huge man in front of him would try to do. As the line coach put up a single finger to signal that they were going on one, Parker got down in his stance. The player, having been lambasted by the coach, was now going to be coming across the ball with everything he had.

"Set! HUT!" Parker fired out, but this time, instead of burying his head in the lineman's chest, he shot for the player's left knee and knocked him off his feet. Applause came from the offensive players hanging around and watching the action.

"Way to go, Parker!" yelled Patten. Out of the corner of his eye, Parker had seen Patten, Wesley Rogers, and one or two other players he did not know. They were wrapped up in the action on the field.

"OK, Hamilton, get in there at defensive tackle. That's enough, Manu!" called Beck. Manu Fiatoa looked out of the corner of his eye at Parker, as if to say, 'OK, motherfucker, you won that one, but I'll get you next time!'. Fiatoa headed for the sidelines and got some water.

Hamilton was a Canadian back-up defensive tackle who probably would not have made Parker's college team as a starter. It was obvious to Parker that Beck expected him to dominate the body across the line, and if Parker let this kid make a tackle, he wasn't going to be around long.

"OK, here's the snap count, Thomas!" called Beck.

As Parker got down in his stance and looked into his opponent's eyes, he quickly assessed what he could do. Football players had so many things to remember, but also had to quickly assess what they could do to another player. So much of football was reaction on the run in a matter of milliseconds; often a player's ability to play well was based on his ability to make split-second decisions while a play was in motion. There were a lot of big, strong men in the world, many built like Tarzan, but most of them played like Jane because they couldn't think fast on their feet and had no moves. God had gifted very few of them with the ability to be big and strong and smart, with the reactions of a cat, like Parker Thomas had. He felt special. Parker knew that this defensive lineman was an unpolished player who would come running into him straight on and give him his whole body.

"Set! HUT!" Parker fired out, slamming his helmet into the guy's chest and came ripping up with his arms, punching him underneath his shoulder pads' breast plate, lifted him up practically off the ground, and proceded to drive the player five or six yards off the ball.

"Come on, Hamilton! You played just like that against Winnipeg, and we're not gonna keep you around much longer if you keep letting offensive linemen pile drive you like that!" Parker knew that he had the back-up on the run. And now, he was ready to tee off at him. As Parker got the snap count and got down in his stance, he could see by the way Hamilton's feet were positioned, that he was going to try to take a side and out-guess Parker because he'd just been beaten head on.

"Set! HUT!" Parker fired out, but the center target that he usually aimed for went quickly to the right side. Parker, although missing with his head, was able to slam his huge right arm into the middle of the player's breastplate and maintain contact. Hamilton countered with a slap to Parker's side with his left arm, but did not have the strength to knock Parker off course. He got shoved laterally down the line of scrimmage as the imaginary back easily ran through the hole.

"You gotta come faster with that left hand, Hamilton!" the D-line coach called out, "But keep working on it, it's coming. It will be a good move once you perfect it."

"OK, Manu, get back in there! Give Thomas some good work!" said Beck as he called to the sidelines.

By this time, Parker was practically hyperventillating. He had gone eight or nine plays in a row with very little rest, and this was just as tough as any game would be. He had fought off the two defensive linemen for about five minutes, keeping the huge Samoan to a stalemate and totally dominating Hamilton. Parker didn't know what the coaches were thinking, but he didn't have much time to worry about it since they had run one play right after another.

"OK, guys," said Beck as he blew the whistle, signalling the end of the drill. Coach Beck called the players to gather around him. He spoke directly to Parker Thomas: "OK. Now we're gonna work on some pass blocking. That's not bad so far."

Beck put a yellow dummy where the quarterback would be. The crowd of players who had gathered to watch the battle started getting more fired up. Big Dave Bonarski, who played for the Al's defense, walked up to the line of scrimmage and assumed his position. Bonarski was the league's sack leader and premier pass rusher. This guy was known throughout the NFL and CFL as an absolute bitch to play against. He was big and tall, and strong, and he had tremendous cat-like moves to the quarterback. Parker knew that when a player pass blocked guys like Bonarski, the player could easily be humiliated. That was the part of the job as offensive lineman that sucked. Sometimes a guy like that could beat you with a move and kill your quarterback. A good lineman would battle like hell on every play and bounce back after he had gotten whipped on the play before. The key was to stay on your feet, because even if the guy got past you, you would hope to recover fast enough to push the flying player past the quarterback, providing that the quarterback was enough of an athlete to escape the oncoming rush. Parker had the literal Fear of God running through him.

"Here's the snap count." Beck said.

"Set! HUT!" Bonarski had lined up on Parker's outside shoulder, and rushed up the field, not even engaging Parker. Parker set up in his pass stance, like he had been taught during the Giants' training camp. Bonarski, seeing Parker's set-up, immediately changed his angle and headed straight towards the quarterback and completely whipping Parker inside. Bonarski ran straight for the six-foot yellow dummy that represented the quarterback.

"OK, hold on a minute, Parker," Beck said right after the imaginary humiliating sack.

"You don't have to set up like that. Set up on the line of scrimmage and kick step out to him. And don't give ground. Keep your outside foot between his crotch and the quarterback, and don't turn your hips. Got it? OK, try it again!

"Set! HUT!" This time, Parker tried the footwork that Coach Beck had told him, and he got it halfway right. Bonarski had rushed up the field, and instead of taking the inside, lowered his shoulders and started to run to the outside, pressing toward the dummy. He quickly worked his way past Parker and started to sprint toward the dummy. Parker, almost totally extended and off balance, somehow managed to gather himself up and sprint back, pushing the huge, speeding defensive end off his course as the defensive lineman had just about passed him.

"OK, Parker, that's a little better. We still need to work on that set. That's the pressure. I need a little better job." called Beck. "It's all in the set!" Bonarski, aware of the reputation he had, was now being tested. As Parker came up to the line of scrimmage and looked into Bonarski's eyes, Parker saw the sparks that let him know that this player was a game one. He was going to come out with his best move and prove to everybody on the field that he was 'the man'.

Beck stuck up his fist to signal that the snap count would be on the first sound, hoping to give Parker a slight edge over Bonarski. But Bonarski, being the crafty fox that he was, had guessed what the coach would do in an effort to try to protect his offensive lineman.

"Set!" Bonarski was off the ball in a heartbeat as Parker kickstepped slowly in an effort to try to get the right footwork. Bonarski quickly engaged him, and before Parker could slam his hands into him in an effort to stop his momentum, Bonarski swung his right arm and swam it over as Parker went hurdling to the ground. Bonarski sprinted toward the dummy and smacked it, knocking it to the ground.

"That's a sack, motherfucker," said Bonarski, trying to let everyone on the field know that he had just whipped Parker's ass. The onlooking defensive players hooted and hollered. As Parker looked out of the corner of his eye, he saw Patten lower his head, as if he'd also been beaten.

"OK, Manu, get in there." called Beck. Parker, without even thinking, blurted out, "Come on, coach, give me a couple more reps with this guy. I think I got this pass set down now."

"You ain't got shit, motherfucker, except how to to get whipped!" yelled Bonarski. When Parker looked at Bonarski, the look in his eye was as if he was on some kind of adrenalin drug. Beck was looking for this kind of attitude in his linemen. As an offensive lineman, you were going to get beat once in a while; this was the pro's. What counted was how you bounced back on the next play. Many players, when they got to this level, once they got beat, would just go in the tank and keep getting beaten.

"OK, Parker, you want him, you got him!" snapped Beck. Those next five reps would be a fight for Parker's football life: everything he had ever been taught would have to come into play now. In practice, they always filmed one-on-one. An offensive lineman would watch his set, his footwork, his jam with his hands and his head placement. He would do constant reps and make constant evaluations.

Situations like the one Parker found himself in were part of the beauty of football. It was one of dog eat dog, and Parker would fight this man, even though the defense had a big advantage, knowing it was a pass. Sacking the quarterback was what every defensive lineman lived for. The defensive lineman, the good ones, like it better than sex, or so they said. Parker was going to bounce back and show Coach Beck that he belonged.

"Set! HUT! HUT!" Parker set up and kick stepped out, sinking his weight and firing out his hands underneath the speeding defensive lineman who tried to spin around Parker. It was a pure move designed to either work or fail, and was used maybe once or twice in a game in order to get to the quarterback. As Bonarski tried the spin move, Parker fired out his hands and didn't get over-extended; Parker was easily able to shove Bonarski out of his course. Parker knew Bonarski was conceding that play to him, and that he was merely setting him up for another move that would leave him totally humiliated again.

"Set! HUT!" This time Bonarski kept rushing up the field, and at the last second, instead of spinning outside, spun inside with a vicious head slap to Parker's helmet. He had temporarily beaten Parker to the inside, the cardinal sin of pass blocking. A good lineman would never get beat inside. That was the quickest line to the quarterback. When you battle them, if you're gonna lose them, lose them to the outside. At least your quarterback would have a pocket to step up into!

As Bonarski went by Parker on the inside, Parker slammed his arm on Bonarski's hip and started shoving him down the line of scrimmage. As the onrushing Bonarski lost his balance, Parker's push started to gather speed and the player went crashing to the ground.

"Come on, motherfucker, quit holding me!" Bonarski yelled out in a rage. Bonarski grabbed Parker's face mask and threw a punch. "Don't hold me, motherfucker, or I'll fucking kill you!!!" Parker flared back another punch, and the two men rolled onto the ground.

"All right you guys, that's enough! Break it up!! We're on the same team!!!! What are we gonna do, lose both of you?!?" called Beck. "Take it out on Ottawa Wednesday night, Bonarski!! Save some of that for the game. That's ENOUGH for today!" Beck walked over to Parker and addressed him directly: "Parker, let me talk to you." Parker was so amped up that he couldn't comprehend the first few words Beck said to him: "What did you say, coach?"

"OK, Parker, relax. I saw some good things out there, and I saw some things we need to work on. Tomorrow we'll be out in shorts and helmets, but I want you to come out in full gear and we'll work again after practice. I'm gonna have you work against some other defensive linemen, primarily back-ups, because they need the work and I don't want to get any of my starters hurt. Have you lifted any weights lately?"

"Yeah, I've lifted a litte bit since I got released." lied Parker, thinking of the kegs.

"Well, go get some lifting in, and get showered and head back to the hotel. There will be an itinerary in your locker that will tell you what the next two days will entail. Keep working, big man, It'll come!"

"Thanks, coach." said Parker as he turned and headed for the locker room. There was no one on the field and it was dark out. Parker emerged from the tunnel and into the locker room; all the other players had already split. Parker felt alone and isolated as he went into the weight room and lifted. He pumped for about forty-five minutes until he almost couldn't go anymore, making sure he hit every body part that a football player would use. He quickly showered, got on the Metro, and headed back to the Hampton. He collapsed on the bed in his room and was just about to doze off when there was a knock on the door. It was Wesley Rogers.

"Parker, open up!" Parker got up off the bed and went to the door. He let Wes Rogers into the room.

"Patten and me and some of the other guys are going to get a beer. Wanna come along?"

"Nah, I'm whipped." answered Parker, "And I don't know if I should be out drinking with you guys. I just got here.

"Don't worry about it, Parker, the coaches don't give a shit. Just make sure you don't get drunk and sloppy. They got great steaks at The Longest Yard. One of the former Alouette players owns it, and he takes great care of us."

"Give me a minute and I'll come down to your room. Where are you guys at?"

"We're in 802, down the hall." Parker got himself ready and walked down to 802. The room was full of thick, hazy smoke, and it almost choked Parker as he walked in. Patten, Marcus, and another guy who obviously wasn't a ball player, and two girls were in the room with Wes Rogers. The girls were tenants and lived a few floors down. One was a flight attendant and the other was a waitress. The waitress was extremely well endowed.

"Burnsey called and said he'd be down in a minute with Susie. They're gonna go with us." said Wesley Rogers. "Cheryl, MIchelle, this is Parker Thomas. He just got in today and hopefully, he's gonna be around."

"Nice to meet you. You from the States?" asked Michelle.

"Of course he's from the States! Did you hear him say "EH" yet?" said Patten, who sat on the couch next to the waitress. Michelle laughed.

"Parker, have you met Larry yet?" asked Wes Rogers.

"No, I haven't. Nice to meet you." said Parker to the unfamiliar man who stood up from a chair and exended his hand in Parker's direction.

"Never been to 'dis country before, eh?"

"No, this is my first time here."

"You like Montreal so far, eh?"

"It's got some beautiful scenery!" said Parker as he glanced at Cheryl's chest. There was a knock at the door.

"Let's go, you guys, I'm hungry!" called Joe Burnes from the hall.

"Are Cheryl and Michelle coming too?" asked a female voice in the hall with Burnes. Joe Burnes and his wife Susie came into the room.

"Parker, this is Joe Burnes, our quarterback and the guy who is going to take us to another championship, and another nice pay day. Joe led the league in passing and was second in rushing last year as a quarterback. If the cat ain't open, he just takes off, and man, can he shoot."

"Nice to meet you, Joe." said Parker Thomas.

"Same here. Where'd you go to school?"

"Ivy University." responded Parker.

"Ivy? Holy shit! It's about time we got a smart lineman. Add a little college to the mix. Maybe you can cement that right side. I've taken some serious shots this year from that side."

"That's why I'm here."

"Heard you had a little skirmish with Cybil today."

"Cybil?" asked Parker.

"That's what we call Bonarski. Man, he has a lot of mood swings, but don't ever call him Cybil to his face. He'll go off like a firecracker. He's one intense mother."

"Thanks for the warning, Joe."

"Parker, this is my wife, Susie." said Joe Burnes as the couple stepped in.

"Nice to meet you, Parker." said Susie with a big Texas drawl.

"Come on, you guys, let's go. We'll take my van. We can all fit.!" said Patten as he got up off the couch and pulled a set of keys from his pocket.

As the group got into the elevator and it descended, Parker thought about how nice it was that he had been invited to come along. It sure beat staring at four walls in a hotel room. Parker decided to see what the town had to offer. He just hoped he'd be around long enough to find out. The elevator stopped at the underground parking lot. The gang got off the elevator, loaded into Patten's van, and rolled toward Crescent Street.

"Geez, this is a nice van. Custom. It's got everything!" Parker commented to Patten.

"Thanks, I got it with my signing bonus, and if this van could talk…"

"What would it say, Patten?" asked Cheryl who sat in the front passenger seat.

"It certainly wouldn't say "EH"!" quipped Wesley, who knew about the van's meanderings as a rolling pleasure palace and orgy pad.

Larry's hand appeared in front of Parker's face. It held the fattest joint Parker had ever seen.

"Want a toke of this, man? Gooood shit! From Hong Kong via British Columbia…" Larry coughed into the back of Parker's neck and almost burnt Parker's shirt with the doobie.

"No thanks, I'll pass." said Parker. "Gotta be ready for tomorrow. I still gotta make this club."

"Don't know what you're missing, man!" said Larry as he gasped for breath and waved smoke around in front of his face.

"You mean you're not on the team?" asked Michelle.

"I'm here on a five-day trial to see if they're gonna keep me. Hopefully something will open up." said Parker.

"I met a guy on my flight route that was up here two weeks ago. I think his name is Mark."

"They cut his ass, that sorry son of a bitch!" broke in Patten, who looked in the mirror and called to the back of the van: "OK, we're gonna be there in a second. Larry, blow that stuff out the window, will ya? I don't want us reeking of dope when we get out of the van." The van pulled up in front of the restaurant, and was taken by the valet who did not demand a tip. The maitre d' took the party to a back table away from the crowd of onlookers seated in the restaurant.

\* \* \* \* \* \* \*

The van rolled back into the underground garage and the troops got out, got into the elevator, and headed for the eighth floor of the Hampton. The conversation had been lively, and the meal top shelf, and on the house.

On the way home, Parker had sat next to Michelle, who had invited him to her apartment to watch the game since he would be in town alone while the rest of the team was in Ottawa. When she got off the elevator on the fourth floor, Michelle turned to Parker: "See you at six Wednesday night!" she said

*From the Outhouse to the Penthouse
and Somewhere in Between*

and winked at him over her shoulder as the elevator doors closed. Parker Thomas was back on the rise, headed for the penthouse again.

*Bill Winters and
JoAnne V. McGrath*

# IN AND OUT AND IN AGAIN

Parker Thomas unhooked Michelle's bra as the commentator's voice called out from the colored television set in the bedroom.

"First down and ten, still a lot of yardage left for the Al's to pickup."

"Wait a minute," said Michelle, as she reached beside the bed and dug into her pocketbook.

"I think I left my diaphram at the stewardess base in Chicago. Do you have any condoms, Parker?" asked the wide-eyed blonde.

Hot and naked and ready to go, Parker got up from the bed and walked over to the chair where he had laid his pants earlier. He grabbed the wallet out of his pocket and produced a silver packet. The expression on his face was one of impatience.

"Penalty on the play! Penalty!" called the commentator. "Penalty against the tackle. He'd better watch out. This could cost him big time!"

Parker lay back down next to Michelle and started making his moves. He ran his hands down her sides,over her waist, and cupped her hips. He slipped his thumbs under the waistband of her panties, and gently tugged them down over her crotch.

"The Als are getting closer to scoring with every maneuver on the field. If they keep moving like this, they should be in the end zone soon!" Michelle sighed and moaned a little as Parker slipped her panties down over her knees, past her shins and over her ankles. Michelle shifted her feet to make the action a little easier for Parker, and to let him know that she was getting ready. Parker tossed the panties over his shoulder and they landed on the floor.

"There goes a flag on the play. Yes, it's a flag!" said the tv voice. Michelle spread her legs and Parker put his hands around her waist. She grasped him and coupled him in her hands as she guided him into her.

"It's up! It's good!" called the commentator from the screen. Parker thrust himseelf into her and began pulling in and out, in and out.

"Did you see the move on that play?" called the commentator. Michelle writhed in ecstacy under his weight as they went at it. Their momentum together became more urgent. Parker pushed his mouth over hers, and their tongues flicked deep and rhythmically to Parker's thrusts.

"Touchdown! Touchdown! What a score!" called the commentator. Parker rolled over on the side of the bed, and

Michelle snuggled into his arms. She had been with some players before, but not anyone like Parker Thomas. His good looks and supreme physical condition made him a champion among champions under the sheets that night.

"End of the first half, stay tuned. We've got a lot more action to go!" called the commentator on camera. Parker and Michelle snuggled against one another.

"If the Alouettes score here, they'll go home victorious. A field goal won't do it! They've got to score again! First down for the Als. Wait a minute, there's a penalty on the play. The right tackle, Bennet, number sixty-nine, has jumped off sides. Now it's first and fifteen. The quarterback drops back to pass. Complete! First down. But there's another flag on the play. Holding! Sixty-nine! Holding!"

"Shit!" said Parker, "The team's self-destructing!" Parker realized what the coach had talked about the day they met.

"First and twenty-five, the Al's have really dug themselves into a hole now. Let's see if they can get out of it. Patterson, number twenty-seven, is in to replace Bennet." Parker saw the rookie run off the field, and the line coach ranting and raving and screaming. There was no place for the kid to hide.

"Burnes back to throw. And he's gonna be sacked! Fumble! Fumble! Ottawa has the ball!! Ottawa recovers!! This should be the game!!"

"Damn," said Parker. "They need some help up front!"

"I could use some help up front now too, Parker!" said Michelle as she tugged on his arm and tried to coax him to lie down again. Parker turned and passionately put his mouth over hers.

"I'll take care of that business tomorrow!" Parker thought to himself.

\* \* \* \* \* \* \*

The next day at the team meeting, the mood was solemn. Ottawa beat Montreal 20 to 14. When the game film was over and the players were getting ready for practice, Coach Beck came up to Parker Thomas.

"Parker, I'm gona start you this Sunday against Toronto. Hopefully, you can get the offensive line to jell. We're gonna cut the other two linemen, providing you sign the contract that's in your locker. I don't know what management is offering, but if you want to start Sunday, I suggest you sign it." Parker knew he was not in a position to negotiate. Management had him by the balls. He would sign if the contract was fair. Parker went downstairs, in anticipation of what the offer would be. Inside his locker was a contract for fifty thousand for the remainder of the season. That was almost twice what the Giants had paid him, and it was Canadian funny money. Parker had learned the the Canadian dollar was worth $1.07 in United States dollars. He looked at the incentive money, and figured he could hit half the incentives. That, together with the play-off money and hopefuly a Grey Cup share, would mean some serious money for the rest of the season. Parker quickly signed the contract, for it looked just like the standard players contract he had seen in the NFL. For the first time, Parker Thomas felt that he was really wanted and that the team was willing to pay for him. Parker ran the contract up to the management offices. As Parker bounded back down to the locker room, he noticed that his locker had been moved and that the two players that had sat in front of him in team meeting had been released. As he put on his shoulder pads and pulled his jersey over his neck, he was amped up like he had never been before. His joy for himself was mixed with sorrow of watching the two other players get released. He was sad for them, but happy for himself. Football was a cold and impersonal business. You either did the job or you didn't. And if you didn't, you were gone in a heartbeat.

\* \* \* \* \* \* \*

It was late in the fourth quarter. Parker Thomas had his helmet pulled up and his chin strap unbuttoned as the trainer came out and squirted water into Parker's mouth. The clock was winding down, and the game had been decided. Montreal had blown out Toronto 38 to nothing with a vicious ground game. Parker had had his number called on almost three-quarters of the running plays, and had opened up holes that a truck could drive through. He had dominated the man in front of him and the two back-ups that had been put in after him. The guys were all loose and laughing, as the Toronto players stood across the field with an ass-kicked look on their faces.

"Good job, O-line," Burnes the quarterback had said as the team huddled. "One more play and we're outta here. Double tight. Kill the clock. On the first sound." As Parker slowly strutted to the line of scrimmage, he looked around to the sixty thousand fans that were in the stands. They were silent, with the exception of a few boos hurled here and there. It was one of the sweetest thrills in the game for an offensive lineman. Parker had often joked about what a shit job being an offensive lineman was; when you won, the publicity always went to the quarterbacks and receivers, or what they called 'the skilled guys'. The only time an offensive lineman's name was mentioned individually was when he screwed up and made a penalty or allowed the quarterback to get sacked. Then the offensive lineman's name would get blasted out over the public address system. But once in a blue moon, the offensive line would play so well together as a unit, like they had in Toronto, and dominate so badly that you would hear a pin drop in the stadium, and get the fans actually booing at their own team.

*Bill Winters and
JoAnne V. McGrath*

Parker looked over at the Toronto bench and saw the head coach drop his head and take on a look like a blind, whipped puppy dog. Earlier in the game, the Toronto head coach, Ted Kalil, had been yelling at his defense and threatening them, and screaming at Montreal about how they were going to get their asses kicked. This seemed a bit out of character for a head coach, Parker thought. Toronto had upset the Western Division leading Edmonton Eskimos the week before, and they were cocky, thinking themselves better than they actually were. Montreal had thrown down a quick screen to the Toronto sideline, and Parker had sprinted down the line of scrimmage and knocked the charging supporting D.B. off his feet and into their head coach, knocking him down to the ground and knocking off the coach's glasses in the process. Roberts, the tailback, had run right by Parker and had gotten tackled into the Toronto bench area. As the Toronto coach got to his feet and scrambled for his glasses, the Toronto players were screaming cures at Montreal. As Roberts and Parker got up at the same time, Parker nocticed the Toronto coach's glasses at his feet. He put his turf shoes onto the glasses and smashed the lenses into shards as the coach said, "Fuck you!" to Parker. Parker turned to the coach and said, "No, Fuck you!" As the chain crew went out to measure to see if the Alouettes made the first down, Wes Roberts patted Parker on the ass as they jogged back to the huddle.

"You're fucking crazy, Parker! I fuckin' love it!" yelled Wes Roberts. Seeing the crew still busy measuring, Wesley said to the players in the huddle, "Hey, look over at the Toronto bench!" The Montreal players looked at the Toronto bench.

"Parker stepped on the coach's glasses! He can't see shit now!" Montreal players put their hands in the air and shouted toward the Toronto coach: "How many fingers do I have up?!?" Most of the Montreal players had just one finger up, the middle one. That mean act had ignited the offense, and the Alouettes took over the game, rushing for some 350 yards. Montreal threw only six passes the entire game. In a victorious locker room, the players were sky high. They knew they could get it going and make the play-offs: after all, they were the defending champions.

Very rarely does an individual offensive lineman get a game ball, and when a ball is presented, usually it is given to the entire offensive line because the line has to play as a unit. Harley Fennell, Monteal's middle linebacker and team captain, called Parker Thomas up in front of the team and presented him with the game ball. Everybody with the team, from Red the equipment man, to the administrative assistants, congratulated Parker. He was now an integral part of the team and back in the penthouse.

Since the Montreal victory was so one-sided and since the team was exhausted after having two games in one week, the coach gave the team the next day off. Instead of taking the bus home with the team, Parker, Patten, and Wesley Roberts rode back with Michelle, Cheryl and another girl who had driven to the game in Patten's van. Larry was in the van too. Led Zep's 'Whole Lotta Love' cranked from the quad speakers in the vehicle so loudly that it was hard to keep up a conversation. As the van rolled down the highway and headed back toward Montreal, the party rolled too. Larry thrust a cold LaBatts into Parker's hand and proceeded to roll up a fat doobie on the console of the van. As the joint was passed around, everyone took a hit or two. When the joint hit Parker's fingers, he thought back to what the coach had said before the team exited the locker room: "Take care of your bodies, men, and they'll take care of you. Go out and have some fun tonight, but don't over do it!" Parker took one big toke off the joint and coughed as the harsh resin hit the back of his throat. Everybody else in the van looked at him and, in unison, said, "Yeeeah! Eh?"

## I GOT THE BELT!!!

Parker Thomas woke up groggy and rolled over in his bed. He saw long blonde hair streaming over the pillow next to his, but he had to blink his eyes a few times and take a moment to focus before he saw the other woman lying next to her. Parker had been introduced to her, but couldn't remember her name; she was the other girl in the van. Parker sat up a little and looked for another body in the room. Had Larry spent the night too? Nobody else was there. The blonde rolled over and planted her mouth on Parker's mouth, and her tongue went across the roof of his mouth behind his back teeth.

"That's not Michelle!" Parker thought to himself as the blonde had him in a mouth lock. "Michelle must be the other blonde!" The woman who had Parker's lips locked up rolled on top of him, and then over to his other side. Parker was in the middle of a blonde sandwich, and he loved being the meat. As they started to get it on, Michelle woke up. Parker stuffed the head of the blonde on his right under the sheets, figuring that Michelle might blow a fuse or think he didn't like her if she woke up and found Parker doing someone else. As Michelle leaned over to kiss Parker, he felt a warm and wet sensation between his legs.

"Oh, Parker," said the voice under the sheet, "You're so bad!" Parker, in absolute fear, looked into Michelle's eyes.

"It's OK, baby," Michelle said, "You earned it. Better than a game ball, ain't it?" The phone rang and Parker reached an arm over Michelle to answer it.

"Hello?"

"Parker, we're coming over to get you. We're going to brunch at The Forge."

"Wait, wait!" Parker tried to respond, but his voice didn't get across the phone line too clearly because his body was preoccupied by what was happening under the sheets.

"Make it an hour, will you?" Parker managed to choke out. As the no-name blonde worked Parker under the sheets, Michelle got on top of Parker and straddled his chin. She stuck her muff near his mouth, and Parker flicked his tongue into it. Michelle started to moan in pleasure.

BANG! BANG! BANG! Three massive hands hammered on the door to Parker's room.

"We ain't waitin' no fuckin' hour to go eat! Get your big ass out here! What's the matter, got a bad hangover?" called the husky voices that waited outside.

Parker's eyes popped as he saw the door strain from its hinges and the chain lock rattle with the impounds.

The girls jumped up and ran into the bathroom. Parker quickly stuffed the bras and panties that had been lying on the bed under his pillow, and threw on a pair of shorts. He didn't know which of the players the other blonde belonged to, but he sure didn't want to find out.

As Parker opened the door, Wes, Patten and Cheryl, and Burnes and Susie walked into the room.

"Come on, we're gonna go eat." said Patten.

"Did you pull anything last night, Parker?" asked Wes Rogers.

"Probably had too much and passed out!" said Cheryl.

"Come on, we're gonna get you some today, Parker," said Wes. "There's some really outrageous broads at this happy hour, and the singer is a reall looker too. It's about time you got some trim, Parker!" Parker went over to the bed and pulled the spread up over the pillows. He sauntered into the bathroom and hopped into the shower. The girls were standing in the tub behind the shower curtain, and the three of them silently took a shower. Parker walked out of the bathroom after showering and dressing, and said to the group waiting for him: "Come on, let's go. I'm starving. I need some food to kill this hangover."

"Wait a minute. I gotta take a piss!" said Patten.

"You don't want to go in there now," said Parker to Patten.

"Why not?" asked Patten with a quizzical look on his face.

"I just cut the cheese, and believe me, you don't want to go in there! That LaBatts really put me on fire!"

"Thanks for the warning!"

The group marched out of Parker Thomas' room and headed toward the elevator. The van rolled through the Mount Royal section of the city, pulled into a parking lot, and the passengers went into the back door of The Forge. They headed for the lounge and sat at a reserved table.

"You guys are gonna eat, right?" smiled the waitress as she fixed her eyes on Parker. "You guys want a couple of pitchers too, eh?"

"Hey Junie, let me introduce you to our newest player, Parker Thomas." Wes said as he noticed where the waitress' attention was focused.

"I know who he is," said Junie back to Wes. "The announcer said his name at least twenty times during the game." Junie looked at Parker and continued.

"Great game the other day! You guys were super!"

"Hey Junie, when you bring the pitchers, can you bring us a couple of newspapers?" asked Wes Rogers.

"The usual?" asked Junie, "The Post and The Telegram, and a couple pitchers of LaBatts?" Wes looked at Parker when Junie mentioned the LaBatts, but nodded at Junie to let her know their order was the usual one.

"Hey Parker, I think that waitress likes you!" said a man who approached the table and went right for Parker.

"Who are you?" asked Parker.

"Bill Bartone, Montreal Telegram. Getting off to a good start, eh?" pressed the reporter.

Parker's media paranoia hit him in the gut, and his discomfort showed in his face.

"Relax, Parker," said Patten, "Bill's one of us. A lot of time me and him get together here at the bar and knock out his columns." Parker immediately let his guard down after the assurance that came from his team mate.

"How'd you feel about the game?" asked Bartone, again directing his question straight at Parker.

"I'm pumped. We played well on both sides of the ball, and hopefully we've made a statement out there on the field. I think we're ready to make our run."

"How about Kalil? Got anything to say about him?"

"No, not really." gulped Parker as he projected forward and produced the next day's sports headline: THOMAS FLIPS BIRD AND BLINDS COACH.

"Nothing to say about the fact that Toronto shit-canned him?"

"No comment." said Parker, and he sighed with relief.

"Well, gotta go! Deadline is an hour and a half away. Nice game, guys. Nice to meet you too, Parker." the reporter called over his shoulder as he walked away from the table.

As Parker surveyed the bar, he thought to himself: "It doesn't get any better than this!" Montreal had won the game. Parker had gotten the game ball. He had his team-mates for friends, and he had earned their respect. Pay day was tomorrow, and they had the rest of the day to screw around. Hell, they even had the media in their pocket. The only thing missing was the championship. Parker wondered if he had a long-term lease on the penthouse.

"Holy shit, Parker, look at this!" said Patten as he handed Parker a copy of the Montreal Telegram. "Here's a picture of you knocking down one of the Toronto players as Wes is scoring. God, you could frame this one! You got the belt now, Big Guy!"

*From the Outhouse to the Penthouse
and Somewhere in Between*

## A ROUGE IS A ROUGE IS A ROUGE

The weeks rushed by as Montreal reeled off six wins and a tie. Parker had received extensive publicity in the States, and the Shrewsbury Gazette, Parker's hometown newspaper, printed the picture that had appeared in the Montreal Telegram. A hometown reporter had called Parker and done a phone interview with him. Parker had been amazed at the results of the interview that appeared in the hometown news. Fan mail poured in. Cooper, Buzzie, Shea, Tracey, and Herb had stayed in touch, and were talking about coming up to one of the play-off games, or even the championship game. The team was running on all cylinders and had stayed away from serious injuries. Parker was making a name for himself in Montreal, and everywhere he went, the service and attention he received was carte blanche. Tracey and Lori had written several letters, and Parker had barely enough time to write back. The weeks had virtually flown by with meetings and practices, and the way the coaches were working the Montreal team in practices, the team was too tired to hit the streets. But when they did go out, they had a great time. The booze and the drugs were always abundant, if players cared to partake, but Parker exercised extreme control when he was out running with the pack. Parker had gone out a few times with Junie and her girlfriends, and was a very different person than the lonely boy who once lived in a spartan basement room and hit day after day on a rusted sled.

Playing in The Canadian Football League had turned Parker into a seasoned veteran. Parker thought he had witnessed every conceivable thing that a gnarly lineman could experience in football, both on the field and off. Although he was dinged up, he was still healthy and playing football, and his team was winning. To Parker, that's how an offensive lineman was judged. It was either kill or be killed, and Montreal was winning their battles. If the O-line was doing their job up front, the team would win. But on Canadian Thanksgiving, a very cold and windy day that year in Saskatchewan, Parker saw the hilarity in the game, and how the cruel bounce of a ball could seal a team's fate. The unpredictability – that was one of the reasons he loved the game so much. The real world was predictable – people would work each day, collected their pay checks, nobody cared what they did, and then they went home to wives and kids. But every time teams teed up a football, the people would pour into a stadium and virtually live their lives through the players who were out on the gridiron. Screaming and yelling, and many times booing, fans got rid of their frustrations with their mundane and sedentary lives. Football was life on the edge, and that's the way Parker wanted it.

It must have been in his blood. Parker's father had been a top-gun pilot and had done two tours in Nam. He had even been on the cover of Life Magazine, and had almost been killed when he landed a helicopter amid heavy fire during a mission. The V.C. had strafed the belly of the chopper with machine gun bullets and killed the forty or so men in it. Parker's father would himself have been killed, if he had not leaned over and pulled the dead co-pilot off the controls. Football bore the same mentality, but it was surreal. It wasn't life or death.

Parker, deep down in his soul, believed that the secret to his survival in this vicious war of attrition was that he was always able to think clearly. During violent moments in ball games, or when booze or drugs were presented to him on silver platters, when women were throwing themselves at his feet, he always thought about the ramifications of too much self-indulgence. Playing football meant keeping almost the same mentality a military man needed; you had to sacrifice yourself for the squad, for the total good of the squad. And any deviation from that policy would lead to someone getting hurt or someone getting killed. Parker had the same philosophy off the field as he had on the field. When he faced the temptations of drugs, booze, or broads, he would temper his actions and never indulge himself to excess. He wondered if the public really understood what kind of discipline and inteligence and street smarts were needed to play the game.

"We are a cross between entertainers and gladiators." Parker thought to himself. Parker Thomas loved every minute of football, as dearly as he loved every minute of life itself.

For all the serious baggage the game toted, it also carried lighter moments. Saskatchewan had played out their ass that day. They were a last place ball club, but everything went their way. Montreal was losing 28 to 14, with two minutes to go. The Als huddled onto the field and clicked off play after play running the two minute offense. Montreal scored in less than thirty seconds as Joe Burnes hit a streaking Rashid Mohammed for a touchdown. Montreal kicked the extra point, and was down by only seven with a minute twenty-four left in the game. They had been on such a roll, that every Alouette player on the field knew the team could pull out a win. Montreal squib kicked the ball to Saskatchewan, to keep time from clicking off the clock. The Saskatchewan team returned the ball sluggishly to their own thirty. All they had to do was pick up a first down and they would have the game. After two straight running plays, with Montreal calling time-out after each play, Saskatchewan was forced to punt the ball. They angled the ball away from the Al's All–League punt returner, Randy Ready. As the ball was about to be kicked, Randy, sensing that they would, streaked across the outer end of the field and fielded the punt. Through the most amazing set of cuts and on-field shifting and shaking, Ready returned the ball all the way back to the Saskatchewan four yard line and got knocked out of bounds with thirty seconds still left on the clock. Montreal scored on the next play as Burnes rolled around on an option play and pitched to Wes Roberts, the tailback. He bounded in for the touchdown. The Alouettes decided to go for the win, not just the tie, so they tried for the two. Joe Burnes dropped back to throw a fade route to the wide receiver heading to the corner of the end zone, but a the last second tucked the ball and somehow managed to catapult himself into the end zone. He was knocked silly in the process. Montreal was up by one, 29 to 28, and the game was theirs, or so the team thought. Montreal kicked off with a little under fifteen seconds to go. As the kicker approached to kick the football, the wind blew the ball off the tee, just as the kicker hit it with his foot. The ball went bounding, looking like an onsides kick. Saskatchewan deftly caught the muffed kick, ran twenty yards up the field and almost broke the kick for a touchdown. There was now only three seconds to go in the game. Instead of throwing a Hail Mary, they lined up in punt formation. The players on the Alouette team started screaming at the defensive backs: "Get Back!! Get Back!! They're gonna kick it!!"

Parker, thinking the game was over, looked up and said to himself, "What the hell is going on?"

Saskatchewan, which had a shitty team but a great punter, punted the ball, and the ball caught a jet stream. The ball went sailing over the heads of the retreating defensive backs, who were in a full out race for the ball. The ball went bounding into the end zone. The ball had taken such crazy bounces that Randy could not find the handle. The Saskatchewan players were drawing a bead on him. Randy, being the veteran player he was, intelligently was somehow able to field the ball in the end zone and kick it back out, as a puzzled and confused Parker looked on. Saskatchewan had left one or two players back on the forty yard line. As the punt from Ready sailed back, both teams immediately turned around and began sprinting the other way. It looked like a Chinese fire drill. Parker still couldn't figure out what the hell was happening. The Saskatchewan return man ran up and fielded the ball on the Montreal thirty-five yard line. He neatly picked up the ball and shanked the ball into the end zone where they downed it amongst a pile of flailing players who were trying either to down the ball or to knock it out of the end zone. Since the last player who touched the ball would be ruled as the possessing team, Saskatchewan recovered the ball and had a virtual celebration in the end zone. The score board already showing that the time had expired, clicked off a point, showing 29 to 29, and the Saskatchewan fans poured on to the field as if they'd won the championship.

Coach Beck pulled off his headset and just started laughing. When Parker ran up to him, he had a crazed look in his eye.

"What the hell just happened?"

"It's a rouge. It's a fuckin' rouge!" Parker stared at the score board in total disbelief. He imediately thought about how hard Montreal had played and how well the team had performed under intense pressure. But some force had not allowed Montreal to win. The Alouettes had done everything they could as a team, but the cruel hand of fate had dealt the Montreal team a bad hand. What Parker learned on the field that day was that football, although a vicious business, was a fun game and not to be taken seriously. Parker felt he had grown up ten-fold that day, and now he was convinced more than ever that he had seen it all.

The Alouettes' next slated game was with Edmonton, who had already clinched their division title in the Western Conference. The game would be played at home in Montreal, and was already sold out. There was no loss of love between the two teams. Edmonton had an up-and-coming ball club, but had been blown apart by Montreal in the championship game the year before. The game had been played in a twenty-below blizzard, and Montreal had routed Edmonton on their home turf in front of ninety thousand. Wes had gotten drunk one night, and had told Parker in confidence that, during a pre-game warm up a sheet of ice had formed on the astroturf surface after it had been squeegied. Several of the players had put construction staples through the soles of their shoes, thus allowing them to run all over Edmonton on the ice.

"Posi-traction, man," Wes had said, "We posi-tractioned all the way to the bank. We each got 15k for winning the game and a percent of the gate, another 3k. It was larger than a fuckin' Superbowl share!" Wes had just laughed and laughed.

The CFL was a loosely officiated and wild league to play in. A lot of the players were cheap shot artists that got away with a lot because the refs were too stupid to see what the players did. Each team had their own way of trying to screw around with the other teams. Calgary had a horse that was a mascot, and the horse was deliberately kept in the visitors tunnel. Before the games, the horse would be fed well and made so skittish by the buzz in the stadium that it would drop giant turds in the tunnel; the visiting team would then squish through horse shit on their way out to the field. The Hamilton team played their games in an antiquated stadium that had benches like dugouts a quarter or so into the ground beneath the turf. Visiting players had to stay in the dugouts, or they would be pelted with beer and trash thrown from the crazed fans that attended the games. The players used to joke about how they were more like bunkers. B.C. had Crazy George, a fanatical spectator who would parachute onto the field and pound incessantly on a tom-tom. He would hit the drum so hard it could be heard miles away. He would get the fans so jacked up that players couldn't hear the plays being called at the line of scrimmage. Montreal had rolled past the other teams, despite the tactics they employed. Parker was getting over his frustration from his stint with the NFL.

The Edmonton game would serve as a reminder of how vicious football could be. Edmonton had a Canadian wide receiver who was All-League. He kept cracking back on one of Montreal's outside linebackers, Charlie Zapalak. During the half-time in the locker room, while Parker was taking a piss at the urinal, Zapalak stood at the urinal next to him and pissed blood.

"That fucking Farley! I'm gonna kill him. He's cracked back on me five times and I told him if he did it again, I'm gonna fuck him up!" A crack-back block happened when a wide receiver ran a route past the linebackers who had dropped back into coverage. The receiver would then peel back, and slam his helmet into the back of the linebacker, clipping the hell out of him. It was an illegal play and a penalty, but the refs weren't calling it, and the Montreal coaches, as well as the Montreal defense, were going nuts. Zapalak came back to the sidelines early in the third quarter and said, "He did it to me again! I'm gonna fucking kill the bastard!!" Zapalak reached into the trainers' first aid box and pulled out a small pocket knife. A few plays later, when the defense was back on the field, Edmonton called an injury time-out. Farley, the wide receiver, had cracked back on Zapalak again. Zapalak took out the knife and slashed the blade across the receiver's cheek. Blood spurted from the front of his faceguard. Only a handful of players on the Montreal bench had seen Zapalak grab the knife, and the refs saw nothing. The Montreal players' attitude was; "Fuck it! If Edmonton was gonna cheap shot us, and the refs were going to look the other way, we were going to retaliate."

A player could have been killed the way the refs were calling the game that day. There had been several brawls before and after that incident, and the Montreal players later would nickname Zapalak 'The Zodiac Killer', after the California serial murderer who was on the loose at the time of the incident.

Edmonton had beaten the Montreal team earlier in the season, before Parker Thomas had joined the team, but now the Alouettes were more fine-tuned. Parker knew that the key to beating Edmonton was to take away their passing game by controlling the ball on the ground. Montreal had prepared to do just that. Early in the third quarter of the game, an Edmonton defensive tackle had rolled up on Parker's leg, and Parker had to go out with a hyper-extended knee. He sat frustratedly along the sidelines as Edmonton slowly came back from behind. Edmonton had gotten control of the game because Montreal could not control the ball on the ground after Parker had gotten

*From the Outhouse to the Penthouse and Somewhere in Between*

hurt. Montreal did have a great defense, but they eventually wore out and Edmonton won the game. After the game, Parker thought that the coaches would be upset with him personally as well as with the rest of the team because they had lost. Parker was surprised when Coach Beck, in his post-game talk, was not upset enough to personally ream him out. The coach told him to get well, because the team was going to make the play-offs, and they wanted to go into the play-offs full strength. The coaches were confident in what the team could do when it was healthy, and they took the position that they were willing to lose one battle as long as they won the war, the championship. All that mattered was that a team finished the season with an asterisk next to its name in the standings, which denoted that they had secured a play-off spot, preferably with home-field advantage. Parker was pleased that the coaches thought that well of him, and he was determined to lay his ass on the line for them once he got healthy.

The Montreal coaches had conceded the Eastern Division to Ottawa becuase Ottawa had a cupcake schedule the rest of the way and had a two-game lead in the division with three games to go. If the Alouettes won just one out of their three remaining games, they would clinch home-field advantage for the first round of the play-offs. If they advanced, they would meet Ottawa for the Eastern Division Championship at their place as Ottawa had a bid for winning the conference. Montreal would first, however, get to play Ottawa at home in the last game of the regular season. If Montreal dominated them, like Parker thought they could, then the Alouettes would have Ottawa's number and beat them in the conference championship, where they would no doubt meet Edmonton. Montreal had run the tables on Ottawa last year: however, this year, the roles were reversed. Ottawa was first and had beaten them early in the season and figured they would return the favor. The line had Ottawa favored by four and an half points, but Parker knew Montreal was a veteran team and the defending champions, and the Als were a different team now. Parker was thinking that this would help and be a great bargaining chip during off-season contract talks. All they had to do was take apart Ottawa. Montreal had Ottawa's number, and everybody on the Alouettes knew it.

## SO CLOSE, YET SO FAR

Eighty thousand bodies jammed into the Toronto Exhibition Stadium to witness the action of the 90th Coup de Grey. By far the biggest sporting event in Canada, The Grey Cup game had been hyped by all the media, and the fans in the stadium teemed with unbelievable excitement as they anticipated the most important game in The Canadian Football League, and their version of the Superbowl. In the upper-level boxes, lavish parties were going on: champaigne, caviar, lavish buffets, men in Gucci shoes, women in full length mink coats. In the bleachers were young, old, working class, unemployed, families, singles, and representation from every walk of life. This day, where you came from, what you did, or what you owned was of no consequence. The fans were there to see a championship game, and the teams on the field would present a spectacle the fans would carry with them for the rest of their days, as well as relate to succeeding generations. THE EVENT was in front of them.

Montreal had indeed produced for the coaching staff. The Alouettes had beaten Hamilton handily at home in the first round of the play-offs. Hamilton, because of the colors in their uniforms, had been dubbed 'the killer bees' by the Montreal players. Montreal had beaten them twice during the regular season. Hamilton was an over-achieving football team that had played Montreal tough: in the play-off game, Hamilton had played like a swarm of bees. They hung around until late in the fourth quarter when Montreal put them away. Wes Rogers had broken off right tackle, skirted out to the outside, and, with a beautiful cut that left two D.B.'s holding their jocks, raced untouched for the icing touchdown. Parker thought Wes had made the most unbelievable cut he'd ever seen, and Parker had seen some good ones.

In the Ottawa game, for the Eastern Conference final at their place, Montreal won the game in the last minute. Montreal kicked them real good in the final regular season game, but Ottawa had rested most of its players and thought the game meaningless. It was going to be a bell ringer.

The Alouettes had first and goal from the three with three downs to go, after two unsuccessful cracks, one over Patten and one over Parker. The coaches called time-out and were going to kick the field goal on third down for the tying points. CFL teams got three downs to make ten. The coaches had called time-out, and were discussing what they were going to do. Parker, playing for a contract for the next year, started waving and rotating his lower arm to tell the team to run the ball to win the game. When the team elected to run behind Parker

*From the Outhouse to the Penthouse
and Somewhere in Between*

for the winning touchdown, the back had barely gotten in, and it took a few seconds to unpile the heap of bodies clutching, snatching, and clawing for that two or three inches of territory. Wes Rogers had clearly scored, and fist fights and pushing and shoving matches ensued. But Montreal had gotten out of there with a win. Montreal's road to The Grey Cup happened just the way the coaches and Parker had hoped it would. The Alouettes were very confident they could play their game against Edmonton and be repeat winners.

It was a cool, blustery, bright day at Toronto's Exhibition Stadium. The ball would soon sail into the air for the start of the 90th Grey Cup game. In the locker room, Wes Rogers and Parker Thomas looked at one another and nodded, as if to say "Let's go, it's up to us!". The team rolled out of the locker room all amped up for the game. Scarpacci had just given the most inspiring, rousing, and sterling speech Parker had ever heard from a coach. Parker was one of the last players left in the locker room as the team headed out. Wes Rogers grabbed him.

"Come here, Parker, I want to make a toast!" Wes went to his gym bag and took out a bottle of Wild Turkey and two shot glasses. He poured them each a shot. At the same time, he plugged in a casette player. The song 'We are the Champions' by Queen cranked and echoed in the almost empty locker room. Wes held up his shot glass to Parker and said: "Parker, I'm running for the big dollars today! I've rushed for over 2100 yards, and I've been fighting with them all year about what they're gonna pay me next year. So I need to come up big. And I'm counting on you!"

"You'll be all right." said Parker, "Just do what you always do and it will work out. Don't press."

"I promise, Parker, that when I do get this big money, that there will be something in it for you."

"Your red Corvette would do it!" joked Parker. Wes turned down the volume on the casette player, raised his shot glass to Parker, and said: "To us!"

"To us, and to the team!" Parker Thomas saluted. Parker and Wes threw the shots of bourbon down their throats. Voices from the tunnel called out: "Rogers! Thomas! Where the fuck are you? Get your asses out onto the field!" The two players hustled out onto the field when they heard the coaches call for them.

As Parker Thomas bounded out of the tunnel and got onto the field, he looked up to where he had reserved seats for his guests. In the stands were Herb Hanson, Cooper, Buzzie, Mike Shea, and Tracey. It gave Parker a real thrill to know that the people who cared the most about him and his career in its earlier days were now there to see him play. "Friends, the most important people in the world!" thought Parker to himself. Parker joined his team on the bench and waited. 'Oh, Canada' played over the stadium's speakers. Edmonton kicked off.

As the Montreal offensive team huddled up for the first play, Patten and Parker looked at each other, reached out, and joined hands for a second. The Quarterback stepped into the huddle.

"All right, you guys, here we go! Red right. Y motion. Sixteen. Wham. O. On two. Ready? Break!" The huddle broke and the players went to the line of scrimmage. The Edmonton team had a confident, ready eye.

"Blue seventeen! Blue seventeen!" Burnes barked. He was audibling and changed the play because Edmonton had over-shifted and had anticipated the run to the right side. Burnes noticed the shift, and handed the ball off to Wes Rogers, who swept around the left end and ran the ball for fifteen yards. Montreal was pumped!

"Penalty on the play!" called the ref. The Montreal left guard, Ben Patrick, had jumped off-sides. The play was nullified, and Montreal was not off to a good start. Nobody said anything, as the quarterback stepped into the huddle.

"Listen, you guys," he calmly said, "They're over-shifting, so be awake for the audible. Let's go! Blue left. Seventeen. Wham. O. On one. Ready? Break!" The play was run, and Wesley rumbled for eight yards.

"Allright, you guys, better! Better! Better keep it going up front! Red right. Sixteen. Wham. G. O. Play pass. On the first sound!"

"Set!" Burnes faked the action and rolled out looking for an open man. He scrambled around and unloaded the ball to Wes Rogers. But as Wes caught the ball and started streaking, untouched, he lost the handle on the ball! Edmonton recovered and ran the ball to the Montreal thirty. Parker bounded off the field amongst a bunch of cursing on the sidelines. Edmonton, in four plays, was in the end zone and up 7 to 0.

As the offensive team went back onto the field to start the second series, the quarterback called out: "All right! Huddle up! Relax! Relax! Let's play our game! Blue left. Y motion. Eighteen. Toss sweep. On one. Ready? Break!" Burnes pitched the ball to Wes Rogers. Rogers skirted around the right side, but just as he got up field, he got rocked by Ed Jones, Edmonton's All-Pro Safety. Wes Rogers coughed up the ball. An Edmonton linebacker scooped it up and ran the ball to the five yard line. Edmonton scored on the next play, and had Montreal on the run. Wes Rogers just lay there, stunned from the hit. After a minute or so, he limped off the field to a rousing cheer. Parker felt bad for Wes Rogers. He had so much on the line, and was getting off to a tough start. Montreal had dug themselves into a hole, and it would be tough for a ground-oriented offense to get back in the game. The Alouettes knew it would take a lot of poise, patience and execution to climb back in it, but they were up to the task. Parker Thomas went over to Wes Rogers.

"You all right, man?"

"I'm blowin' it, man!"

"Relax, Wesley, we got plenty of time. Patten and I will get you going!" Wes gave Parker an appreciative look.

The rest of the game, until late in the fourth quarter, had gone the same way. Montreal was down 20 to 14, as Edmonton had kicked two field goals in the second half, and Montreal had scored on two long, penalty-driven drives, running over Patten and Parker Thomas. Wes Rogers had coughed up the ball one more time during a key drive early in the third quarter, and had blown a fuse. The coaches sat him down and put a back-up into the game until Wesley could get a hold on himself. The ballclub would surely use this against him in contract negotiations. Twenty-one hundred yards, a CFL title, and a new rushing record – even with all those statistics, Wes was showing up bad in the 'What have you done for us lately?' world of pro football. Even as badly as Montreal had played, the defense was keeping them in the game. Parker knew the defense would get a turn-over and give the offense a chance to go down the field and win the game. Late in the fourth quarter, with about three minutes to go, the Al's defense got the ball back as Edmonton fumbled. Montreal had forty yards to go to win the game. The Alouettes knew they could do it. As Burnes stepped into the huddle, he looked up at the Montreal players, and with confidence in his eyes and in his voice said, very calmly, "Let's put these guys away and go home. We can do it. Red right. Eighteen. Toss sweep. On one. Ready? Break!"

"Set! Hut!" Burnes pitched the ball to Felton Straiter, Wesley's back-up. Straiter ripped off a gain of nine yards. The fans went beserk! Players were going back to the huddle with a look of victory in their eyes. It was more of the same as Montreal methodically drove the ball to the fifteen yard line and the clock wound down.

"First and ten." the ref said, as Montreal came up to the line of scrimmage to run the next play.

"Set! Hut... hut... hut!" Burnes rolled out to the left, reversed his field, scrambled back across the field, and then calmly set up and drilled a strike to Mohammed, who had hooked five yards in front of the goal line. He caught the ball and was immediately popped, causing the ball to squirt into the air. Parker, sprinting downfield, saw the ball coming his way. As he bounded towards the ball in an effort to catch it, Parker felt a helmet knock his ankles out from underneath him. He crashed to the ground and landed just a yard away from the ball. When the pile of bodies was unheaped, Edmonton had recovered the ball. Parker could not believe how loud the cracking of bodies against each other had been. He heard bones crunch and helments crackle over the uproar of the rocking stadium. It was as if he had heard the sounds for the first timne, and comprehended their meaning. This was a vicious sport played at an intensity level second to none. As Edmonton whooped and hollered, Parker got up. His ankle was killing him. Parker hoped it wasn't broken. Edmonton ran out the clock and won The Grey Cup.

*Bill Winters and
JoAnne V. McGrath*

# THE ONE THAT GOT AWAY

The red Corvette sped down Interstate 95. Destination: Florida Keys.

"Want some more wine?" Wes Rogers asked.

"No, I've had enough. I've got a buzz."

"Well, that bag of goodies Larry gave us will put you over the top!" said Wes. Parker Thomas knew Wes felt that is was his fault that Montreal had lost the game.

"I'm trippin'! I don't know how I could have dropped that pass!" said Wes, "And fumbled those balls!"

"Look, Wesley, you didn't lose the game for us. So get that shit out of your head. We win as a team, and we lose as a team. You're the one that got us there!"

"Thanks, buddy. I'm really, really sorry. Hey, reach into the console and break out that stash. I need something to kill the pain, and this wine ain't cuttin' it. Hey Parker, did you know I got two kids and a woman?" Parker Thomas stared at Wes in total disbelief. All the time he had known Wes Rogers, Wes never said anything about family. In fact, when the Montreal pack was on the prowl, Wes Rogers pulled more broads than any other player. He had the title.

"Guess you never know what's not right in front of you," Parker mused to himself as he pulled a packet from the dashboard. "Things are never really what they seem to be."

"You know, Parker, I really needed to score that contract so I could take care of the two kids." continued Wes.

"Well, what about your wife?" asked Parker.

"We're friends, but she's really not my wife, just my old lady."

"Don't worry, they'll give you your money." said Parker.

"I don't know. Straiter ran pretty good when they took me out. They're groomin him. You know, if they can find somebody just as good, they don't have to shell out the dollars. My ass might be history."

"Come on, Wes, you know you're 'the man'. As you go, we go."

"Yeah, well if they thought that, they would have been talking to my agent. They won't even return his phone calls." said a distraught Wes Rogers.

Everybody knew that contracts had option years. In the option year, when new negotiations were supposed to take place, a ball club would typically wait until the last minute to do any talking. And when they did talk, the offer was insultingly low. A player virtually had no bargaining power because of the tremendous supply of players and so few jobs. Even when a player had them by the balls, like Wesley did, they would not negotiate in good faith, getting a real bang for the buck, while the player was playing with the hopes of bigger dollars later. Wesley had carried the rock the whole season and never said a word. Parker knew it had to have been hard on him. It was a shitty part of the business.

Attempting to change the subject and lighten the mood, Parker asked, "Hey, what time is it?"

"Oh, it's about five thrity. Where are we on the map?"

"Just south of Miami."

"Good, we'll have time to pull over and get some more booze. God, that sunset is beautiful, isn't it?"

"Sure is." agreed Parker, hoping Wes was less despondent. "This is where I want to live when I retire. Get myself a crib on the water, put a boat out in the back yard, be able to just kick back and drop a hook in the water or write, or do whatever I want.."

"Hey, put that Pink Floyd tape in, will ya." Wes said, "and pass me the wine. What time do we have to be at the marina?"

"We'll have to be there by eleven. Herb and Cooper and everybody else are meeting us down there."

"That was real nice of your friends to charter the boat for us. I just can't wait to sit back, get in a couple of days of fishing, and rest, and down a few cases of Bud." said Wes as he took a guzzle and emptied the wine bottle.

*From the Outhouse to the Penthouse and Somewhere in Between*

\* \* \* \* \* \* \*

Later that evening, the Corvette pulled into the Palm Key Marina parking lot. Wes and Parker got up out of the Corvette and stretched their arms. They were sore from the season, and from the twenty-six hour marathon down the interstates.

"Fuckin' A...!" bellowed Parker Thomas, as a pair of arms set about his waist in an almost tackle. Parker's weight went down onto his ankle. The stress fracture sent bolts of pain up his shin and into his spine.

"A? What, are you Canadian or something?" said the voice behind Parker.

"God Damn it, Coop!"

"Well, at least I don't have a squirt gun!" Then Cooper looked down and saw the white cast on Parker's leg.

"Sorry about that, buddy. Didn't know how bad a hit you'd taken!"

"No problem. Good to see you, man. The boat ready?"

"All set. Let's get your gear stowed and we're off." said Cooper to both men.

"Are the rest of the gang here? Is Herb with you?"

"Yeah, him and Tracey came with Shea and Buzzie yesterday. I drove with the others. Even Ryan Corbett came along. You remember him don't you, Parker? They're all on the boat, and we're just waiting on the two of you. Let's hit it!"

"Damn, I haven't seen Ryan for years. What's he doing now?"

"He's got your old job loading beer trucks." said Cooper with a smile. "Only he uses the two-wheeler when he brings in the kegs!"

The three men walked down the pier toward the 'Crazy Lady', the sixty-foot pleasure craft they had chartered. As they walked up the gangplank, they were met by Captain Ron. He was almost as big as Parker Thomas, and had huge tattoos over his arms. He had a big space between his two front teeth, and had retired from the navy and set up a charter business in the Keys. He lived for his boat, and for his dog, Hangover.

"Welcome aboard. Rough seas on the way out tonight. Front just blew through. We're gonna have twelve foot swells all the way out. If you're gonna ride astern and drop a line tonight, better buckle into the chairs. If you need anything, I'll be on the bridge. Hope you enjoy the cruise. Stow the gear below, and make sure it's fast."

Wes and Parker went below to their tiny cabins, changed over, and went back up on deck. They seated themselves in the fighting chairs in the rear of the boat. Parker harnessed in and put his leg with the cast on it up on the transom to take the pressure off it. Even though it was close to midnight, the balmy temperatures made him glad that he had decided to put on a pair of shorts. The sub-tropical weather of Palm Key was much easier to tolerate than the cold Canadian climate they had just left. Wes leaned over in his chair and looked at the case of Bud that the mate had set out for him. He reached down, grabbed a can, and popped the top. The mate gave them rods and efficiently baited them. The two men looked out over the Atlantic as the boat make its way out to sea.

After a few hours of drinking and hitting Larry's goody bag, the girls had gone to bed. Herb had passed out, and Tracey had gone below to tend to Jennifer, who always got seasick, but wouldn't miss a party if her life depended on it.

"You know," said Cooper, "They're starting a new football league, Parker. The United States Football League. They're gonna play their games in the spring, and they got a big television contract. A lot of the cities that want NFL teams and haven't been able to get them are getting teams in the new league. I bet that in a couple of years, there's some kind of merger. Remember the old ABA with Dr. J.? There's some major players in this deal, like Donald Trump. He's supposed to get the New Jersey – New York franchise. And John Bassett, who owns the Toronto Tribune, he's getting a team in Tampa. And there's a players' agent, Jerry Argovitz, you know him, he's a doctor and has all those dental clinics, well, he's gonna get the Houston franchise. Don't know if all these things have been in the papers up in Canada, but it's big news here. They're going after the top players in the draft, and they're going to try to steal some guys from the NFL and CFL."

Parker Thomas was half asleep as the voices next to him rattled on, but he was awake enough to ask a question.

"What are they gonna pay the players?"

Mike Shea joined the conversation: "They're gonna pay the players all the same, at least what you're making in Canada, and they're gonna give unlimited salaries to two players every year. I hear they're gonna be paying Herschel a couple of million. You know they got a t.v. contract, and a lot of guys with a lot of jack who want in." Parker looked over at Wes, who was sitting next to him. He wasn't on the same planet. He seemed preoccupied and just kept popping can tabs and looking at the wake left by the 'Crazy Lady'.

"You know," added Ryan Corbett, "They got some big time coaches who are supposed to be leaving the NFL or college ranks. It was in the Times a couple of weeks ago."

Parker thought back to his Giants' training camp days when he worked against a lot of the Memphis players from the defunct World Football League, and how good some of them had been. Parker thought there were plenty of players around that could stockpile teams and make the league competitive, like expansion teams in the NFL. And with two impact players coming on every year from either the NFL or the first pick of the draft, who knew, maybe there would be a merger. Hell, the New

Jersey Nets with Dr. J. and Billie Paultz had done it, and a lot of the World League players had made the NFL after their league's demise. Maybe this would present a perfect opportunity for Parker. A lot of further thought would depend on what Montreal offered him in his option year and on what some of these new teams may offer him as well.

"Man, if I could play," said Ryan Corbett, "I'd play football here down in Florida on a nice grass field and retire and hope I'd get the opportunity to make the big big money in the States when the merger happens. It sure would beat loading those frozen kegs in the dead of winter and working for somebody else!"

Parker Thomas turned and stared at Ryan Corbett. Even though they were miles apart in what they did and what they made, they had been boyhood pals. And Ryan had been smart enough to come up to Parker and tell him to try out for the Rhinos. Ryan, although being a good player himself in high school and dreaming of going on to play college ball, never got an opportunity. He had been virtually relegated to accepting his place in life. Parker saw the love of the game through his eyes, and was thankful that at least he had been given the opportunity to live the dream. Maybe Parker would get a job down in Florida and prolong his career by playing on a grass surface rather than an astroturf field, move his mom down, and hook up with Herb and Cooper in a few years, as they were always talking about retiring in Florida. Hell, maybe they'd get together and open a juice joint and... and... zzzzzz... zzzzzzz.

* * * * * * *

"Parker! You're burning up!" Parker Thomas snapped his eyes open, and standing next to him was Tracey. He looked around and blinked, as the mid-moring sun glimmered off the water. Tracey squirted a blob of suntan lotion into her palm, and rubbed Parker's shin above his cast, working her hands over his knee and up his thigh under his shorts. Parker Thomas had fallen asleep in the fighting chair. When he looked around for the other guys who had been up into the wee hours of the morning, all he saw was Wesley Roger's half empty case of Bud on the deck next to his chair.

"Where are the other guys, Tracey?"

"Must be down below sleeping it off. They were all pretty loaded when I went to bed at three." Parker looked out over the water, and inhaled deeply, trying to wake up and take in the salt air. He scrunched his nose.

"Why do I smell bleach, or lysol, or something?"

"Oh, the mate was up earlier," said Tracey. "Somebody puked up and the mate had to swab up. Who was sitting next to you, Parker?"

"Oh, that was Wes. Yeah, he's had it kind of rough lately, and he's been overdoing for the past couple of days."

"He'll feel better when he sleeps it off." said Tracey. Parker took a good look at Tracey's breasts, slightly sunburned, as they bulged out of her bikini top.

"Hey Tracey, why don't we go down to the cabin and you can finish putting on the rest of my lotion down there?"

"Sounds good to me!" beamed Tracey. Parker unsnapped his safety harness, and Tracey helped him move his cast off the transom of the fishing boat. They walked down the five steps to the guest quarters, and then they went into their tiny cabin.

The single berth that pulled out of the wall was only six feet long.

"This ought to be interesting." thought Parker as he dropped his shorts to the floor and stepped out of them.

"How are we gonna do this?" asked Tracey. "Are you going to have to lay down because of your cast?"

"You'd better do the work this time." Parker answered as he lay on the small bunk. Parker maneuvered himself under the chains that held the berth to its support pins and lay on the berth with his left foot sticking over the edge. His right foot was on the floor, and he tried to keep his knee bent to keep the pressure off his ankle.

Just as Tracey climbed on top of him, the boat pitched to starboard, and Tracey went flying onto the floor. The boat rolled to the other side. Tracey banged her head on the bottom of the berth. She got to her feet and tried to climb onto Parker again, but the boat once again heaved, and she went slamming into the cabin wall.

"Remind me to bring my helmet for you next time!" Parker quipped.

"Parker, I don't think this is going to work. Not like this."

"Forget it, Tracey. I'll just catch a nap for now and see you out on deck later.

"I hope you're not disappointed, Parker." said Tracey with a sincere tone of apology in her voice.

"No Problem," responded Parker. "Hey, Tracey, hand me my shorts, will ya? I think I got a couple of pain killers in my pocket. Wes gave them to me last night."

Tracey walked over to get Parker's shorts, and as she picked them up, a car key fell out of the pocket. It made a little pinging noise as it hit the cabin floor.

"What was that?" asked Parker.

"Just your car key." nonchalantly answered Tracey.

"That's not my key." answered Parker Thomas, and then the light bulb went on in his head.

"What cabin is Wes in?" asked Parker as he got up from the berth and hobbled into his shorts.

*From the Outhouse to the Penthouse and Somewhere in Between*

"Next one." said Tracey. "What's the big deal?" Without answering, Parker limped out of his cabin and banged on the door of the cabin next to his.

"Wes! Wes! Get up!!" hollered Parker, hoping against hope that his guess was wrong. Not waiting long for an answer, Parker Thomas pushed open the cabin door and walked inside. Wes was not there. The berth was still made, so it had not been slept on. A piece of yellow paper lay under it on the floor. Parker picked up the yellow paper and read it.

"RE: YOUR INQUIRY. RELEASED FROM CONTRACT. BEST OF LUCK." The Montreal ballclub had cut Wesley Rogers. Parker stuffed the ship-to-shore-gram into his pocket and headed for the deck. Herb and Jennifer were catching some rays on the forward deck, and Cooper, Buzzie, and Shea were in the chairs at the stern and listening to Ryan Corbett tell one of his infamous 'Rhinos' great moments' stories. Wesley Rogers was nowhere in the picture.

Parker climbed the five stairs to the bridge, where Captain Ron was trying his best to keep the boat under control in the massive Atlantic swells. Parker told him that he had found the cablegram in Wesley Rogers' cabin, and that he had searched the boat for Wes and couldn't find him.

"What time did that cablegram come?" pressed Parker.

"About four thirty this morning." replied the mate, who was also up on the bridge and was busy feeding the dog.

"Search the ship!" ordered the Captain, "Bow to stern!"

"I don't think I need to, sir," said the mate. "About five this morning when I was on watch and the weather started getting rough, I was cutting bait, getting ready for today. I heard a big splash, and thought maybe someone had gone over, but no one yelled, so I just kept cutting bait. Didn't give it a second thought at the time. Hangover never barked. That was just a couple of minutes after I delivered the cablegram."

"Nooo! NO! NO! WES! MY GOD! OH NO!!!!" wailed Parker Thomas as he clutched the key to the red Corvette in the palm of his hand and stared out over the wild and frothy Atlantic.

*From the Outhouse to the Penthouse
and Somewhere in Between*

## THE DOCTRINE OF FOOTBALL

Parker Thomas bounded out of his office, got into his car, drove down West Shore Boulevard and headed to the Tampa Bay Bandits office. He was excited because today he was to sign a contract that hopefully would execute the game plan Ryan Corbett had mentioned on their fishing trip thirteen months earlier. The time that had gone by since the day of the fishing trip had been a long haul for Parker Thomas. He had taken a financial consultant job with a brokerage firm in a small town outside of Tampa. He had rented, on a lease option, a house on the water, had recovered sufficiently from his broken ankle, and had been training and working out, and was in great shape. The wonderful Florida weather had allowed him to heal up and improve from the last time he had played. Tampa Bay had called him several months earlier while he had been negotiating with Montreal. The Tampa team had told him that they would buy out his option with Montreal if he would play for them.

Montreal refused the buy-out, as many of the CFL players were jumping to the new league. The Bandits were going to give Parker a nice bonus, the day after his contract with

Montreal expired, which was January first. The general manager, Buddy Edwards, had been the general manager with the B.C. team of the CFL and was familiar with Parker's ability. Everything had been lined up: now all Parker had to do was take care of business. He had been there before, and he knew what he had to do.

\* \* \* \* \* \* \*

As the team stood in the tunnel, Smokey the horse, the Bandits' mascot, backed up and dropped huge turds. This was the first regular season game and kick-off in the league history. The Governor of Florida was at the stadium, as well as the many celebrities who had invested in the ball club. Parker thought about the horse, how he had been there before, and how he was truly a veteran, assuming a leadership role. Parker Thomas felt a great sense of accomplishment with the fact that he had executed his game plan, and he knew that getting off the ball and making that first contact with the opponent would just be an affirmation of all his beliefs. Life is what happens while you sit around planning for it! Parker was not content to just plan; he spent his time executing.

Parker would be starting at left guard and back-up at center and tackle and tight end. He would also back-up for punts and field goals. This was a role he had played before. The Bandits would carry seven linemen instead of eight or nine like other teams, and would feature a passing attack which no league had ever seen the likes of before. Whereas Parker had been on teams before that had put a premium on running the football and playing smash mouth, the Bandits would air it out and play a wide opened brand of football. The Bandits would carry an extra wide receiver, as opposed to an extra lineman.

"And now, laides and gentlemen, the starting line-up for the Tampa Bay Bandits!" blared the public address announcer. Parker waited for his name to be called, and he was totally jacked up, yet retained the composure that came only with being a veteran of the game.

The game was a nip and tuck affair and a hardily fought contest. Tampa had moved the ball well and scored fourteen points. But Boston had run the ball and played well, and managed to go ahead with a field goal late in the fourth quarter. Boston had a free safety that had been making practically every play after the Bandits had caught the ball, and Tampa had not been able to hit any big pass plays for touch downs. What had made the situation worse was, that after making several vicious tackles, Tommy Hoag, the free safety would talk trash at the young receivers. They were getting intimidated. As the Bandits were in the huddle, Reed, the quarterback, who was a veteran of the NFL and had jumped ship to play with the new league, tried to calm down the wide receivers. He looked at them and said, "When you catch the ball, make sure they don't strip you." Parker immediately flashed back to the Grey Cup game when Mohammed had dropped the ball when Montreal was going in for the winning score. Parker had seen it before, so he took it upon himself to trail the play down the field. In case of a fumble, he would have a chance to be in on the recovery. His instinct had taken over. Tampa had thrown the ball fifty times, with thirty-six completions and no fumble. Statistics told Parker that one was due, and he was going to do his damnedest not to let Boston get the ball when it did.

The Bandits moved the ball down the field with three consecutive pass plays for first downs. Parker kept runing down the field as most of his other team mates on the O-line looked at him as if he was a nut job. Parker had felt the effect of his rigorous training again on the sled with Herb Hanson as they prepared for the season and still had plenty of gas left in his tank. On the next play, his conditioning paid off as Willie Williams, the Tampa wide receiver, fumbled the ball after taking a hit from Hoag, the Boston free safety who had been hitting on Williams all that day. The players were all yelling and screaming and clawing for the ball. The crowd went crazy as Parker Thomas emerged from the pile of bodies with the ball in his hands. Parker tossed the ball to the ref as Tommy Hoag and several of the other D.B.'s, with crazed looks in their eyes, screamed out: "You better not send another motherfucker across the middle, because if you do, we'll get the next one. You lucky motherfuckers!"

As Tampa rehuddled, Reed, the quarterback looked at Parker and said, "Good hustle, man, good hustle. All right, let's take it in! Trips! Eighty-six. X hook. Y post. Z corner. On the first sound. Ready? Break!" Tampa had forty yards to go and less than a minute left. Parker, as he got down in his stance, said to himself: "I've been here before."

As the quarterbasck dropped back into the pocket amidst a fierce rush by the Boston Breakers, he dodged the grasp of a blitzing middle linebacker, hurriedly set up, and delivered a ten-yard completion to the tight end who had hooked. The defensive backs, as they tackled him, were holding him up in an effort to try to lay a lick on him and strip the football. Parker, flying downfield and getting pissed off and seeing this brutal tactic, zeroed in on Hoag just as Smith, the tight end, went down. Wham! Parker delivered a knock-out blow to the breastplate of Hoag, the free safety, just as the whistle blew and before Hoag could open his mouth again. An injury time-out was called. Hoag was carried off the field, K.O'ed from the game. Parker could hear the screaming of the entire Bandits team: "Great fucking hit! Holy shit! Did you see that? He's a mad man!" The entire Tampa team appeared to have been shot with adrenalin as they got back into the huddle. David Jones, a wide receiver fresh off the bench and who had just been put in the game, caught a corner route on the next play, handily beating Hoag's replacement and a tired defensive secondary, for the winning touchdown. The fans went nuts and the Tampa defense stopped Boston cold. With only twenty seconds to go, Boston saw their quarterback get sacked three times. Tampa had won the game, and Parker knew that they had a good ball club. Parker had wondered what the caliber of play would be going in, and saw that the Bandits were two or three players away from being as good as a winning NFL team. Parker had made the right decision to play for the Bandits.

Parker felt that he had become a team leader that day, and his hustle had been instrumental in the win. He knew he had been an unsung hero that day, a familiar role that every offensive lineman feels.

The Tampa team reeled off its next four wins in a row and was easily the class of the league. With their winning record came media attention that allowed the entire country to evaluate the new league.

As the league proved to be a rousing success in most of the cities, the Bandits were still cutting and releasing a few players, and signing other ones in an attempt to get better. Even though the team was winning and Parker was playing every snap, the team always seemed to have lined up in the wings players who felt they were better than what Tampa already had, and the coaches wanted to look at a few of them. There was a rumor of an impending NFL strike, and many players were looking for a try-out. Parker, although ecstatic that he was playing and fulfilling his mission, realized that no one's job was secure.

It didn't matter if you had gone through six weeks of a two-a-days and three exhibition games, and four regular season games and proven yourself: this was pro football, and the concept of team, even in a new league, didn't matter – it was business. Parker Thomas was hurt, but not surprised, when, in the fifth game, they sat him on the bench for the entire game and started Steven Geary in Parker's left guard position. Geary was a high-round draft choice out of a big school, Parker didn't know which one, and a silver spoon. Tampa had signed him amidst the hype of the NFL draft, and the coaches seemed to like him. During the game, Geary got beat for four sacks, and Tampa got routed by Greg Arden's Chicago Blitz as Lonnie Radley, an All-Pro and veteran out of Notre Dame, intercepted the Bandits six times, setting a modern pro-football record. The Chicago team had the Washington Redskins philisophy of playing only proven veterans, even in a new league. Parker was inserted back into the line-up the following week as Geary was outright released. Parker felt he solidified his job in the next game, as Tampa beat 4-and-1 Denver on Monday night in a nationally televised game on ESPN. The Bandits had thrown the ball sixty-two times without a sack, thus setting a pro-football record. The game had gone into overtime, and the

Tampa team ran off the left side on a draw over Parker for the winning touchdown. The game had been an exhausting one, and the team had had a difficult time adjusting to the thin air. At times, Parker's heart felt like it was going to explode. Parker would make the Bandits pay for their lack of faith in the off-season during contract talks. Parker thought of Wes Rogers and said, "If they're gonna pay me to produce, they're gonna pay me now, not later." Where was the value system going? People were out on the streets starving, families were homeless, the inner city kids were joining gangs because they didn't have any facilities. The season ticket holder couldn't even afford to take his wife and 2.7 children to a game – the tab was more than his weekly paycheck. Hell, the NFL's Tampa Bay Buccaneers, who had three first-round picks on their offensive line, couldn't even win a game! Didn't it make more sense to pay these high-round draft picks and impact players only a little more money than the guys in-between who were proving it every day on the field, and give that extra money when they actually produced and hit the incentives in their contract for performance on the field, and take those millions left over and pump them back into the community – feed the hungry, shelter the homeless, build rec centers and ball fields for the inner city kids, and reward the fans and the community for supporting a team. That philosophy would create a better performance on the field – a better product and a happier fan, and a lot more happy football players. Parker's Ivy education had taught him that great empires had crumbled after hundreds of years of existence over this very issue of wealth. The have-nots would rebel against the haves, and then start all over again. The sport was becoming big business and not a sport, and the fan would, no doubt, become alienated. Hell, Parker felt guilty for making what he did for a living compared to what Ryan Corbett made. He felt happy he was earning his money, but he knew the teams were not paying near what he was worth. The media always talked about the few players with the big money contracts, and the public perception was that all players were paid like silver spoons. He felt very uncomfortable with the public perception.

Parker was kind of happy to see the coaching staff get slapped back into reality and go with proven players, and if they wanted to look at younger players, they were going to have to wait until the end of the season. Parker would keep his mouth shut and prove to them that they'd better keep him around. As Parker sat out of the game, he thought, "What the hell were they looking for? This Geary kid has no experience, can play only one position, can't snap for punts and field goals, and had been with the team for only a week. Plus, he looked soft. I wonder if he'd spent four months of two-a-days on the sled?"

Parker tried not to take it personally, but sometimes he wondered. The game Parker spent on the bench motivated him not only to play harder, but also to play for himself. Tampa had a two game lead in their division, and Parker would do everything in his power to keep them there. He knew the young players would see how he reacted, and even though the coaches might not know, the younger players looked up to Parker. A lot of the coaches were rookies themselves, having never coached in the pro's. Parker did not take his sitting out during that game as a personal affront – it was business. The team, as it approached the Oakland game, was the starship franchise of the league. Tampa led the league in attendance and wins, and the team threw the ball like no team ever had thrown it before.

As the course of the season wound down, Parker, with four games to go, had established himself as a team leader. Ben Dyne, the center, had cracked his ribs earlier in the season. Parker, in practice, would run with the first and second units, as well as back-up for snaps and field goals, and the mileage started to pile up on his body. The coaching staff, turned on by how well the team was doing, instead of letting go of the reins, started cracking the whip. Tuesdays and Wednesdays, as well as sometimes Thursdays, the Bandits were in full gear and hitting like it was a game. Everything was the same, except the tackling. And the injuries started to pile up, particularly on the younger players.

*From the Outhouse to the Penthouse and Somewhere in Between*

The younger players, especially the ones who had gone high in the draft, sat out and got rested as their back-ups ran their spots. The team had two impact players making over a million: one was the NFL total sack leader, raided from the Packers, that ultimately caused the head coach to lose his job, and the other was one of the top running backs in the first round of the draft out of college. Both were immediately given penthouse status and preferential treatment. This was a familiar theme that Parker had experienced in every ball club he had played on in the pro's. There were the haves and the have-nots, and those guys in-between, and those guys in-between were the backbone of a football team. It would fire Parker up, for although Parker knew it was business and he was happy for his teammates that could get whatever they could get, and that he wasn't a have-not in front of a television set either, it seemed that if you got your education from an academically oriented school and came through the back door, something that was encouraged when you were young, that you constantly had to prove yourself while other players were able to kick back when they were hurt because of either their press clippings and what they had done in college or because of how much money was invested in them. It was sort of a lie.

A lot of times these guys never had degrees and had majored in advanced basket weaving. Rumor had it that there was a guy on the Bandits who couldn't even read. With a hot league competing against the NFL for players, salaries were starting to go haywire. A few of the owners, during the middle of the season, in order to get better clubs, started paying astronomical amounts of money to unproven college players. Their test scores at the combines and their performance in college would dictate that they would get contracts with twenty-six million dollars over five years. The owners' business philosophy was more people would come to see these marquee players play. Parker felt that football was football, that people came to see a winning performance, and that computers didn't play football – men with hearts and character did.

Parker also believed in getting an opportunity, and in what you did when you got your chance. You either deliver or you don't. Prove it on the field, in front of the fan, and then get your money. And, give back!

The season rolled by as the Bandits kept their division lead and had only four games to go. These thoughts stayed in Parker's subconscious as the nagging injuries piled up on his body. He had been living on Napacin, as did practically the whole team. It had been handed out in cups, and had been put in each player's locker along with salt tablets. The synthetic cortisone, most widely given to horses, was so potent that the players had to get off of it after three weeks and give their bodies a rest before using any more. Continued use could cause an eating away of joints and potential liver damage. Parker himself had taken three injections in his right shoulder for chronic bursitis, because there were days he rolled out of bed that he couldn't raise his hands over his head or raise them in front of him. A player needed to use his hands and arms and his shoulders, as well as the rest of his body in order to survive.

Parker had gotten a turf-toe injury and had to be shot up a couple of times before the game so that he could play. He had an extreme inflamation of the tendon in the big toe area caused by a hyper-extension of the toe due to the astroturf. A rookie offensive lineman had watched Parker get shot up in the shoulder, then in the toe with cortisone in order to kill the pain. Even the shots were painful. The rookie didn't seem phased when the team doctor told Parker that the toe would have to be drained before he could give Parker the shot. In addition to 'turf toe', Parder had 'black toe', a severe swelling under the big toe nail caused by blood building up in the toe after it had been smashed. The doctors would have to drain the toe to take away some of the pressure in order to shoot him up. For weeks the toe had been so sore that when it was stepped on in practice the pain was excruciating. The doctor took a power drill and reamed a hole in Parker's big toe nail. Blood and puss came squirting up like a geyser, and the rookie got sick. The doctor and Parker just laughed. As Parker went back into the locker room with his new toe and shoulder, and felt brand new as the drug worked its way into the injured areas, Parker passed the gagging rookie leaning over the commode. Parker waved to him and called out,"Science!". The rookie looked at Parker as if he were crazy.

As Tampa prepared to play Oakland, Parker felt his right ankle, which he had injured in Montreal, start to bother him. He had gone to the team physician and trainers, complaining to them that it was hurting and that he wanted to get an x-ray to see what was wrong. The x-rays had come back showing no damage and nothing broken. Parker had even tried using DMSO, a metal solvent many times used on horses to kill pain. The ache in his ankle had started to nag him, but it had not caused him to miss any games or practices. In the Oakland game, late in the third quarter, as Parker set up to pass block, he heard a snap. Parker knew that he had broken his leg, and he had to come out of the game on a stretcher and be taken underneath the stadium to be x-rayed. As the team doctors came in to examine him, the doctor was immediately interrupted to take care of an Oakland player. The player, brought in on a stretcher, was a former All-Pro tight end in the NFL. He had gotten hit running across the middle by one of the Bandits' backers and had been knocked out cold. Both team doctors and several trainers feverishly tried to revive him. As he lay next to Parker on a stretcher with his hands across his chest and with a cervical collar on, he looked as if he had been laid out in a coffin. He hadn't woken up despite the doctors attempts for ten minutes. Parker wondered if the player was dead. After ten minutes or so, the player started to moan, but overheard the team doctors, who were looking at his x-rays, say, "He's done. That's his career. He's broken his neck, but I don't think he's paralyzed." Parker felt as if he had been in a war. The only differerce was that instead of bomb noise, there was crowd noise.

When Parker was finally able to be looked at, having had his gear cut off with hedge clippers, the results of his x-rays had been 'no break'. They gave him a pair of crutches and told him to go shower and to watch the rest of the game inside the locker room on the monitor. They told him that he would probably be out a couple of days, and that he had a severely sprained ankle. Hell, Parker had broken it once before – he knew what it felt like, but this was ten times worse. He knew he would have to fight them to get a second opinion – it was all part of the game. Parker, the following week, watched practice on crutches until Thrusday, when the coaches told him that if he didn't go suit up, he wouldn't start.

"We're not gonna let you sit back. If you're only hurt, you play. If your injured, you don't play!" Parker knew that he had one of the highest pain tolerances on the team, because the trainer had told him that when he had his physical earlier in the year. Parker always gave his all until he couldn't go any more, and then some, because that is what a 'tweener' did.

As Parker suited up for practice that Thursday and got the start the following week, he lasted until late in the second quarter. As he attempted to get himself back in the line-up, it was obvious to him that he couldn't go. The coaches looked at him like he was trying to take a vacation. But when they gave him a more detailed x-ray, a bone scan, they found out that he had a seven-inch stress fracture in his shin. That had not shown up in the first x-ray. Parker felt vindicated that at least he was right about his injury, and that he had given the team everything he had. He hoped that the coaches and management would reward him for his efforts – after all, the team was in first place. Parker had played every snap in every game except one, and in that game they got blown out. He'd run every play in practice with the first and the second units during those Tuesday, Wednesday and Thursday practices like each was a ballgame. Hopefully, coaches and management would reward him in the off-season for his efforts and remember him, not forget him. This is why a tweener had to go balls-out: it was a matter of character. The love of the game, a lunch-bucket, blue collar, come-to-practice and play-every-day attitude by himself and by his team mates that had gotten the team to first place.

*From the Outhouse to the Penthouse
and Somewhere in Between*

Would they remember or would they treat him like a disposable unit and give the money to someone else, either an impact NFL player that they say attracted people to the games, or to some hot-shot rookie who had only the potential to play?

Parker Thomas watched the Bandits lose three out of their last four games and go from first place to last place, and miss the play-offs. He watched several of his team mates drop like flies, many in the same boat as he. Parker Thomas watched the games while he was in a plaster cast up to his gonads. He was through. He was done for the year, and so was the team.

Bill Winters and
JoAnne V. McGrath

# DOLLARS AND SENSE

"Call on line two, Parker."

"Thanks, Pru. I'll pick up." said Parker Thomas to his sales assistant. Parker Thomas picked up the receiver of the phone on his desk at RLS Securities, a brokerage firm just outside of Tampa. As he sat looking out the window of his eleventh floor office, he scanned Tampa Bay and the skyline in front of him.

"Parker Thomas. How may I help you?"

"Parker, this is Helen Greer." said the voice on the other end of the phone. Helen Greer was the wife of one of the highest paid players in pro-football. She and her husband had a splendid estate on a peninsula that jutted out into the Bay. Paul Greer had helped Parker launch his second career by giving him some money to invest a year back. Parker did a lot of nertworking with his football contacts and had built up a clientele that had made him a top producer at the small, struggling investment firm that he how worked for.

"Parker, I want you to withdraw twenty thousand out of our annuity and send the check to us."

"Well, I wouldn't advise doing that. There's a penalty for the withdrawal, and it's pretty stiff. Plus, because the money is growing tax-deferred, the IRS is gonna clip you another ten percent above your regular tax bracket. Besides, the investment's been doing real good. Can't you get the money somewhere else? I'd hate to see you take a hit like that if you don't have to."

"There is nowhere else. Paul sold the last of his General Motors a couple of months ago. I need the money to put into the checking account so that we can meet our mortgage payment and cover credit card bills. They're really piling up and past due."

"OK, I can get you a check in four days. But you and Paul will have to stop in the office and sign a withdrawal form."

"Four days? We can't wait four days!"

"Come on in and sign the papers today. I'll get the company to overnight the money into your account. It can be in there by noon tomorrow." Over the phone, Parker heard the screams and yelling of the Greer children in the background. He had been over the Greer house many times, and had often witnessed the hell-raising and commotion the five children were capable of.

"I can't get over there. The kids are home, the nanny is on vacation, and the only vehicle in the garage is the Triumph."

"Well, why don't I come over. What time is good? What time will Paul be home?"

"I don't know. He took one of the boats out earlier, and he didn't tell me what time he'd be back."

"Call me as soon as he gets in. You have my pager number. I'll get the paperwork ready to go and have it with me. I'll take care of everything."

"Thanks, Parker. I'll page you as soon as Paul gets in."

Parker Thomas hung up the phone. He had been a friend of Paul Greer for many years and knew his lifestyle. Like many other players, Greer had signed for the big bucks and was living large, thinking that the money would come in forever. Parker had become appalled at how the agents, who were just labor negotiators, had taken their four or five percent, and somehow managed to convince players that they also managed money as part of their roles. Many times the agent had a broker in his pocket, and would put players into shit deals, like bars and restaurants and limited partnerships, and businesses that the agent usually had a hand in. The commissions were large for the agents and brokers, and the investments, Parker thought, weren't suitable for what a player needed to have for after he retired. Parker had learned this by calling over nine hundred NFL ball players at home during the NFL strike. About a third of them were really hurting because all their money was tied up and nothing was coming in. Parker had gotten a list of players to call from a big agent who had formerly been a judge: he had encouraged Parker to try to give back to the game. Parker felt he knew what went through a player's mind better than an agent or a broker, who often times invested money and left the player with limited cash flow. A lot of bar and restaurant deals and other business ventures went under. And the government had changed the tax laws, so that limited partnerships became virtually worthless as a tax-advantage item. When the player retired and was hit with this stark reality and making a living in the real world, the agents were gone, setting their sights on the naive rookies coming into the league.

If only a handful of checks weren't coming in during the strike and a player couldn't meet his day to day living expenses now, what the hell would a player do when he really retired from football and had to go out into the real world, work, and prove himself all over again? A lot of players had told Parker that they had lost a lot of money, and told him that they had to play a lot longer to make up for the losses they had already incurred. Parker convinced some of them to start running their own money, with him giving advice and service, and eliminate the middle man, the agent with the broker in his pocket.

Additionally, Parker had told a lot of players that he personally felt that they really didn't need an agent. He had always negotiated his own contracts, and had always gotten bonus money and a base salary with incentives. He had been told when he signed his first pro contract that management looked at the draft as the garbage pail of football. Some unproven player was going to come in and tell them what he was going to make. Most of the teams ranked their linemen one through ten, number one making this, number ten making that. An agent would just take the offer the club made and go back and tell the player he had cut a hell of a deal. Parker felt that unless you were a top pick in the first few rounds of the draft, you had no bargaining power. The NFL had already proved that with free agency. Marquee players, playing out their option, would test themselves on the market and find no takers. The reason for this was simple – the compensation to sign a marquee player from another team would require the marquee player's team to be compensated with draft picks from the other team. The better the player was, the more players they had to give up to get him. The NFL had things covered. They owned the players.

Parker's middle-class background had taught him the value of a dollar. Playing pro football afforded him the opportunity to make a damned good living right out of college, and Parker realized how fortunate he was. He still played for the love of the game, but pro football had been reduced to playing for the dollars. He had seen how his mother had struggled to raise him and how she had sacrificed following his father's death. The government, in its wisdom, had decided to cut back Parker's mother's widow pension, and if it weren't for Parker's help, she would not have been able to meet even her modest living expenses. Parker remembered going home one day and finding a letter from the bank on the coffee table in the living room. He found out that his mother missed a mortgage payment and the bank had notified her that they were starting foreclosure. Parker immediately withdrew money from his savings account and paid off the entire eight thousand dollar mortgage. She had made payments faithfully for twenty years on the loan, and the situation she was in was her thanks for giving the bank tens of thousands of dollars in interest above her original loan amount. Parker vowed he would never let himself be put into a situation like that. He knew the value of a dollar and was thankful that he had been able to save and invest. His investments had doubled, and he felt that over the next ten years, if the growth continued, he would have enough money to start a family and start to work on writing, something that Parker found that he liked to do. Since that night on the boat when Wes disappeared, Parker found the only way to cope with the pain that he felt was to put it down on paper. The more he wrote, the more he learned about himself and the way he felt about the world. Putting his thoughts down on paper forced him to think clearly, so in times of stress and turmoil, Parker often would pick up a pen. Parker was not going to make his exit like Wes, who had jumped ship so that his kids could get through college on the two hundred thousand dollar life insurance policy he left them. There was life after football, and Parker intended to live it.

Parker had always worked in the off-season, but he felt discriminated against when he looked for work. He had gambled on his future to go after a dream, rather than run the traditional route of working for the man, and having limited control over his future. Parker felt that that route led only to the outhouse. He also knew that working for the man wasn't secure either. Parker felt playing pro football was a privilege, and with that came responsibilities to be a role model on and off the field. He fought hard to get these teams to pay for that way of life.

The major brokerage firms wouldn't hire Parker because his job was seasonal, and they claimed it wasn't fair to others at the firm who worked year round. Parker had felt that his Ivy education and the fact that he was a pro ballplayer counted for something, and that he should at least be given an opportunity to work as an apprentice, and continue to work as an apprentice until he retired from pro football and started to work full time. Since Parker hadn't gone to law school or med school, he had been directed to to into the borkerage industry because he could make a good living and have unlimited upside financial potential. It was also a career that allowed him to train, lift the weights, run the miles and sprints, and hit the sled in order to play pro football. If he had worked a nine-to-five job, the employer wouldn't go for that. He had learned that when loading kegs for Rhinegold. Parker had worked as a doorman until six o'clock in the morning two or three nights a week for one of his friends, and had hustled during the day until he convinced a small, independent brokerage firm to give him an opportunity. Parker further had to sell a product he believed in to players that he loved and to retirees who were banking on him to do the right thing. Ivy's academics had little relevance to pro football, and Parker thought that college, no matter what school, only prepared people to learn to teach themselves. He felt a great deal of appreciation just to get hired by the firm that he now worked for. And there was another kind of pressure, that of gathering assets and investing them properly and not lose the client so that when he retired he'd still have them. This was not an easy task if you were gone six or seven months out of the year. If Parker could do this, he might be able to keep up with his fraternity brothers who were in the real world going the traditional route. Lawton Biddle had already established a successful surgical practice, and Mack Warren was a rising star in a major Philadelphia law firm. Mike Brennan's government career had taken him all over the globe, and Lenny Silverman was already a vice president at IBM's world headquarters. Parker Thomas did not see himself showing up at an Ivy reunion twenty years in the future to tell the rest of the Tau

Kappa Epsilon guys that he was the captain of a keg crew or painting houses for a living.

Even though Parker deeply admired men who took the traditional route to success, he was glad to have the opportunity to do something that everyone wished they could do. Parker Thomas was content in his own rite. His idea of the penthouse was to be able to do what he had dreamed about, and to love what he was doing. How many other people out there really loved what they did? All the carte blanche he received was only a perk.

As Parker Thomas got ready for the upcoming season, his brokerage firm job allowed him to train and to put in the many hours he needed to stay in shape. And with the impending NFL USFL anti-trust case, Parker was now preparing to play some twenty-something ball games in the spring, get a few weeks off in the summer, and then play in the fall until the merger would take place. If the merger happened, the union had said that salaries would increase dramatically. Parker had to prepare in the hopes that the merger would take place, as well as keep afloat the reality of taking care of business in the here and now. It would be a long haul playing another twenty-plus games in the fall. If Parker survived in one piece, the management might be forced to admit that he was one hell of a player and that they were willing to put their money where their mouth was. This served as Parker's motivation to get up in the morning before work and train, work all day, and then go lift in the weight room to build himself up. There was nothing glamorous about his routine, but Parker Thomas would be ready to face his future. This was the run for the money.

Bill Winters and
JoAnne V. McGrath

# ALL DRESSED UP AND NO PLACE TO GO

The Tampa Bay Bandits' spring training camp was a virtual revolving door. A few new teams had been added to the league as expansion teams, because the rousing success of the USFL's first season had proven that many cities deserved pro football teams. Cities like Jacksonville, Baltimore, Memphis, Oakland, and Orlando were ready to go. The cities that thought they had a good shot at getting an NFL team committed the dollars to NFL players who had played out their options and were on the market. There were a lot of proven players available, and players' salaries in both leagues started to skyrocket. The ony roadblock was the on-going court case to find out if the NFL was guilty of anti-trust, and if their monopoly could be broken. The case was the biggest and most expensive anti-trust case in the history of the United States.

Parker was quietly optimistic that the USFL would win the case and that there would be some kind of merger. He believed that America had been built on the free enterprise system, and that the NFL monopoly would be busted. A lot of the owners had put twenty to thirty million dollars into their USFL teams, and in legal fees. Anti-trust cases paid triple damages, so if the

USFL won, the award by a jury, if it came down at a billion dollars, would become three billion, and the NFL would have to pay out.

The NFL would not be able to come up with that much money, and instead of spending more money on legal fees and on countless appeals and judgements for further damages, would capitulate and merge the league, and pick up those markets that were ready to go.

The Bandits players used to joke about playing the Bucs in a winner-take-all, loser-leave-town game with the whole city watching. The loser would then go to Orlando. The NFL powers would never let that happen. The Bandits would probably merge with the new Orlando expansion team and play in Orlando. Parker felt that something good had to come out of this scenario, and that anything that happened to him would be a bonus. All Parker could do was control what he could control by playing solid football and hope not to get hurt.

In training camp, Parker started out at his familiar left guard spot. The team won its first two exhibition games. He had seen the influx of talent from the year before when the competition was fierce, and there were a handful of players who were now playing on the juice. Players now coming in were bigger and faster than ever, and it was obvious that they were on performance enhancing drugs. The most widely used drug was Simobol, a synthetic gorilla hormone that had been making the rounds via the Mexican pipeline. If players used Simobol, they could pack on a good fifteen or twenty pounds, and get stronger and faster much more quickly than by traditional workouts. The problem was that they had to stay on the drug, and Simobol had long-term health effects.

Drug testing was a joke: players easily got around the limited testing. The leagues were at a loss at how to even test for Simobol since it so closely resembled natural human hormones, and they were also unsure how to handle a situation if a player was caught using it. The owners were also caught up in the improved product on the field as more players started to use the drug. Parker, in his surgery with the Giants, had been given a form of this drug by the hospital doctor in an effort to get him onto the field faster. He had noticed a change in his body, and although physically addicting, the drug had made him very ill. Parker believed that once he got himself back to where he was naturally, that he would get too big on that stuff. And there was an old axiom he had been taught – you can only get so big and so strong; sooner or later it boiled down to how quick you are and how fast you can play the game. He struggled as he worked against some of the guys on Simobol in camp. They were a bitch to play against, and many times one of the side effects, the rage, would manifest itself. Parker remembered a story told by one of his old CFL team mates who now played in the USFL. He had mistakenly cut blocked their

*From the Outhouse to the Penthouse and Somewhere in Between*

All-Pro defensive end one time in practice. The defensive end, having had four knee operations, went ballistic and grabbed him by the facemask and literally ripped the facemask off of his helmet. He flew into a rage that scared the shit out of the entire team. The way he told the story that day was funnier than hell, but Parker thought himself crazy enough when he was on the field, and he didn't want to take some drug that might make him blow a fuse. Parker factored that into the equation, and for the time being, decided not to live by the needle. He had gotten this far under his own power, but thought about what he'd do if the big dollars really presented themselves.

As Parker got up the next day and was reading the sports page over the shitter before practice, in bold headlines was: BANDITS SIGN FORMER REDSKINS' OFFENSIVE GUARD STEVE SCHMEEL. Schmeel had gotten a half million dollar signing bonus and a guaranteed two year contract. Immediately, Parker Thomas knew that he had been put out of his starting job. Schmeel's claim to fame was that he had been a back-up offensive guard for the Redskins when they went to the Superbowl. Bandits' management figured that Schmeel would draw more people to the games because of his m.o., and that would justify the contract. It made good copy. Parker, after seeing Schmeel play, became incensed because he felt that he was better than Schmeel, plus could play a number of different positions. But all that aside, Schmeel came into camp in terrible shape. "What the hell were the coaches thinking?" Parker asked himself out loud.

It became clear as the nose on Parker's face that the Bandits didn't think too much of him. Parker thought of Wesley, and didn't take the team's decision personally – after all, football was business. As to Schmeel, Parker thought, "If he was lucky enough to put himself in that position, great. The Superbowl really did mean something." As usual, Parker minimalized the situation, because he had seen this happen to other players in the league. Again he spoke to himself out loud: "Well, I can play center. That's really my best position. Maybe they'll give me a chance there."

As training camp wound down, Parker agonized over his back-up status and the lack of reps. Although Parker made the final cut, all his former linemen from the year before got released. He knew it would be just a matter of time before they cut him too. The press was already talking about how the Bandits were going to sign a center who was a back-up for the Rams. The center was a former All-Pro. Parker was merely around for insurance – to back up the offensive line and also to back-up for punts and field goals.

As the team won its first game at home, Parker sat on the bench and was just relegated to the wedge on kick-off team. When he drove to practice following that game, the new offensive line coach of the Bandits called to him just before team meetings and said: "Parker, you got a minute? Bring your play book."

Parker knew he was getting the axe. The coach said: "We've signed Craig Killbourne, and I want to thank you for helping establish the team. I think you can still play in this league, so perhaps you'll get picked up. I want to thank you for your attitude and committment, but we're gonna go with the younger players that we have."

"OK, coach." said Parker. He could get no other words out of his mouth. He was in shock.

Parker didn't agree with their decision, and inside he was furious. But he was in too much of a shock to argue or plead his case. After Parker left the office, he immediately got on the phone and started calling other teams. The Jacksonville team, an expansion team, was having their opener Saturday night. And one of his former team mates was on the squad. Parker gave him a call, and Ted was happy to hear from Parker. He told Parker that he would talk to the offensive line coach about setting up a meeting between him and Parker after the game. After much pleading to the coach, the player called Parker back. He told Parker that the coach would see him, but not to get his hopes up. On Saturday, Parker got into the red Corvette he had put into storage and headed for Jacksonville. He had woked too hard to get where he was, and once again would try to beat the politics and big money of pro football.

*Bill Winters and
JoAnne V. McGrath*

# DO THE FOOTBALL LIMBO!

Parker Thomas sat in the stands and watched Jacksonville easily rout the Washington Federals, the worst team in the league. By looking at the program, Parker knew immediately that he could help this team. He watched as his buddy Ted played. He couldn't believe how much bigger and stronger his friend had gotten since Giants' camp. Ted was obviously on the juice.

From the stands, Parker looked around and assessed the entire situation. He studied the program for a while, and later when he looked up, he saw one of the Jacksonville cheerleaders standing near the tunnel checking him out. He watched the rest of the game, and after it was over, went over to find Ted and meet the coach. As he was looking for them, Parker bumped into a body. He turned around. It was the same cheerleader who had checked him out earlier.

"Oh, excuse me." said the cheerleader.

"No problem." said Parker as he took a look at her classic features and perfect figure.

"Do you know Ted Jamison? I'm supposed to meet him here." said Parker in an effort to keep the conversation going.

"Sure. I know all the players. He should be right out. Are you going out with him after the game?"

"Where does the team usually go?" asked Parker, who really didn't care where the team went. He just wanted to know where the gorgeous brunette in front of him was heading so that he could catch up with her.

"We go to Mulligan's. Maybe I'll see you there!" Parker knew he would not have a problem getting her phone number, and that she was as hot for him as he was for her. As a matter of fact, he knew that she would wait at Mulligan's until he got there, and that the phone number wouldn't be the only thing he would get.

"Thanks. By the way, what's your name?" Parker asked the cheerleader.

"Terry. What's yours?"

"I'm Parker Thomas. Maybe I'll see you at Mulligan's."

"Tell you what, meet me right here after you get done with your business, and we'll talk for a while."

"That would be great! I'm supposed to talk with the line coach. My buddy Ted is gonna introduce me to him, hopefully. So look for me as soon as I'm done."

Parker hoped that she would not interrupt the conversation, which had to be all business. He know how sometimes coaches were really funny about women. Parker thought back to one of his old team mates, Tommy, who had moved into Parker's waterfront house and helped out with the payments. They had a lot of fun together chasing skirts, and Parker used to joke about how much fun it was to run with Tommy because he was such a lady killer. There were always good looking cast offs, and Parker was always happy to be back-up. But Tommy's matinee idol looks blew up in his face one day. On the team plane on the way to play Oakland, Parker and Tommy sat in the very last row and listened to their walkmans, as they usually did on road trips. An absolutely stunning stewardess went up and down the aisle and quickly zeroed in on Tommy. It was difficult for her to hide her strong attraction to him in front of the team, because she was such a looker that everyone else on the plane had focused their attention on her and literally drooled as she walked by. She was like a piece of meat in front of a pack of starving wolves. Even the coaches and managers up front in first class made a few passes at her.

For the first two hours of the flight, she kept coming to the back of the plane and talking to Tommy, jamming him up and making him very uncomfortable with the situation. While she was in the rear of the plane making plays on Tommy, one of the team's major investors, a good friend of the owner, went to the back of the plane.

He said he was headed for the rest room, but the real reason he was there was to hit on the stewardess. He had alread been partying it up in first class, and it was pretty obvious that the rest room was not his destination. He was not happy when the stewardess made it quite apparent that she preferred Tommy over him. As the flight continued, a lot of the players had droned off into a sleep and the cabin lights were low. Tommy got up to use the rest room. The stewardess noticed that he was not in his seat, and she headed for the lavatory compartment. As Tommy opened the lavatory door to head back to his seat, the stewardess whispered a few words to him. Tommy tapped Parker on the shoulder and asked him to keep an eye out as he joined the mile high club. Parker stood up, and, pretending to be waiting to use the rest room next, kept guard at the door while behind him he could hear the banging around and throes of passion that were going on in the tiny, cramped compartment.

"Oh... again! Yes! Tommy! Yes! Lower!... Oh... again!" Parker tried to keep a straight look on his face as he waited ten minutes for the couple to emerge. Tommy and the stewardess got out of the lavatory, and Tommy walked back to his seat. Parker stepped into the lavatory, waited two minutes, and then came out and sat down next to Tommy.

"So," said Parker as he settled into his seat, "Did you join the mile high club?"

"I just got a real frequent flyer bonus, pal!" Tommy said with a huge grin. The rest of the flight was uneventful.

As the team was getting off the plane, Parker and Tommy were the last two passengers to exit the craft. The stewardess grabbed Tommy and whispered to him: "I'm staying at the same hotel you guys are, and I've been invited to a party with the coaches and owners. I'll call you." At the baggage grab, a lot of the players gave Tommy the 'way to go!' look. Tommy looked like a guy thrashing and drowning in water with no one around to help out. Amid the heckles and oohing of the players, Tommy noticed that the coaches and managers did not share the same amusement with his situation.

That night, as Tommy and Parker went across the street to get a bite for dinner before the team meeting and bed-check, Tommy said to Parker: "Damn! Do you think I should have done that? She was infatuated with me, and you know I can't help myself. The reason I'm over here across the street and not in the hotel lounge with everybody else is so that I can hide. She's already called the room twice! I'm trying to avoid her until we get locked in tonight after bed check."

A approximately eleven thirty that night, there was a knock at the hotel room door. Tommy got up out of bed, threw a towel on, and went over to the door.

"Who is it?" Tommy asked.

"Tommy, oh Tommy! Is that you?" Tommy recognized the voice – it was the stewardess from the flight.

*From the Outhouse to the Penthouse  
and Somewhere in Between*

"Open UP!" she drunkenly blurted out. "I've been… hiccup!… downstaris at the party with the owners and coaches. Hiccup!… What a bunch of big Lame-O's! Hiccup! Tommy, please let me in!!"

"Monica, get out of here. The coaches are doing bed check. If they catch you up here, whatever you do, don't tell them my name or why you came up here! Now please, get back on the elevator and get out of here!" Monica kept knocking at the door.

"Hiccup! Please, Tommy… let me come in… hiccup!" Buddy Edwards, the general manager of the Bandits got off the elevator and came down the hall for bed check. He had one of the trainers with him.

"Miss, you're going to have to leave and go downstairs." Edwards snapped.

"Oh, Buddy, darling, is that… hiccup!… you?" Buddy Edwards turned to the trainer who was with him and said: "Take Monica downstairs, back to the party, Hobie!" The trainer ushered the stewardess back down the hall and into the elevator. Buddy Edwards pounded on the hotel room door: "Thomas! Norton! Are you both in there?"

"Yes sir!" answered Parker.

"Open up now!" Parker Thomas got out of bed and opened the door. Edwards was fuming.

"Norton asleep?" Edwards demanded as he made sure ther eas a body in Tommy Norton's bed. Then he truned to Parker

Thomas and said: "Thomas, you ready for the game tomorrow?"

"Yes, Buddy." Parker answered. Buddy Edwards gave Parker Thomas a steely-eyed look.

"I like you, Parker, and I like your pal Tommy, too, but you better tell him to cool it with that stewardess! A couple of the coaches and owners are really pissed off!"

"He's been trying to avoid her. He's not doing anything! In fact, she's been stalking him!"

"Well, Parker, he'd better watch his step, for his own good!"

The Bandits team defeated Oakland the next day and flew back to Florida. Tommy, on the flight home, had been relieved that Monica did not work the return flight. Something was up, but he didn't dwell on it very much because he had been smashed in the mouth during the game when he went to make a tackle on a run play. He had bitten through his tongue so badly when he made the tackle that it had to be stitched. His face was all swollen, and he was in terrible pain. He was in no shape to have Monica see him or to handle her on the ride home.

The team members had been busting his balls since the beginning of the flight home. They had been making quip after quip, saying things like: "I bet little darling would get turned on with those stitches between her legs!" and: "How are you gonna French kiss like that, Pal?" and: "What was the name of that

Greek motherfucker in mythology that had his tongue cut out because he pulled too many broads? Lapp-a-nipple-us?"

"No, stupid! It was Suk-a-muff-adies!"

"You're both wrong, motherfuckers! It was Clit-a-lick-adus!" The team roared all through the flight, and Tommy wished that he had an eject button in the arm of his seat.

Pro football players were some of the best stand-up comics and one-upsmanship artists on the planet. Humor took the boredom out of road trips; it took the edge off a solemn mood if a team lost, and it often took away the pain from injuries sustained in games.

The following morning, before Parker and Tommy headed for practice, the phone rang.

"I've got it!" Tommy called out, and picked up the receiver.

As Parker got out of the shower, he yelled to Tommy: "Where are you! Who was on the phone?" There was no answer. Parker looked into the living room. Tommy was sitting on the couch, just staring into space.

"I just got cut." said Tommy.

"They can't cut you, you're hurt."

"They're giving me my last two game checks, and that's it."

"You'll be healed up by then."

"When I asked them why they were cutting me, they said I lacked aggressiveness on the field." Tommy incredulously stated.

"That's fucking bullshit! You're one of our headhunters back there!" said Parker.

"Well, I did get beat for that touchdown."

Parker thought to himself: even though that wasn't really the reason, management would always find a way to justify their decisions, and with media, the truth surely wouldn't come out.

Parker and Tommy both knew why Tommy had been cut: management and the coaches were going to dictate policy to the players. And when a player went on the road, he'd better be focused on the game. Disrespect of management was a heavy sin, even if it was the mere appearance of it.

Parker looked at Tommy's face and the blood crusted scar near his mouth.

"What a fucking sport!" Parker thought to himself, "Cold blooded!"

\* \* \* \* \* \* \*

"Hey, Teddy!" said Parker Thomas to his pal after he had come through the tunnel. Ted had showered and shaved after the game and had signed a few programs for the fans. Parker, standing there waiting to be introduced to the line coach, felt like an autograph seeker himself.

"Hey, Parker."

"You did all right out there."

"Yeah, but I didn't play much." Parker noticed that Teddy had a serious mood swing and looked like a manic depressive. "Probably coming off the Simobol." Parker thought to himself.

"Yeah, the coach said he'd come out and talk to you for a few minutes. But Parker, it doesn't look good. The coaches are really happy with the way the offensive line played. It's gonna be tough to get in."

"Well, you know the Feds are the worst team in the league. I hope they don't think every game is going to be like that. That line coach, he's a rookie in this league. They just don't know that much about the competition at this point."

"Yeah, well try to tell them that!" Teddy said. "I know what you can do. Well, listen, Parker, why don't you stop by Mulligan's. I won't hang out long 'cause I'm tired. Just gonna grab a few beers and head home."

"Teddy, are you all right?"

"Yeah, I always feel kind of nauseous after the games lately. And me and Lisa haven't been getting along too good. Fighting a lot." That didn't make sense to Parker. He had met Lisa and thought her to be on the timid side. Parker kept the conversation rolling: "You still seeing Lisa?"

"Yeah, we're engaged. Hey Parker, here's the coach coming now. Coach Young, this is Parker Thomas, the guy I was telling you about."

"Hey, Parker, Paul Young." said the line coach as he extended a right hand in Parker's direction. "Parker, we're not looking at anybody right now. So th best thing I can tell you to do is call Monday and leave your information with my secretary. I'll put you in the file."

"You guys played well today, but the rest of the league isn't like the Feds. I know I can help your team. I can play center, guard, tackle, and even tight end. Plus, I can snap for punts and field goals."

"Yeah, I'm familiar with you, Parker. If anybody goes down, I'll give you a call. But for right now, I'm going with who we got." Parker knew enough when to lay off. The last way he wanted to sound was desperate, even though everybody knew he was.

"Well listen, Parker, I've gotta go. Good luck to you." Paul Young turned to Ted: "Ted, you'll be in the weight room first thing in the morning, right?"

"Yeah, coach. I'll be there."

"You're getting a lot bigger and stronger, Ted. We gotta get you in there."

"Thanks, coach." Paul Young strolled away from the two football players to a family that was waiting for him in a green car.

"Parker, I gotta go. I gotta show at Mulligan's. They're having some kind of party there. I'm beat."

*From the Outhouse to the Penthouse and Somewhere in Between*

"Hey, man, stay in touch with me. You know, if you ever need anybody to talk to, just give me a call." Teddy looked into Parker's eyes with a sorrowful look. Maybe Parker was reading into things too much, or maybe Teddy really had been using heavy. Parker dismissed his thoughts.

"Good luck, Parker." said Teddy as he gave his pal a hug. He turned and walked down the tunnel. Parker felt a tap on his shoulder.

"Hi, Parker."

"Oh, hi Terry."

"What did the coach say? Is he gonna give you a chance?"

"Nah, not right now."

"You know, I know who you are. I saw you play two games last year at Tampa Stadium. You were a good player. I like the way you played. Plus, you had one of the tightest butts on the team."

"Would you mind getting a cup of coffee with me?" Parker asked in an embarrassed yet encouraged tone.

"Well you can come to Mulligan's too with the rest of us."

"Nah, be like brown-nosing."

"OK, I know this place around the corner from where I live. I've gotta stop home and change before I go to Mulligan's. Just follow me back to my place." Parker followed Terry back to her apartment in his red Corvette. As he pulled up in front of her building, she said, "Why don't you put it in park and come on up. I'll be a couple of minutes." Parker followed Terry up to her apartment and they went inside.

"Get yourself a beer, Parker, if you want one. In the fridge." Terry went into the bedroom to change. Parker stood in the kitchen, then walked out to the living room.

"Parker, do you smoke pot?" Terry called from the bedroom.

"Yeah, once in a blue moon. After the season is over and I'm all beat to shit."

"Well, would you mind rolling a joint for me? Why don't you turn on the stereo and put on 103.9?" Parker went over to the stereo cabinet and put on the music. Terry called again from the bedroom.

"Parker, what are you gonna do now?"

"I guess I'll drive home and wait for the phone to ring." Parker Thomas was in no man's land. Maybe he'd hang out at his mother's new house. He had just bought it for her and moved her into a house around the corner from his. She wanted him to repaint a couple of rooms for her. As far as football was concerned, Parker was on the outside looking in. He still had plenty of mileage left, but no road to drive down. Terry emerged from the bedroom. She had on a pair of gym shorts and a football jersey.

"Parker, why don't you stay with me tonight? We'll do something, even just hang out. I don't feel like going to the party now. And if I catch my second wind, I can go later." Terry grabbed the freshly rolled joint from Parker and fired it up.

"I'm not that great a roller." said Parker. She passed the joint to Parker, and he took a big hit off it. Parker felt totally unemployed and null and void.

"You know, you can stay here tonight if you'd like. It's a long drive back to Tampa and it's getting late."

"That would be great. Mind if I use the phone to call home? Just need to let my mom know where I am and check my messages, if I have any."

"Sure, Parker, go ahead. The phone's right there." Parker made his call and hung up the phone. He took a few more hits of the weed. An old Gino Vanelli tune came across the radio, as if to set the mood.

"Parker, you want a rub down or something, to kind of relax a little?" Parker felt the joint kicking in, and the thought of this beautiful brunette rubbing her hands all over him would be the best drug he could ever have.

"You know, I'm studying massage, and I hope to become a masseuse, so I'd be glad if you'd let me practice on you."

"Well, as long as you don't feel like I'm coming on to you." Parker Thomas said.

"It's cool, Parker. I trust you. You're a good guy. I kind of like you. You're so sweet for a big, tough football player. You're just a big teddy bear."

Parker took off his shoes, pulled off his shirt, and lay on the bed with his jeans still on.

"Parker, I'm gonna give you a full body massage, so those jeans will have to come off. You want me to do it right, don't you?"

"Damn, I've died and gone to heaven!" Parker thought to himself as he took off his jeans and got back onto the bed. Terry put some lotion from a bottle on her bedside table into the palm of her hand. She rubbed both her hands together, then started working on Parker's feet and ankles. She took her time and pressed her palms and thumbs into his skin. Parker tried to make conversation as she worked her way up his shins.

"Hey, Terry, did I ever tell you the five things that are wrong with a penis?

"Of course not, Parker! We just met. But tell me, what are they?" Terry asked as she rubbed his back and his shoulders.

"He had a hole in his head. He has ring around the collar. His two best friends are nuts. His neighbor is an asshole. And just when you really need him, he throws up and passes out." Parker and Terry were both so stoned by that time that they laughed really hard. Terry lost her balance, slipped off the bed, and fell onto the floor. As Parker reached out his hand to pull her up onto the bed, as soon as she got to her feet, she jumped, as if to tackle him. She landed on the bed next to him and rolled over. She presed her lips passionately onto his.

*   *   *   *   *   *   *

The next morning, as Terry and Parker lay in bed together, the phone rang. Terry answered the phone.

"Yes, he's here. Just a moment." Terry put the phone down. Parker, it's for you. It's the Bandits." Parker took the phone from Terry and said hello.

"Parker, this is Coach Sperling. We need you back. Do you want to come back and play?"

"How did you find me?" Parker asked.

"I called your mom and she gave me a phone number where you could be reached. What are you doing in Jacksonville?"

"Staying with Ted Jamison, one of the Bulls players and a buddy of mine, and his girlfriend. I'm trying to get a try-out with Jacksonvile."

"So his girlfriend answered the phone?"

"Yes, coach."

"Well, be back here tomorrow for practice. We'll have your gear up for you and we'll resign you. One of our offenive linemen went down. Don't sign with Jacksonville. We need you."

"Thanks, coach. I'll be there tomorrow." said Parker, then he continued, "I see you guys won."

"Yeah, we did OK. We'll see you tomorrow, Parker."

"You can count on me." said Parker Thomas, and then he hung up the phone.

Fort the next three weeks, Parker Thomas sat on the bench, playing only on special teams as a kick-off return man on the wedge. He had gotten very few reps in practice and felt that he was nothing more than an insurance policy in case someone else went down. Parker felt like a taxi squad member or a developmental roster player. Management and coaches could take a player up and down that roster, and if a player went on that list, he got only a thousand dollars a week. But the Bandits offered him his old contract back, so they hadn't totally grinded him. Parker sat during those games collecting his paycheck, and half the time, he felt like sticking a book inside his helmet so he could look down and read as he sat on the bench. He was on the team, but he wasn't a part of the team.

*From the Outhouse to the Penthouse
and Somewhere in Between*

## DEEP IN THE HEART OF TEXAS

Parker Thomas flipped a tape into the casette player as he drove toward Tampa International Airport. He boarded a flight for San Antonio, Texas. The Tampa Bay Bandits had released him because they had reactivated the injured lineman who had gotten hurt a couple of weeks earlier. The San Antonio team, the last USFL expansion team, had claimed Parker on waivers. The Gunslingers were supposedly the league's worst team, full of renegade football payers. The team had a cast of characters, from the front office to the ball boy. They had an All-Pro defensive end who had received national publicity after branishing a firearm on the field and who was arrested and escorted off to jail after threatening the head coach when the coach had tried to release him. The Gunslingers had a rookie quarterback who had played only a senior year of college football, and had a back-up whose claim to fame was that he had played on the local semi-pro team in San Antonio. The team had picked up these players in a supplemental expansion draft when they were a new team in the league and not given much chance to win. They had the lowest payroll in the league and had spent virtually no money on impact players, so even though they were called the Gunslingers, they weren't playing with a fully loaded gun. There had been a laughable rumor in the league that a couple of special team players that ran down in the kick-off were Mexicans and playing for a couple hundred a game. It was a Mexican version of Texas A&M's 'twelfth man'.

Parker Thomas had joked during his three-game paid vacation with Tampa about being shipped to San Antonio, which would be like a foreign legionnaire going to a last outpost, only with Spanish lessons thrown in. Crazy rumors had circulated about the league that the owner was a crook and never paid his bills. He had had a semi-pro team in San Antonio and had gotten the Gunslingers because he was able to secure a huge loan for the franchise at the last minute. The USFL had needed an eighteenth team to round out the league schedule, and they had given him the franchise. Rumor had it that he was under federal indictment for fraud to creditors, and was dubbed in South Texas as 'the man with the black hat'.

As Tampa Bay had been a starship franchise, San Antonio was looked at like a sinking frigate, and they hadn't yet set sail. They were the last team granted a franchise and barely had their players and coaching staff intact. They lost their first four games, and had been routed in their last game by the Houston Gamblers' Jimmy Kelly and their high powered offense. The lights had been shut off by Gulf Power late in the third quarter during a game that was nationally televised, and they played in a stadium that reminded Parker of a high school field. It seated thirty thousand and was the smallest stadium in the league.

Football was football to Parker Thomas, and even though all those seemingly negative forces loomed over the San Antonio franchise, he had been encouraged by the phone call he had received from the offensive line coach, Ike Perry.

"We'll be glad to have you. I'm gonna start you at center, the position you're best at. That's the place we really need help." Perry had been an assistant NFL coach and had seen Parker Thomas develop as a player.

"I think Tampa Bay is crazy to let you go. But here you will have a chance to start and help this football team win. If we can start to run the ball, we could surprise a lot of people. We're better than a lot of people think we are. We've made reservations for you at the Prince Henry Hotel. It's where all the oil barons stay, and it's the nicest place in town. Hell, the maids even put a mint on the pillows after they make up the beds! What more could a guy ask for? I don't know what management is planning to pay you, but it will be fair. The coaches and I want you here, so we'll tell management to take care of you. Are you gonna come? Are you gonna play any more ball? We're zero and four, and, to be honest, some of our jobs are on the line. I'll have someone come by the hotel and pick you up. Be at my office for eight. I'll meet you in the morning at the stadium and we'll watch some film. The way I look at it Parker, you need to keep playing, so you need us to get what you deserve in this league, and I need you to keep my job and get this offense going. Since we don't have any big play guys, since management refuses to spend the money, we're gonna run the ball and try to stay in every game. With a little luck, we'll win some of them that we're not supposed to. I think we have a great defense and a lot of these guys are trying to prove something to their old teams and to the league. We could have won two of the last four games we played, if we had just gotten some movement at the nose. The guy we got in there now has been getting stuffed, and our guards haven't been able to get around and trap anybody. Plus, the guy we got in there now can't snap for the shotgun. Parker, I'm looking for you to get some movement on the nose so we can run our offense and stay in these games. We need some leadership up front."

Parker Thomas, for the first time, felt needed and wanted. Even though he was being sent to an allegedly sinking ship, maybe the coach was right. Parker had played on a lot of winning football teams, but they only seemed to win when he was in there. He watched the Giants go in the tank and the Bandits go in the tank after he had gotten hurt. Even though the public didn't know it, Parker felt in his mind at times that he was important, and he would try to make the most of this opportunity. After all, that's what the game was all about — delivering when you had the opportunity.

As the players stood in the tunnel for player introduction to a capacity crowd at Alamo Field, Parker looked across the stadium and surveyed his new yard. It was so hot on the astroturf surface that day, well over one hundred ten degrees, you could have fried an egg on the field. It had immediately reminded him of the Dallas game a few years back. For some ridiculous reason, San Antonio was wearing their dark purple jerseys, and those shirts were really sucking up the heat. There was virtually no air, and Parker started to panic because he couldn't fill his lungs. Parker looked around at several players making small sucking sounds in order to take in the little air that was available, and with all of them standing together in a group, there wasn't much air to be had.

The cheerleaders, as they lined up for form a gauntlet for the players to run through, had made a banner that the players were supposed to break as they came running on the field. It had already been broken and had been masking taped back into one piece right in the middle of the spelling of the team's name. Parker found the whole scene ironic, like he was in the middle of some fractured fairy tale. He could smell the booze in the air from the already drunken and rowdy fans, many of the Mexicans who spoke little, if any, English. The cheerleaders were dressed like hussies, with purple silky low-cut saloon girl costumes complete with fishnet stockings and garter belts, and feathers in their headbands. Parker thought they all looked like a bunch of hookers, and cheap ones at that.

But somehow, all this diversity had made the team come together. All the guys appeared to be team ball players who loved the game, just like Parker. Parker Thomas had been impressed by their offensive line, just like coach Ike Perry had said, and now, with their being able to use the shotgun and run the ball up the middle, they just might open up their weak passing attack. They didn't have any running backs that could break it, but they did have a bunch of hard-nosed blocking grinders who played hard. It was as if they were all out to make a statement. The players, for a variety of reasons, had would up on this team, and although the guys were loose and funny in the locker room and at the practices before the game, the team had taken on a unified and keyed-up temperment that Parker liked. There were no big stars, no high-round draft choices, no impact players, no established NFL players with years of experience – just a bunch of tweeners, a group of blue-collar football players. If they won, they would win ugly. And a win would be a win.

When San Antonio presented Parker with his contract, they had sent one of their gofers over to the hotel with a fair offer. But Parker said he would sign the contract only if it did not include an option year and he would be an unrestricted free agent at the end of the season. He had learned this lesson with Montreal because when they had brought him up and paid him for the remainder games of the season, they all but owned him for a year after that with the option year and never came across with another fair offer. Thank God the Bandits wanted him and were willing to wait for the option to expire. If the anti-trust case that was in the courts played out, San Antonio would probably be merged with Orlando, and Orlando would be given an NFL team. There was no way management would have him under contract during the anticipated player auction. The Gunslingers originally fought Parker's demand. In a fit of heavy emotion, Parker told management: "Fuck it! Same old shit! You really want me but you don't want to pay for me. I'll tell you what. I'm going home. The only way you are going to get me is with a no-option clause and the hotel for the rest of the season. You tell them that!" The gofer left shaking in his boots but returned a few hours later with the contract the way Parker wanted and the hotel room covered. Parker signed the contract and knew Joey Rucker would have been proud. If Parker stuck out the season and did a good job, there could be some good dollars in his future.

A gust of air came whipping through the stadium and revitalized Parker. That's what the opportunity to play felt like to Parker. He would be all right. He would just go out and play, and let the chips fall where they may. He could only control what he could control.

As Parker's name was called, he ran out onto the field. He was back in the league, and as a starter, where he felt he belonged. One never knew what was around the corner in pro football. Just like with the bounce of a football, strange things cold happen.

It was late in the fourth quarter. The team had played just as Ike Perry had said – close, but with no offense. Although San Antonio had run up and down the field, they could not score when they got in the red zone. Oakland, a struggling team as well, but a more established team, was leading nine to three. They had scored a touchdown and had tackled the Gunslingers' punter for a safety.

As Parker and the rest of the San Antonio offense bounded onto the field, Parker could feel the offensive line gelling. He knew they could score if they could just relax and stay together. They were the better team. But the Gunslinger players were starting to get uptight. A lot of bitching went down in the huddle. As the rookie quarterback stood outside the huddle and watched the offensive coordinator's play signal, Parker calmly took on his role of being a team leader and in a controlled tone said to the players in the huddle: "I've played these guys three times and we've always whipped them. And I'm not about to lose to them now. I'm killing that fucker in front of me, and I

*From the Outhouse to the Penthouse and Somewhere in Between*

know the rest of you guys up front are too. Let's quit the fucking bitching and listen to the play and concentrate on our assignments. We've been beating ourselves with the freakin' false starts and holding calls. The defense has been playing their guts out, and we're letting them down. Let's come together and quit fucking around."

The whole team stared at Parker Thomas in disbelief, as if something that had long needed to be said finally had been stated. Ron Gurvin, the offensive guard who had played for the Philadelphia Stars, the defending league champs, and who had come to the Gunslingers in the expansion draft, popped Parker on the side of his helmet and started yelling: "That's what I'm talking about! Let's get fucking going and win this game!" His words made Parker flood back to the huddle in Montreal. Parker decided that he would remain in control and play his best not only for himself, but also for the memory of Wes Rogers. Players clapped their hands together and started cheering and chanting: "Fuck 'em up! Fuck 'em up!' Avery Tillerman, a right guard who had gone off-sides several times during the game and who was obviously amped up on bennies said: "OK, guys, on three – Fuck 'em up! Fuck 'em up! One, two, three..." and all the players put their hands on top of Gurvin's hands and shouted in unison: "FUCK 'EM UP! FUCK 'EM UP!"

The team methodically started to move the ball down the field. As the team started from its own thirty, with about a minute and a half to play, they started ripping off five and eight yard runs and ran the ball when any other team would have been passing. And Oakland couldn't stop them! Oakland was a small and quick team, but the were wilting in the heat for having been out there so long amid the Gunslingers' long, yet scoreless drives. San Antonio got down to the nine yard line with thirty seconds to go. San Antonio called their last time-out. Both teams were wilting under the heat. Parker knew with their five up front, that the Gunslingers were wearing Oakland down because they weren't saying much and had the 'we know we can't stop you' look in their eyes. Parker looked over to the sidelines and watched as the coaches fought amongst themselves about what play they were going to call. As San Antonio came into the huddle, the quarterback, Rick Newell, called a pass play. Every player in the huddle looked at Newell as if he were nuts. The team had just driven some sixty yards, running what amounted to be a two-minute offense, on the ground. Why deviate from what was working?

"Brown right. Thirty-two. Trap pass. X hook. Y corner. Z flag. On two. Ready? Break!" As Parker bounded up to the line of scrimmage, he could see that Oakland was going to blitz; they were desperate to stop San Antonio. A pass play would flow right into their hands.

"Set! Red Eighty! Red Eighty! Set! Hut! Hut!" Newell faked the play action and rolled out and set up to throw. He was immediately sacked from behind with a crushing blind side hit by the blitzing linebacker from the back side. Newell coughed up the ball. Lucky for San Antonio they were covered and only lost a couple of yards. Parker blew a fuse!

"Tell the fucking coaches to run the goddamned football! Up the middle!" Newell just looked at Parker with a frightened look in his eyes as he was recovering from the vicious hit he had just taken.

"Calm down! Calm down!" Newell said, more talking to himself than to anybody else. As the next play came in from the bench, the quarterback called: "Brown right. Eighteen. Half back. Pass." Now Parker, along with the rest of the offensive line, was really getting pissed off.

"Here we fucking go again! Fucking coaches!" Avery Tillerman said. "Everytime we get into a fucking position to win, the fucking coaches fuck it up with some fucking bullshit call!"

"Shut the fuck up, Tillerman!" Parker said as Gurvin stepped in-between the two of them. It looked like they were going to come to blows, even though they never would, and to Parker, it was the ultimate heat of battle. It was as if their lives were on the line. Everybody was shell shocked. The pass fell incomplete, and the clock stopped with eleven seconds left. As the Gunslingers' players huddled up, it was as if they had to take the game out of the hands of the coaches and do it themselves. It was third and eleven, and the Gunslingers would come together as a team. Their rookie quarterback instantly became a veteran and proved to the team that he could lead.

Newell had been factoring information from both sides, the coaches and the line, and was stuck in the middle. He just looked at Parker as if to say, "Get these guys calmed down!"

"All right, quiet! Let the quarterback call the play!" said Parker.

"All right, listen you guys up front. The coaches want me to pass. But I tell you what we're gonna do. Can you guys show pass, and then run a trap like a 32 up front for me? Well, I'm gonna drop back like a pass, and I'm gonna run a quarterback draw up the middle of the hole that you're gonna make for me. You want the ball up the middle? You got it!" As they broke the huddle, Parker could hear Ronnie Gurvin screaming, "That's what I'm fuckin' talkin' about! That's what I'm fuckin' talkin' about!" As Newell started barking out the signals, having spread the Oakland defense out with an obvious passing formation, the coaches were screaming: "WHAT THE FUCK ARE THEY DOING?!?" You could hear them clear as a bell, even above the uproar of the stadium fans who were now on their feet and going nuts.

"Set. Blue sixty. Blue sixty…"

*From the Outhouse to the Penthouse and Somewhere in Between*

At the last second, the Oakland defense shifted from a thirty front, where a man had been over Parker's nose the whole game, to a forty front, with a linebacker now over him and the guards both covered. The Gunslingers were ad-libbing their assignments already, and now their blocking scheme up front was being altered.

Avery, Parker, and Gurvin would have to adjust on the run, and Parker hoped that they were true veterans. A true veteran was somebody who had a lot of reps, could adjust on the run, and communicate in such a way that the guy next to him knew what he meant. Sometimes it was as simple as reaching out and pointing at the man and saying, "I got 51. You got 72." All Parker had said to Tillerman and Gurvin before they ran on the field was: "If we get jammed up there on the line of scrimmage, and we don't know our assignment, say something. Avery, you be A. Gurvin, you be G. I'll be just plain old Parker."

As Newell barked the signals, Parker quickly looked to his left and said, "G, you got 72 over A. Parker's got the man over you."

Then Parker turned his head to the right and said: "A, you got 51 the backer. G's got the man over you." As he snapped the ball, Parker folded on the guy over Gurvin. Tillerman showed pass and then went up on the linebacker, and Gurvin easily trapped Avery's man, who had taken an outside rush toward the quarterback and had run himself out of the play. A hole that you could drive a truck through opened up, and Newell dropped back to pass, but tucked the ball and ran the ball right up the middle through the gaping hole, getting tattooed at the six-inch line.

The clock was winding down to under five seconds. Visibly dazed from the hit, Newell got up.

"Red right. Just line up! Line up! Quarterback sneak, on the first sound."

"Set!" Parker snapped the ball just as time expired, and Rick barely got in over the pinching Oakland defense as an Oakland defender arrogantly slapped the ball out of Rick's hands, as if to make it look like a fumble. The ball bounded toward the back of the end zone, and an Oakland D.B. scooped up the ball and started to run as if he was going to run one hundred nine yards the other way for a touchdown.

"Touchdown!" called the ref. Half theSan Antonio team was bounding out onto the field as time had expired.

"Get back! Get back! Extra point team!" the coaches yelled. The San Antonio fans went beserk! Parker had lit out for the defensive back and clotheslined him, knocking him silly and from the football. It was a chickenshit attempt by the back, so Parker was going to make him pay for it. The D.B. wasn't going to rain on the Gunslingers' parade! Or even think he could! The San Antonio mascot came running into the end zone shooting off blanks out of a revolver as the offensive line just looked at one another as if to say, "Let's just make this fucking point, or I'm gonna use that gun!" Parker picked up the football and handed it to the ref, and the refs were pretty occupied with the San Antonio bench. Parker didn't know what made him do that. It was as if his subconscious had told him, 'we're not taking any more of this shit'.

Parker, as he lined up to snap the ball for the extra point, zeroed in on his target and saw the quarterback's face a bloody mess. Oakland had literally gouged his face as Newell had snuck it in, and they had taken it out on him. Parker snapped the ball with his head on a swivel to avoid the impending cheap shot that he knew he was going to get. Stick a fork in them! They were done!

The ball sailed through the uprights. San Antonio had won 10 to 9.

As the Gunslingers' mascot came out with blazing six-shooters, Parker bounded off the field. Coach Ike Perry jumped into Parker's arms and was an absolute lunatic. He screamed: "I knew you guys could do it!!!" After he got off Parker, he said, "I saw the clothesline on that guy. You're fucking out of your mind! I don't care if you do that shit, do what you gotta do. But if you get caught with a flag, your ass is mine!"

"Don't worry, coach, it ain't gonna happen!" roared Parker Thomas with a shit-eating grin on his face.

As the team went into the locker room, their attitude was as if they had won the league championship. Players were high-fiving one another, and shaking up soda cans and exploding them all over. Gil Steinway was the oldest coach to ever coach a professional football team. He'd been out of the game for a few years, but because of his legendary status as a college coach in Texas, he had been talked into becoming head coach of the team. He had been smart enough to surround himself with some hellacious assistants. The guys were all joking in the locker room: "Don't hoot and holler too much! We don't want the coach to have a heart attack and die on our first win!" Gurvin just kept screaming.

"That's what I'm fuckin' talkin' about!!! That's what I'm fuckin' talkin' about!!!" Parker hardly knew half the guys on the team, especially the defense, but they all got a chance to meet each other as the team came together and knew that football was going to be fun. Jefferson Anthony, the middle linebacker and captain, or Doctor Doom, as he liked to call himself, got up to present the game ball.

"I'd like to give this ball to the offensive line, for the job they did. You guys did a hell of a job out there at the end of the game. And we're glad to have Parker Thomas, our new center."

Parker was the focus of attention. He called out, like Gurvin did: "That's what I'm fuckin' talkin' about!" And the locker room just exploded with laughter.

*From the Outhouse to the Penthouse and Somewhere in Between*

## TUCK THIS IN YOUR FILE!

As the San Antonio Gunslingers readied for practice the next week, a new feeling of confidence overtook them. All they had needed was that first win, and they had gotten it. Parker Thomas and the offensive line became confident in their ability to execute up front, having proven their abilities in the ad-libbed play against Oakland. The coaches had been split amongst themselves in a power struggle about how the offense should be run, and the ridiculous play calling down at the goal line at the end of the Oakland game brought the problem to a head. The offensive coordinator was fired. Ike Perry and the offensive coaches were now going to call the plays by committee, and run the offense the way Perry had told Parker they could when he had spoken to Parker on the phone.

Mark Osbourne, who had been a part-time starter with Newell but who had gotten hurt and was helping the offense during practice, was brought in as a coach. He became a liason to the players because he had been one of them and had run with them. And the coaches, who used to drink with the team members after the games, took a lot of information from Osbourne about what plays would work and about what the players were really thinking. Parker, in all his days of football, had never seen a situation like that. He thought it was very unique and a great idea.

The entire organization was a loose ship, with the coaches and players almost being like one. On all the other teams Parker had been on, the coaches and players rarely hung out together unless they were invited to some stuffy social affair where players were afraid to let their hair down. It was the exact opposite in San Antonio, but it immediately made Parker feel comfortable. Additionally, Parker felt with the faith the coaches had in him and the lack of evasiveness from the coaching staff, the players would really play better on the field.

As the Gunslingers left to go on the road to play Chicago, Parker felt confident they could win. While sitting in the familiar back seat of the airplane, Parker had a squatty girl with purple hair and purple eye make-up come bounding to the back of the plane to meet him. Her eyeliner was so thick that she looked like the Bride of Frankenstein.

"I'm Mary Lou! Mary Lou Monges! You must be Parker Thomas. How y'all doin'?" Mary Lou Monges was the daughter of the owner of the team. She was a spoiled girl who was dumpy and odd looking. The only thing she had going for her was that her daddy paid all the team bills and, of course, Parker's sixty-thousand dollar salary.

"You're our newest player, aren't you? You're cute!" Mary Lou pressed on. Parker Thomas merely smiled and was as polite as he could be given the circumstances. She was like something out of a carnival side show, and Parker recognized her as the girl that had sung the national anthem before the Oakland game. Unfortunately, she was off-key and had screeched for most of the song. Her purple make-up, bat-like eyes, and crew cut scared Parker half to death. He gasped when he saw that her fingernails were painted black.

"And I thought the cheerleaders were bad!" Parker thought to himself. Because Mary Lou had decided to make Parker her center of attention for two hours during the plane ride, after she went back up to first class, the team started busting Parker's balls.

"Parker and Drucilla, and kids!" one player called out.

"Get a paper bag for her head during the honeymoon, Parker!" added another.

"A German shepherd would be better for you, Parker." yet another called out.

"How about a pound of moustache hair remover for the bride?" At one point, Tod Simpson walked up to Parker and said: "It ain't so bad – look at the nice shirt she bought me when I went out with her!"

"But you only got her after I gave her up!' added Joe Bob Miller, the free safety. "But watch out, Parker, you won't get shit in the divorce settlement!" The team roared, and the comments continued all the way to O'Hare Airport. Parker's fate had been sealed. He had been 'glued' to Mary Lou and an object of team jabs for the rest of the season. A day wouldn't go by without some barb or comment being hurled at Parker. But Parker was not intimidated by the coaches: He didn't worry about what they might think if he and Mary Lou were rumored to be an allegedly hot item, and if those rumors spread up the ranks. Parker was much more laid back now, and he let a lot more slide than he used to. Parker knew that no one would fuck with him, and for the first time, he could relax. Parker thought about what had happened with Tommy and Monica, the stewardess, but he didn't worry about his being associated with Mary Lou. He was secure in his job, and, barring injury, he would get a chance to shoot for that penthouse money that may lie somewhere down the road.

But just as Parker was starting to feel secure, that feeling was taken away from him. Late in the third quarter of the Chicago game, Parker had snapped the ball and sprinted out for a quick screen. As Parker had chopped down the D.B. in front of him, he caught a helmet on the thigh, and his leg exploded with a huge contusion. Parker had to come out of the game, as his leg blew up into a purple mass from his ankle to his ass. The team lost against Chicago by a touchdown; the Gunslingers couldn't move the ball at all.

*From the Outhouse to the Penthouse and Somewhere in Between*

Parker felt totally frustrated, knowing that his getting hurt was why San Antonio lost the game. Chicago was a team San Antonio could easily have beaten if the Gunslingers' offensive line had stayed intact. Parker was further frustrated as the Gunslingers lost to the Michigan Panthers the following week. San Antonio was one and six, and the guys were getting antsy. The San Antonio team buoyed Parker's confidence by doing everything possible to get him back in the line-up. He was getting treatments twice a day at the team facility, and the team sent a trainer over to Parker's hotel twice at night for yet more treatments. As the swelling in Parker's leg went down, the team also brought in an accupuncturist, and even a faith healer. Parker would never forget the day that Dame Astra showed up at his hotel room. She was about seventy years old and dressed in royal blue silk garments. She had a gold bag full of potions and powders that she sprinkled and threw all over Parker as she did spins around his room and around his bed, while chanting something like, 'Jugetso clabmal doristo vukmiro abtormala', some secret cult language she used in her treatments. All Parker knew was that when she left the room, he had to call maid service to clean up the mess and change the bed so that he wouldn't have to sleep in fragments of animal bones and feathers she had thrown on him during her ritual. Parker thought it was the weirdest shit he had ever seen. His injury was a contusion; outside of the normal medical treatments, the others were circus-like, just like the owner's daughter.

Parker had promised Ike Perry that he would be back and ready to go for the Jacksonville game, a game Parker wouldn't miss for the world. The game would be at Jacksonville, and their park was leading the league in attendance with seventy thousand fans showing up for each game. Parker was going to make Jacksonville pay for not giving him a try-out. Jacksonville had lost their previous game to Oakland, and Parker knew that with the Jacksonville 'we're better than anyone else' attitude, and their expecting to easily beat the Gunslingers, he was ready to rip them a new asshole. Paybacks were a bitch in any football league. One of the greatest challenges to any pro player was to go back and play against a former team that for whatever reason had let him go. It was a way for a player to establish himself in a league. And as Parker was starting to see opponents, although many of them new faces, for the second and third time, he now knew players' weaknesses and could really step up his performance and establish himself and his team as a force to be reckoned with. Once management saw that you were an impact player for your team, that kind of reputation could keep you around for many years. It was all what you did with the opportunity, and a little luck. Parker felt lucky to have the opportunity, as the Gunslingers bounded onto the field to play Jacksonville.

"All right. Huddle up!" called Newell. "Blue left. Thirty base. On one. Ready? Break!"

"Eleven yards. First down." called the ref.

"Way to go, guys up front!" said Newell as he got into the huddle again. "Blue left. Thirty base. On one. Ready? Break!" The back skirted through the hole for thirteen yards.

"Red right. Thirty base. On one. Ready? Break!" barked Newell in the next huddle.

"Set! Hut!"

"Sixteen yards up the middle. First down!" called the ref. The boisterous crowd was getting antsy, as was the Jacksonville team, after San Antonio had made three running plays right up the middle with big yardage. The crowd was already being taken out of the game as a dead silence started to fall across the stadium.

"OK, you guys," Newell said in the huddle. "Red right. Thirty-four. Pass. X hook. Y corner. Z fly. On two... Before Newell could break the huddle, Parker yelled out: "Rick, hold up, hold up! Run the ball up the middle, god damn it! I'm gonna kill the nose that just signed for a half million dollars. This is his first start. I wanna kill that son of a bitch!"

"All right, you guys, hold up." said Newell, "Red right. Thirty base. On the first sound. Ready? Break!"

"Set!" The back ripped up the middle and bounced it to the outside, and ran twenty-four yards.

"First down!" called the ref. The Jacksonville coaches started yelling at their defense: "Come on, you guys. Shit! Get the hell going! They're kicking your asses!"

Parker was sky high! He had met Teddy right before the game to say hello outside the locker room, and Teddy told Parker that he was glad that he had found a job and was getting a chance to start. Parker had been shocked at how much bigger Teddy had gotten since Parker had last seen him. If anything, a football player, during the course of a season, was lucky if he could maintain what he had brought into camp. Games ground players into a nub. But this guy was getting bigger and faster and stronger.

"Ted, you look great. Are you on the juice?" asked Parker.

"Yeah." he responded.

"How much of that shit are you taking?"

"Three c.c.'s of Simobol a week."

"Don't you think that's a lot? You know what they say – live by the needle, die by the needle!"

"I'm not getting that much playing time, and the only way I can stay around is if I get bigger and stronger. I don't have a choice!"

"Come on, Ted, you just need playing time, man. Don't play that game. It's just not worth it!!" Articles had been coming out in the press about players needing heart transplants and developing complications following use of steroids. Players were getting arrested for domestic disputes with wives and girl friends, as well as getting busted for having the stuff in their possession. Parker felt steroids played a large part in these things happening. The drugs were readily available in any locker room or trainer's kit. Players were being boxed into situations where they felt forced to take the drug. Parker knew a football player's mentality was 'do whatever it takes to stay around'. It was bred into the beast. Parker wasn't so sure that in a few years he wouldn't be on it, as his body started going on him. But for now, he didn't have to stand at that crossroads.

"Are you still with Lisa, Teddy?" Parker asked his friend.

"No, she left me. Listen, Parker, that new nose guard that you're gonna play against, this is his first start. Can you believe it? They gave that son of a bitch half a million to sign, and a three hundred thousand dollar salary."

"You gotta be fuckin' kiddin' me!"

"He's some big college player out of FSU. Supposed to go high in the draft, but he ain't shown me nothin'."

"That's the fucking game, Teddy. That's the fucking game. They give these unproven guys all the money and play around with the guys who are out there delivering. It just doesn't make sense to me. Shit like this really pisses me off!" Ted Jamison looked Parker straight in the eye and said: "Oh no, I know how you can get when you get pissed! You're gonna punish that guy, aren't you?"

"I'm gonna make that guy wish he'd never set foot on the field. And I'm gonna shove the ball up your coach's ass for not giving me a look!"

"Hey, I love you, Parker. I'll see you after the game. Good luck!" Parker and Ted hugged each other and slapped one another on the shoulder pads. Even though they would be opponents that day, they each wished the other well.

The Gunslingers had their first and ten at the Jacksonville fourteen. The only noise in the stadium was the shouts of the San Antonio team and their bus driver.

"All right, huddle up!" Newell barked. "Red right. Eighteen sweep. On one. Ready? Break!"

Parker knew Jacksonville would take away the inside, so San Antonio would run outside. Stocker, the Gunslinger's halfback, took the ball around right end while Parker fired out and knocked the Jacksonville linebacker right off his feet. He had hit the linebacker by his ankles, and the guy literally flipped up and landed on his head. After Stocker got knocked out of bounds on the seven yard line, he came rushing back to the huddle and patted Parker on the ass and yelled, "Nice fucking block, Parker!"

"Second and three!" yelled the ref as Newell stepped into the huddle.

"Red right. Thrity-two trap. On three. Ready? Break!" Parker bounded up to the offensive line. He noticed that Jacksonville had taken the rookie and put him down over Gurvin. Parker started to foam at the mouth. He'd been kicking the rookie's ass straight on, and now Parker would get a chance to fold down on the rookie as Gurvin pulled out the trap. Parker figured the rookie wouldn't see him coming. A good veteran defensive tackle would smell it and not give Parker a clean shot at him. But Parker knew that he was going to pile drive and blow him out of there.

"Black sixty. Black sixty. Set! Hut! Hut! Hut!" Parker fired out, and just as he had figured, the rookie was standing there and not closing the trap as Gurvin pulled. Parker burried his helmet into the guy's ribs, and punching with his arms, lifted the defensive tackle up off his feet and into the air. Parker started running with him and bounced the player onto his back with the full weight of his body. It was a beautiful pancake block. Parker could feel the air go right out of him and the player go limp.

"You fucking motherfucker! I'm going to kill you!" said Parker as he slammed the player to the ground, and Parker felt that he just might have.

Parker got up and stood over the unconscious player. The ref said, "All right, you guys! Break it up!"

At the same time, Parker heard the other ref call: "Touchdown! Touchdown!" As Parker bounded back to form the huddle and the extra point team came on the field, the coaches yelled, "Way to block, Parker! Way to block!!"

He heard them over the booing of the fans. Jacksonville called an injury time-out as the defensive tackle was taken off the field on a stretcher. Parker would later find out that the player cracked his ribs and would be out for the rest of the season. Parker was glad to give him a paid vacation. He didn't feel the player deserved to be out on the field; he sucked!"

The rest of the game was a day off for Parker, as San Antonio ran up and down the field totally dominating the Bulls team. It was the kind of football game Parker loved; even though they called these types of games ugly, the were beautiful in Parker's mind. The Gunslingers had 200 yards of rushing by half-time and had not thrown the ball once. By the time the ref blew the final whistle, most of the crowd had gone home. They had gotten tired of constantly booing their home team.

Parker was interviewed on the radio after the game. The Jacksonville media and even some Tampa reporters were covering the game. Parker used all the general statements, like, "We came to play today." and," I think we caught them a little flat." He was totally lying, but that is what you did for the media. You never insulted teams or talked trash. Whether a team won or lost, you always gave the other team credit. It was part of the game. Parker knew that no one else really gave a shit except him and his team mates, and that was who he played for. The thrill of going into a packed house on national

*From the Outhouse to the Penthouse and Somewhere in Between*

t.v. at another team's ball park and dominate them to the point where all he heard was booing and the only cheering heard was from his own side lines, that was worth the world to Parker. Those kinds of games were flat out fun. San Antinio had shut out Jacksonville thirty to nothing.

What Parker Thomas had really wanted to say to the media was: "We kicked their fucking ass and in their own back yard! Tell your coach, Paul Young, to tuck that in his file, Jacksonville!" To the Tampa reporter who was there, Parker wanted to say, "Hey, we're gonna play you guys too! And, we're gonna do the same thing!" But instead, Parker said the usual cannon phrases he stuck with.

As the San Antonio team boarded the airplane, the mood was really up-beat, because the defending champion Philadelphia Stars were coming to the Gunslingers' corral to play later that week. The game would be ABC's game of the week, and it would be played in front of a national audience. This would be a make-up of their first nationally televised game when the lights had gone out.

Parker got onto the plane and was soon seated in the back. He heard a voice.

"I bought these for you, Parker. You're so handsome. Why don't you try these on and see if they fit."

It was Mary Lou again, and she was standing over Parker with four boxes neatly wrapped in purple foil paper with gold bows on each box.

"Oh, Parker, these are the same color as your eyes!" said a thrilled Mary Lou as she opened up one of the presents and held up a pair of silk boxer shrots for everyone on the plane to see. The guys grabbed their guts and rocked in their seats.

"Oh, thanks, Mary Lou." said a blushing Parker Thomas. He was very uneasy, but managed to add: "These are real nice, but don't do this any more, please. My girlfriend usually helps me shop." Even though Parker was not seeing anyone on a regular basis and he was willing to risk the wrath of the young coquette in front of him, he had to say something to get her off his back. Little did Parker Thomas realize it would take about six of these very same types of encounters before she would take the hint and he would be able to get the message across to her. As soon as Mary Lou went back up to first class to join her daddy, the team started in on Parker Thomas and the cute little boxes that sat on the seat next to him: "Gonna put on a private modeling session for her, Parker?"

"What color are the condoms in the little box, Parker? Purple to match her hair?"

"Bet you got a bottle of Hai Karate in there too! It's her favorite!" Parker turned to Joe Bob and called out, as he held up the silk boxers: I like these better that that silver g-string she bought for you!"

"I knew he was an exotic dancer! I knew it!" called out another player.

"Yeah, he's one of them dick swingers!"

"Hey, Joe Bob, what's your stage name? Johnny Thrust?"

"No, he's named after that Greek god. They call him Joe Bob-Adonis, King of Cream."

One of the players whipped out a dollar bill and before long the aisle was filled with palyers waving dollar bills. The players were totally off the walls. Another one of them got up in the aisle and started swiveling his hips and waving his arms.

"Is this how your dance goes, Big Wad?" Another player got up in the aisle and started a different version with a little more grind to it. He put both his hands on the top of his head and thrust his hips side to side.

"No, it's like this. You got to push, push, push your hips into it!"

"Hey, Joe Bob, check out my Butt! Think you can get me a job too?"

"Nah, my butt is tighter than yours, lard ass!" The players threw more money, and some danced all the way home to San Antonio. Parker started living not only for the football wins, but also for the plane rides home.

Bill Winters and
JoAnne V. McGrath

# DO THE DOOMIE DANCE!

The San Antonio team ran through the tunnel and out onto the field. The stadium was packed, and extra lawnchairs were set up to accommodate the over-flow crowd. The ABC cameras rolled as they covered their USFL Game of the Week. Parker knew the game would be a nip and tuck affair. Both teams had big offensive lines and played great defense. Their offenses ran the ball with vicious ground attacks, only throwing when they had to.

The Philadelphia Stars had Calvin Hyatt, their leading rusher in the league. He went into the USFL for big bucks instead of the NFL when he got out of college. This game was San Antonio's chance to one-up the Philly number-one rated offensive line, and to prove that the Gunslingers were the best. Additionally, a couple of the San Antonio players were former Stars players, and the Gunslingers were really jacked up. Parker hoped today would be a day of vindication for them, just as he had had in Jacksonville.

The game was a back and forth affair until late in the fourth quarter. Philadelphia was leading 20 to 14. With about four minutes to go, San Antonio got the ball back on their own thirty.

Parker and the offensive line had become increasingly frustrated during the course of the game. All of them, at one time or another, had opened up huge holes that put the backs into the secondary, but they kept getting run down from behind by the Philadelphia D.B.'s. Parker felt that the score should have been more like 40 to 20, and if the Gunslingers had had a back like Calvin Hyatt, had ownership opened their wallets as did all the other teams, the San Antonio team would have won going away.

San Antonio ran the ball down to the Stars' twenty, and the Gunslingers could see that Philadelphia was on the run. The Gunslingers had run inside and outside all day, gaining five or six yards at a pop. The announcers in the booth said that if the Gunslingers could score, they would pull off the biggest upset of the year. The Stars would be taken down by an up-start expansion team that wasn't playing like an expansion team any more. The commentators let the American public know that the game that day was high caliber football. The USFL had arrived. They made a few comments about the anti-trust case in the courts, then returned to the scene in front of them.

"I sure would pay money to see these USFL teams play!" said one of the ABC sportscasters.

Rick Newell stepped into the huddle.

"All right, you guys, let's go. Red right slot. Thirty-two. Trap. On two. Ready? Break!"

"Set! Hut! Hut!"

The back ran up the gut and gained eight yards. The guys in the huddle got more up-tight in anticipation of going in for the winning score.

"Blue left. Nineteen. Toss. Sweep. On the first sound! Ready? Break!" Newell reverse pivoted and tossed the ball to the halfback, who got around the corner and looked like he might score. As it looked like he might cross the goal line, the ball was punched out of his grab, and Philadelphia pounced on the loose ball.

"Fumble! Fumble! First down! Philadelphia!" called the ref. Philadelphia had gotten lucky. They had bent, but not broken. As the Stars' quarterback took a knee and ran out the clock, the gun sounded. All the players on the Gunslingers' team were saying to each other, "We should have beaten those guys!" The Gunslingers, now two and seven, knew that most people would be writing them off. The San Antonio team felt like they had given a good account of themselves, and they could still back into the play-offs. The Gunslingers had come so close, but just like in any good pro football game, the team that makes the most mistakes usually loses.

Parker started to feel hate toward management. Most of the other teams were signing even more impact players for big dollars than the two they had originally started with. A couple of high-round draft choices that had just been drafted had compared offers from the NFL and then joined the USFL teams for more dollars. San Antonio didn't have any. No matter how well the Gunslingers played up front, how were they going to compete? Parker felt like a punched-out boxer ready for a title shot, but with no chance. The rest of the team felt the same way.

As the Gunslingers bounded out onto the field to play Arizona the next week, the San Antonio team had a look in their eyes as if they were going to take out their frustrations on Arizona. Coach Ike Perry had had a personal feud going on with the line coach of the Arizona team. Perry had not told his Gunslingers exactly what had happened, only that the offensive line coach of the Arizona team had stuck a dagger in his back. Ike Perry couldn't think of a better way to pay back the deed than for San Antonio to go down there and kick them in their own yard.

The game was another nip and tuck affair, and as Arizona played the run and forced San Antonio to pass, Newell, the rookie quarterback now turned veteran, was runing play action passes off the run and getting time to set up. This extra time allowed Newell to complete some passes in key situations, which allowed San Antonio to sustain some long drives and go up 24 to 23 with about two minutes to go. Arizona was a solid team, and led their division. They had taken the Gunslingers lightly.

As the Arizona team went out onto the field, everybody knew that they didn't deserve to win. But everybody was scared that Arizona might get lucky and score anyway. Football could be cruel sometimes. The Arizona fans in the sold-out stadium were going nuts, even though the game had been changed to a later time that evening due to the heat.

Arizona moved the ball down the field with a couple of pass completions. The San Antonio team had been in so many close games and most of the time come up on the short end, that the entire team was up screaming at the defense to stop Arizona. The Arizona quarterback dropped back to pass. He threw a strike down the middle to a streaking receiver who had raced down the middle of the field and was open. As he caught the ball, Joe Bob Miller, the safety, came up and laid a lick on him that caused the ball to squirt into the air, then into the hands of the Gunslingers' middle linebacker, Dr. Doom. Doom corralled the ball and started racing downfield. The San Antonio bench erupted! As Doom got knocked out of bounds on Arizona's fifteen yard line, he spiked the ball into the turf and did a dance that sort of was a cross between the Funky Chicken and the Texas Two-step. It had been the wildest dance that Parker Thomas had ever seen, and Parker couldn't get over the cast of characters and personalities that pervaded the squad.

In the film room the next day, as the Gunslingers watched the victory, the coaches kept running back Doom's victory dance. When the meeting broke, all the players had to do was go out and run. The coaches gave them the next day and a half off. The spirits in the room were so high that the players were all jumping up onto desk tops and doing their versions of Dr. Doom's dance. The scene rivalled anything Parker had ever seen in an airplane. Even one of the coaches was on top of a desk and waving his hands and shaking his hips. It was something Parker never thought he'd see. The coach got down off the desk top and said, "All right, men, calm down! Just go out and get your running in. And don't drink too much tonight! Let's give a good account of ourselves in these last eight games!"

The San Antonio Gunslingers team was three and seven, and still believed they could make the paly-offs. They had gone through the hard part of their schedule, and believed they could win against the rest of the teams they were slated to play. They had played two of the league's best teams back to back, and had almost won both of the games. All Parker could think about after the coaches ran them really hard at practice was that if he hadn't missed those two earlier games with an injury, the Gunslingers easily would have been in a position to make the play-offs. Now they had dug themselves into a hole; maybe if some breaks went their way, they could easily back in. The team was playing really well. Parker couldn't wait to get himself home and go to sleep. They had gotten in at four in the morning and then had to be back for film and running at ten. Parker Thomas was whipped.

## DIFFERENT TOWN, SAME OLD SAME OLD

The phone rang. It rang again. It rang a third time. Parker Thomas turned over in bed and reached for the receiver.

"AAAAGGGHHHHHHH!!!!!!!!"

Before Parker Thomas could pick up the receiver, he had been rousted out of a deep sleep and greeted by a bloody turkey head on the pillow next to him. He picked up the pillow the turkey head was on and whipped it across the room. Blood blobs flew everywhere.

"What the fuck was that?" yelled Parker Thomas, although there was no one else in the hotel room to answer his question. "Who the hell put that fucking bloody turkey head in my bed?" The phone kept ringing. Parker caught his breath and answered it.

"Hello?"

"Parker, are you all right? You sound out of breath. Got some broad up there with you?" asked Mark Osbourne. Parker caught a snicker in his voice, then put two and two together. Osbourne had set him up.

"Hey Parker, we're gonna come get you. We're gonna get a bite to eat and some beers down at Mr. Chico's Taco Palace.

Then we're goin' to this juice joint to meet some little darlin's. We'll be by to pick you up in fifteen minutes."

"I'll be ready!" said Parker Thomas as he hung up the phone. What he really meant was at the first possible opportunity, he would be ready to execute some type of revenge plot on Mark Osbourne. He knew Osbourne had managed to put the bloody turkey head in his bed because he was one of the players on the team who fished and hunted. On the ride home from the airport after the Arizona game, Osbourne had asked Parker if he wanted to go turkey hunting with some of the guys. Since Parker hadn't gotten any sleep on the trip home and had to show up for practice five hours after the plane touched down, he had declined the invitation.

A big jacked-up four-by-four truck pulled up outside Parker's hotel. The horn honked, then honked again and again. Parker looked out the window and headed out to meet his ride. On his way down to the lobby, Parker thought about the many diverse cultural experiences he had encountered in the five previous years. In Montreal, the players used le metro and went out to pubs. They'd voulez-vous the mademoiselles. In Tampa, players drove around in high performance cars and went out to nightclubs. They cruised for bikinis. And in San Antonio, team members drove all-terrain vehicles and carried shot guns on racks in the back windows. When they weren't hunting prey, they were on the prowl in saloons and juice joints looking for fillies and little darlin's. Despite the different terminology used, the bottom line was that the players usually did the same things when they weren't on the field. They went out in packs and bonded their camaraderie over a few brews and looked for a little skirt action. Today, that action would hopefully take place at Mr. Chico's Taco Palace.

Parker and the Gunslinger pack piled out of the four-by-four, then strutted into the jam-packed restaurant. They were immediately escorted to a reserved table in the room, just like the carte blanche treatment Parker had gotten so many times before. As Parker Thomas looked around the room, all he could see were white cowboy hats – tall ones, shorter ones, everybody had them on. And boots! The men and all the little darlin's had boots on. Some of the boots were black, some were white, some were brown, and some were even a yellowish snake skin. All the boots had two-inch heels. On the bar he saw posted a big cardboard schedule of the San Antonio team's games. A big 'L' was penned in next to the first four games, but the rest of the schedule had no marks next to it. Parker asked the waitress for a black magic marker, and after she came back with one, he strode on up to the bar. He took the marker and chitted off game scores and had the pleasure of putting three 'W's' on the card.

"There's gonna be about eight more of these W's that I'm gonna write in in the next couple of weeks! You can count on it!" said Parker to the bartender.

"Espero, senor! I hope so!" the bartender said back to Parker.

"Pretty sure of yourself, aint't cha!" said a sweet young voice with a heavy Texas drawl.

Parker Thomas turned around and looked into the most beautiful eyes he had ever seen. The long brown curls that cascaded out from under the white hat, the bountiful clevage teeming under a v-neck pull-over, and a pair of thin, tanned thighs running from a fringed mini skirt and into high white boots were a total turn-on for Parker. The girl's wide, bright smile and her fleshy, gloss ruby lips put an extra twinkle in Parker Thomas' eyes.

"You're not from around these parts, are ya?" said the woman.

"How can you tell?" asked Parker, still dazzled by her.

"Well, for one thing, you're not wearing a hat. And you've got on those Gucci loafers, not boots like the rest of us." she said as she teased him.

Before Parker could say any more, one of the players butted in. Obviously he had his eye on the same sweet young thing who had just targeted Parker.

*From the Outhouse to the Penthouse and Somewhere in Between*

"Honey, leave him alone. He's from New Jersey. Can't you tell from his Puerto Rican pimp shoes?" The little darlin' dismissed the other player's comment with a smile and continued as she put out a right hand in Parker's direction.

"I'm Katie. Born and raised right here in San Antonio. What's your name?"

"I'm Parker Thomas. I play for the Gunslingers." said Parker as he clutched the extended hand and held onto it. "Can I buy you a drink?"

"Oh, a Gunslinger, hey? I haven't seen you in here before."

"Only been here a month or so. Want a beer or something?"

"Sure, I'll have a Corona."

"Two Corona's," Parker called to the bartender, who placed two bottles and two wedges of lime in front of him on the bar.

"I've never heard of Corona before." said Parker, trying to make conversation.

The other player butted in again: "It's Mexican piss in a bottle. You gotta stick a lime in it to make it drinkable." Parker followed Katie's lead. He stuck a wedge of lime into the bottle, turned the bottle upside down, watched the lime float up, then turned the bottle back upright. He stared into Katie's deep green eyes as she wrapped her luscious lips around the long neck of the bottle and tipped it up.

"Yeah, big Parker," the other player butted in again, "He's not used to how we do things down here. He's probably never ridden a horse in his life, and he probably never fished or hunted either!"

"Ever ridden a horse, Parker?" Katie asked.

"Once, when I was a kid. I rode a pony at a birthday party. That's about it.."

"Parker, you haven't lived until you've ridden a horse. Tell you what, my ranch is just a few miles from here. I have a couple of horses. Would you like to come on out and ride with me sometime?" Parker had riding on his mind, but it sure wasn't the horseback kind.

"Sure, I'd like to try you, er, I mean it. You know, horse riding."

"Well, I'll look forward to having you out to my place sometime, then." said Katie with a really big smile and fluttering eye lashes.

"How far do you live from Thousand Pines Apartments?" asked Parker.

"About a mile, maybe less. Why?"

"Tell you what. Let's step outside for a minute. I'd like to get to know you a little better, but it's just too rowdy in here to really talk."

"Sounds good to me." said Katie as she took his elbow and left the bar.

# YOU NEVER REALLY KNOW WHO YOUR FRIENDS ARE

Mark Osbourn's phone rang at eight o'clock the next morning. It rang again. It rang a third time. He snorted and shook his head as he groped for the receiver.

"Hello?" said Osbourne with a throaty voice. His head was banging.

"Mark, this is Parker. Be over if fifteen minutes to pick you up for practice."

"What the hell time is it?"

"Time to rock and roll, big guy. I'll be there in fifteen minutes."

"Parker, what the hell are you talking about? I got my own wheels."

"What time did you leave Mr. Chico's last night?"

"Closed the fuckin' place out. Got home about three or so, and I swear I'll never do shots of tequilla again! I don't remember too much, and I know this is gonna sound really fuckin' nuts, but I could swear I saw a horse in my bedroom last night before I passed out."

"Probably ate the worm from the bottle, Osbourne." said Parker Thomas.

"Yeah, must have been fuckin' hallucinating." croaked Osbourne.

"Sure you don't need a ride?" Parker pressed one more time.

"I'm all set, buddy. See you at practice." Mark Osbourne hung up the phone and put his fingers to his temples. He started rubbing them to clear his blurred vision. Then he got that feeling in the pit of his stomach that told him that he had better run for the bathroom.

As Mark Osbourne shifted his body to the side of the bed, he slipped his feet onto the floor. Both feet went smack dab squishing into a pile of horse shit. On the run to the bathroom, he stepped in two or three more giant flops and proceeded to heave up his guts.

"I'll get that fuckin' Parker Thomas for this!" gagged Osbourne, who was sure that this was pay-back for the turkey head prank he had played on Parker the day before.

Most of the team had already assembled in the locker room for the team meeting, and Osbourne was one of the last to straggle in. He went over to his locker and sat down on a bench. He needed to get dressed for practice, so he reached for some of the gear in his mesh bag.

"AAAGGGHHHH!" Osbourne screamed, and the entire team turned around to find out what the outburst was about.

"Who put this fuckin' bloody turkey head in my mesh bag?"

"What's the matter with the great hunter? A little under the weather this morning?" called out one of the players.

"Can't take the sight of blood this early?" called yet another player.

"I told you to wash that mesh bag. Now you got shit growing in it!" jabbed another.

The team set onto Osbourne with the usual barbs and smart alec comments. Osbourne took the turkey head and flung it aross the locker room. It hit a player in the back of the head. The player next to him picked it up and whipped it back at Osbourne. Another player took a pair of dirty socks and whipped them through the air. Someone tossed a jock across the room. The turkey head flew through the locker room for a good two minutes. It looked like a grade school cafeteria food fight scene.

"Parker, I'll fuckin' kill you for this! How did that horse get in my apartment?"

"What horse, Mark?" asked Parker, hardly able to keep a straight face.

"He's seeing horses when he's zonked! Next thing he'll be seeing is pink elephants!"

"Nah, that was the broad he was trying to suck up to last night at Chico's!"

"Better get off the sauce, Ozzie!" said one of the players who picked up the turkey head and zinged it toward the locker room door.

"What the hell is going on in here?!? Settle down, you bunch of apes!" yelled one of the coaches as he looked at the bloody turkey head that hit him and landed at his feet.

"Knock it OFF! Get to your meetings!" called another of the coaches. The players stopped their horse play and went into their meeting across the hall.

Gil Steinway and his assistants walked into the players' meeting. Steinway's mere presence commanded silence in the room, and the team knew it. Steinway spoke: "An eleven and seven record would surely get us into the play-offs. And a nine and nine record might get us in too. Just keep playing hard every snap and execute your assignments. Men, we can beat Denver. We lost to them once before, but we had a couple of key guys out with injuries. So let's take them one at a time."

As soon as Steinway mentioned the Denver game, all of the players started laughing and looking at each other. Hell, they were going to play Chicago, not Denver. Didn't the coach know that? The guys started propping up their play books and hiding their faces in them. Parker had noticed that during side line conferences at key situations in the games, that the coach had gotten flustered. His age and the fact that he had been out of the game for several years was a stumbling block to the Gunslingers. Parker wondered if the coach wasn't part senile. Even though this negative thought flowed through Parker's mind, he suppressed it. It didn't matter who the coaches were. If you had the horses, you could win. And winning at football was fun, even if you were playing for a team in an antiquated stadium and for a coach who didn't have a clue. But football was a business if you lost. And Parker was determined to take care of business, as was the rest of the team. The San Antonio team, at home, took Chicago. The 30 to 21 game once again reaffirmed to the coaching staff and to the team that they had to have Parker in the line-up in order to win.

Then the Gunslingers, again at home, beat the real Denver team, the one the head coach thought they were going to play, 27 to 20. The game had been considered somewhat of an upset because Denver was a very high scoring ball club, running the run and shoot, an offense that didn't use a tight end and sent out everybody on passes on almost every play. San Antonio had beaten Denver by controlling the ball on the ground, like they always did, and with an ever-improving passing attack off the run.

The San Antonio team was climbing back into the play-offs, and all the other teams noticed that the Gunslingers were getting stronger and winning more games, particularly at home.

*Bill Winters and
JoAnne V. McGrath*

During those weeks, the turkey head circulated around the locker room and was found in different players' mesh bags before each practice. The players thought of the turkey head as a talisman, some sort of good luck symbol. They became very superstitious about it. The team finally gave the turkey head its own mesh bag and hung it in a place of honor in the locker room. They would touch the mesh bag with the turkey head in it before going out of the locker room before every game. The equipment manager was instructed never to wash the turkey head's mesh bag; the team feared losing the karma the turkey head exuded. The team did not want their rhythm broken.

As the team went into their fourteenth game, against the lowly Washington Federals at RFK, Parker knew he would have a war on his hands. He was going to be playing against one of his old buddies, Dave Bonarski, the guy he had broken into Montreal with. The wiley old veteran, like Parker, had gone from the CFL to the USFL. He had wound up with the Feds. Parker had noticed in watching game films of the Feds that they had moved Bonarski inside and he seemed bigger and stronger and faster than Parker had remmbered him. He wondered if Bonarski had tured into a steroid stallion. Parker had thought that Bonarski was a bitch to play against, and now that he was bigger and stronger, he would be worse to face. Bonarski had worked against Parker a lot in practice during their season together in Montreal. This would be a slobberknocker affair.

And even thought the guys were friends, Parker knew that the minute the whistle blew for the game, Bonarski would try to take Parker to school, as he had during Parker's Montreal try-out. Paarker hoped that San Antonio would be able to run the ball on the ground and keep out of passing situations, because Bonarski could be an absolute terror on a pass rush.

As the Gunslingers ran out onto the field at RFK amisdst a torrential downpour, there were only a few thousand fans in the stadium. Most of the people had opted to stay home and watch the game on television. San Antonio just could not lose to Washington. It would undo their momentum and put the team back into the funk they had been in before Parker had joined the team. The Feds were a good team, even though they were in last place: they played everybody tough. The Feds felt it was a game they could win, and when the two teams ran out onto the field, the Feds were further buoyed by the fact that the driving rain had caused the field to flood with six inches of water. The field being underwater would serve as a great equalizer – it would be tough for San Antonio to control the ball on the ground in six inches of muck.

As Parker came to the line of scrimmage, he couldn't believe how much Bonarski had changed physically. He was as big as Ted, but knew how to play the game. The game was a virtual stalemate, as neither team could score in the rain. It was a real bell ringer up front, as Parker and the offensive line tried to run in the mud. Bonarski's play that day had made Parker think without a doubt that Bonarski was on the juice. He was talking trash during every play, as if on some kind of speed. He had cheap-shotted Parker a few times, and had pissed off Parker to the point where he didn't think they would be friends any more. The game was winding down, and San Antonio was down by three points. Washington had mustered a field goal.

Parker, many of the times, had felt he was on skates when he was playing on that field. He had been stalemated at the line of scrimmage, where he normally would have gotten movement. San Antonio's inside game was shut down. Plus, Bonarski had knocked Gurvin, Parker's left guard, out of the game with a wicked hit. The Feds were taking no prisoners up front. The rookie guard who replaced Gurvin was shitting bricks, and had make numerous penalties during the course of the game. The kid was going up to the line of scrimmage and forgetting the snap count, and Parker had to keep telling him, which only made it worse up front as Bonarski teed off.

On the next play, the rookie guard fired out and got his right foot caught in the metal fishnet that had been laid underneath the now washed away sod. The back came running through the hole, and Bonarski tackled him, rolling the back up into the rookie guard's back leg. The snap of his leg could be heard all through the stadium. Morris, the rookie, just lay thre screaming bloody murder as the trainers rushed out onto the field. The

*From the Outhouse to the Penthouse
and Somewhere in Between*

trainers needed fiften mninutes to get Morris off the field because of the seriousness of his leg injury. As they carried him off the field, his leg was in a blow-up cast, and Morris kept screaming "No! No! No!" to end a very ugly scene.

Parker thought right back to when a similar thing had happened to him, but Morris' break was a lot worse and looked career-ending. Bonarski had KO'ed two of San Antonio's best players, and the Washington Federals had started to smell victory. Gurvin came back into the game, but could not remember anything but the snap count. As the team huddled up to get ready to run the ball the thirty yards that separated them from victory, Parker and Gurvin spoke: "G, you all right?" Parker asked.

"Yeah. I'm OK. I can go. Just tell me what to do."

As Newell called the play and the team came up to the line of scrimmage, Parker's assignment was to block down on Bonarski. He told Gurvin to pull right. As he snapped the ball and his team ran around right end on a sweep, Parker found a piece of sod that game him firm footing and slammed into Bonarski. Parker fought him until a little bit after the whistle blew. And with that, Bonarski yelled: "Get off me, you motherfucker!" Bonarski turned around and punched Parker right in the face... The refs threw a flag, signalling personal foul. As the referee marked off the infraction to put the

Gunslingers at the Fed's ten yard line, Parker looked up at the clock and saw that there was less than a minnute to go.

"I'm gonna kill you, Parker, you motherfucker!" Bonarski said again. Before he said any more, the ref warned Bonarski that if his trash talk continued, he would throw another flag. Parker watched as Bonarski blew into a rage, no doubt caused by the juice that he was on. His team mates had to restrain him for fear of having another flag thrown. They said to him: "Come on, Bonarski, don't get us another flag!"

"Keep it under control. We have to finish this!" As Newell stepped into the huddle, he said, "All right, guys, let's get this over with. Let's get in. Blue left. Thirty-five man. On two. Ready? Break!"

As Parker came up to the line of scrimmage, his assignment was to double team Bonarski with Gurvin, and then one of them would peel off and try to block the linebacker that was flowing to the play. Both teams were muddy, and the game was practically being played under water at the line of scrimmage.

As the ball was snapped, Parker fired into Bonarski, along with Gurvin. Parker saw Gurvin and the entire left side were stuffed at the point of attack. The back came bounding into the hole, and Parker could feel him slam into his back. As Parker started to go down, he grabbed Bonarski and the pile of men he was entwined with, and the entire pile dropped onto the slippery field. The back, still on his feet, slipped to his right and ran the remaining distance for the winning touch down.

As Bonarski got up from the pile, he just hauled off and punched Parker. A team melee ensued. Both benches emptied, and everyone started throwing punches.

"He was fuckin' holding me, ref! He was fuckin' holding me!" Bonarski said to the ref as he was tossed out of the game. "He fuckin' held me! You guys don't see shit! You fuckin' blind bunch of fuckin' refs!"

Parker knew that most good linemen held once in a while, and if it wasn't called by the ref, it wasn't holding, even though it was. If a lineman was going to hold, he'd better do it with his hands inside a player's numbers and not outside the numbers. Parker had his hands closely inside Bonarski's numbers when he pulled him to the ground, and the refs missed the hold. The muddy field and the muddy players and pile of bodies had made the ref miss the call. San Antonio kicked the extra point, and had gotten out or town with a 7 to 3 win.

On the team plane ride home that night, Parker learned that Morris' leg had been so badly mangled that his career was over. Parker once again was reminded of the brutality of the game. In the back row of the plane, Parker fell asleep after reading the sports page. He had just read the accounts of the trial of the anti-trust case. Things were looking good, and

Parker's final thought as he drifted off was that he hoped these battles would pay off.

*From the Outhouse to the Penthouse
and Somewhere in Between*

# THE LONG TRIP HOME

San Antonio was one game from 500, and the play-offs looked like reality. That seeming reality, though, got derailed when the Gunslingers went down to play Memphis in the Liberty Bowl in front of a packed house.

From what Parker had seen, Memphis, like Jacksonville, was a turn-key franchise. They had gone out and spent some big money for one of the premier defensive linemen in either league, Reggie White, the Minister of Defense. He would be the guy Parker would spend most of his time playing against that day.

On the first pass of the game, the ball was intercepted and returned as a touchdown by Memphis. Since San Antonio was a ball control offense and on the road playing to a packed house, every time they got the ball, they could barely hear the signals. On third down and four, Newell dropped back to pass and threw another interception. This one was run down to the six yard line, and Memphis scored on the next play. The score was then 14 to 0. The game was Parker's worst nightmare. The Showboats and Reggie White would now be playing pass on every down and coming like bats out of hell. They had taken the Gunslingers out of their game very early, and the San Antonio team was in for a long night.

On the next series of plays, San Antonio was three downs and out. Memphis returned the punt, and being jacked up by the crowd, who could now smell the rout ensuing, ran the ball all the way back to the fifteen. The next play, Memphis hit one over the middle, to make the score 21 to nothing. The rout was on. It had been the longest day of Parker's life on a football field, as the Memphis defensive line ran twists and stunts and pressured the San Antonio quarterback all day. Although the Gunslingers were able to score two touch downs, the points were meaningless, since Memphis had already scored thirty-eight points, and the passes San Antonio had completed for touch downs were against second and third string players.

Although Parker was never so happy to get out of a town in his life, he had felt he had given a good account of himself against a player who was the standard of excellence and maybe the best in his position. Reggie was as big and as fast and as quick as they come, with cat-like and instinctual moves. Even though Memphis had kicked San Antonio's ass, Reggie hadn't kicked Parker's.

The next week San Antonio went to Pittsburgh and played an expansion team that came in the same time as the San Antonio team. The Pittsburgh Maulers had spent a lot of money on talent, but for some reason hadn't jelled like the Gunslingers

*From the Outhouse to the Penthouse and Somewhere in Between*

had. As the team gathered in the tunnel for player introductions, Parker looked up and saw Dr. Kline and Lori on one side of the tunnel, and on the other side of the tunnel were Cooper, Shea, Tracey, Ryan Corbett, and a bunch of other people from Parker's home town. They had a banner that said, PARKER, WE LOVE YOU!. The banner had a big heart in the middle of it. Just to the left of them, cheering just as loud, were a couple of Parker's frat buddies from college. They had been nice enough to take time away from their busy schedule and families and businesses to come see Parker play.

Parker smiled when he saw them and yelled up to them: "I'll see you after the game!"

And Ryan Corbett, with a beaming smile yelled back: "Rhinos, yeah!"

San Antonio easily defeated Pittsburgh 21 to 3. They again controlled the game on the ground and totally dominated the Maulers. The game had been televised on ESPN, and the commentators were going on about comparing the two expansion teams. They noted how San Antonio had done so much better as a franchise than Pittsburgh. They considered Pittsburgh just an expansion team, but looked at San Antonio as a real threat to get into the play-offs.

"If San Antonio beats Okalhoma next week and Doug Williams, they'll be at 8 and 8, which is outstanding for an expansion team that wasn't supposed to win a game. With some luck, they might make the play-offs. And since they played the Philadelphia Stars tough, and actually beat themselves down the stretch when they had a chance to win, who knows what could happen in the USFL. We're gonna find out how good San Antonio is next week when they play Houston and Jimmy Kelly, the highest scoring team ever in pro football. If they beat Houston and get into the play-offs, the Gunslingers could be the league's dark horse to get the title."

Parker Thomas, just like the small cable station ESPN, had taken a chance on the USFL. ESPN had taken a gamble and bankrolled the USFL and given each team two million dollars for players' salaries. They were hyping the San Antonio Monday night game against Houston as 'The Showdown in Texas'. ESPN would be showing the game nationally. If the anti-trust case was won by the USFL, there would surely be a merger, and ESPN, just like the USFL, was going to get a big piece of the revenue. They would surely televise NFL games, and just like Parker, get a bigger piece of the pie.

As Parker flew back to San Antonio that night, he looked forward to seeing Katie, who would be picking him up at the airport. They had been seeing a lot of each other lately. They had become great friends, although they hadn't made love. When they had put the horse in Osbourne's room and peered through the window, they both had laughed so hard together when they saw Osbourne wasn't sure whether the horse was real or not because he had been so drunk. That same night, when Parker and Katie rode back to her ranch after retrieving the horse in Osbourne's apartment, Parker had developed really strong feelings for her. He started thinking along the lines that Katie might be the girl that he would spend the rest of his life with. She was the opposite of Parker in almost every way. She really didn't care about football, just about him. She had a love of animals that was peaceful and tranquil. It was a stark contrast to Parker's world of slamming violence and mayhem.

As the ball sailed into the air on the opening kick-off that Monday night at the Astrodome in front of a capacity crowd with a nationwide audience watching, Parker was playing his version of The Superbowl, The USFL Championship Game, The Grey Cup, and everything he'd ever worked for on a football field all rolled up into one. Parker had read in the newspapers about how the league verdict would be handed down in a couple of weeks and how it looked like the USFL had a strong case against the NFL. After the last practice before the Houston game, Parker's coach, Ike Perry, had told him in strict confidence that if the merger went through, San Antonio and Orlando were going to merge and play in Orlando. Perry was going to be given the offensive line job there for the job he had done coaching the Gunslingers. It was a big money contract, and they told Ike that he would be able to bring in three of his best linemen, and that he could offer up to half a million dollars per player to get who he wanted. He added that there would be a substantial bonus up front for the players who signed. He was going to take Parker Thomas with him and make him his center, for he felt he owed Parker for having turned his coaching situation around. That was all the incentive Parker needed. It was like throwing a ravenous dog a bone with meat on it. There was no way San Antonio was going to lose that Houston game, if Parker had anything to say about it.

As Parker bounded out of Ike Perry's office, the coach said: "Go get them, Parker! And, thanks." Parker believed what he was told because of the way they had shared the foxhole. Both men had put their careers in the other's hands, and now it was time to go out and fight for the title. All the training, the roadwork, the lifting of weights, the sweat and conditioning, all the injuries, all the trips on the road, all the bullshit of off-season jobs, all the heartbreaks of watching friends as well as himself get cut, all the countless mind games played with coaches and management – Parker Thomas' entire essence would be laid out on that football field.

As the ball sailed through the air for the opening kick-off, San Antonio bounded out onto the field, first and ten on their own twenty.

"All right, you guys, you know what you gotta do. Let's do it." said Newell, and then he barked out, "Blue left. Thirty-one man.

*From the Outhouse to the Penthouse and Somewhere in Between*

On one. Ready? Break!" The San Antonio team lined up on the line of scrimmage.

"Red seventy! Red seventy! Set! Hut!" The back broke through the middle for a modest three yard gain. The Gunslingers' players had been very nervous going into the game, and that first hit had settled them down. Houston could literally light it up with the most explosive offense in pro football. They ran the run and shot with five receivers who could fly. They had set modern pro football passing records for yardage and receiving, and the papers had talked about their merging with the New Jersey Generals and Herschel Walker. A lot of people thought that with the merger of those two ball clubs, they might perhaps be better than the Bears, who had just won the Superbowl.

San Antonio knew they had to control the ball on the ground for most of the game to have even a shot at winning. They had seen what had happened to them the first time they had played Houston when the lights went out as Houston smoked them 35 to 7. Newell stepped into the huddle: "Red right. Eighteen. Toss. Sweep. On one. Ready? Break!" The Gunslingers lined up on the line of scrimmage.

"Blue seventy. Blue seventy. Set! Hut!" Newell tossed the ball to Stocker, the half-back, and Stocker bounded in for fourteen yards.

"First down!" called the ref.

"Way to go, guys!" Stocker said as he came back to the huddle all pumped up from the long run. Newell took over: "All right, you guys. Blue left. Seventeen. Toss. Sweep. On the first sound. Ready? Break!"

"Set!" Newell pitched the ball again to Stocker, and Stocker nailed the corner around left end, made some sharp cuts, and then broke it with a sixty yard run down to the Houston three yardline. The Gunslingers' offensive line just looked at one another as if to say, "We can get these guys!" The Houston goal line defense came in, and San Antonio went back into the huddle.

"Double tight. Eighty-seven. Sprint pass. X hook. Y hook. Z fade. On one. Ready? Break!" As Rick Newell came up to the line of scrimmage, he could see Houston was goin to blitz from the corners.

"Black! Thirty base! Black! Thirty base!" called Newell as he changed the play at the line of scrimmage. Parker hoped, as he snapped the ball, that the team would pick up the audible because it was very hard to hear over the noise from the crowd.

The back took the hand-off and went right up the gut for the touchdown, almost going in untouched. The Houston defense stared in disbelief: this wasn't the same team they had played before, and they knew it. The extra point was good, and San Antonio was up.

Houston got the ball back, and on the third play, Kelly threw an interception. The San Antonio defense returned it to midfield, and in five consecutive running plays, they were set up first and goal on the three. The announcers up in the booth were going on about how San Antonio was whipping Houston up front and having their way with them. Newell stepped into the huddle.

"Double tight. Thirty-four pass. X hook. Y hook. Z fade. On one. Ready? Break!" Four seconds later, the Gunslingers were in the end zone again as the entire Houston defense took the run fake, and the tight end, who had chopped off after the block, was standing wide open in the end zone and caught the ball for the touch-down.

As Parker Thomas ran off the field, the players on the bench were going crazy.

"Way to go, O-line! Way to go!" Parker, before he had a chance to catch his breath, was back on the field: in a matter of thirty seconds, Houston, after two incomplete passes, had thrown a seventy yard strike for a touch-down. Houston could manufacture points in seconds, as opposed to the Gunslingers, who could only manage points in long minutes.

As San Antonio took the returning kick-off to their own thirty-five yard line, that sense of fear that Parker had seen on the first snap pervaded the huddle. San Antonio, as well as Houston, knew they were in for a dog fight. It was almost like a battle of the old school, and the old style of football versus the new style.

"Red right. Thirty-five. Z motion. On two. Ready? Break!"

"Red eighty! Red eighty! Set! Hut! Hut!" Barns, a running back recently acquired from Pittsburgh, got the ball and darted off left tackle for a sixteen yard gain. San Antonio matriculated the ball down the field with a series of nine running plays as the Houston bench looked on with a 'What are we gonna do to stop these guys?' expression on their faces. The Gunslingers had used up almost ten minutes of the clock and almost the entire second quarter.

The drive stalled on the nine, and San Antonio kicked a field goal. Parker came off the field knowing that they should have scored, and somehow that the field goal would probably come back to haunt San Antonio.

Houston got the ball back and seemed unnerved by the Gunslingers' ground attack. On the fifth play of their drive, Kelly was hit from behind by the San Antonio free safety, Joe Bob Miller. San Antonio got the ball on Houston's forty yard line with about a minute to go. The Gunslingers moved the ball downfield to their own thirty with a series of runs and were forced to take another field goal. The half ended, and San Antonio went in with a 20 to 7 lead.

The players in the locker room were all encouraging one another to keep the momentum going. Everybody felt San

Antonio had a chance to win the second half of the game. The defense was very fresh from not playing much, and the offense knew they had to keep running the ball to keep the defense from going out on the field. That hope was soon dashed early in the second half as Houston, on its first drive, scored on the third play with a sixty yard bomb. Just like that, the score was 20 to 14.

San Antonio got the ball, and after two first downs, was forced to punt. Houston took the punt and ran it all the way back for a touch down. The Houston fans went nuts as the extra point was good, and figured that their team would now blow out the Gunslingers. Houston went up, 21 to 20. San Antonio was no match for Houston's high-powered offense. Houston was scoring at will, and they knew it was a matter of time before they would shut down the Gunslingers' running attack. They had already shut down San Antonio in the air with their big corners.

The Gunslingers' defense came off the field and yelled to the offense: "Don't give up on us! We'll figure out a way to stop them!"

As San Antonio received the kick-off, the back momentarily fumbled the football and San Antonio had to start ninety yards from points. In a fifteen play drive that lasted most of the third quarter and half of the fourth quarter, San Antonio drove the ball all the way down to Houston's seven yard line. The drives had all been runs over each individual lineman up front at several different times. Each guy contributed as the back gained five or six yards at a shot. Parker Thomas had contributed his share because in three different times at third and short, they had run over him and gotten the first down. The drive stalled, however, and San Antonio was forced to kick a field goal. But at least they were in the lead 23 to 21.

Houston, starting to feel tight, had had the living hell scared out of them by that long drive. Every guy on their offense looked clean as a whistle, while the San Antonio offensive players looked dirty as hell from having battled down at the goal line on the baseball infield.

San Antonio was lucky to get the ball back three plays later when Houston was forced to punt as one of their wide open receivers dropped the ball on third and five. San Antonio got the ball in good field position on Houston's thirty-five. The Gunslingers started moving the ball on the ground. Houston was gambling big time up front, sending their defensive line on pinches and slants and all out blitzes. But the Gunslingers were still able to move the ball and kicked a long field goal of almost fifty yards, to go up 26 to 21.

As the Gunslingers' offensive team came off the field, they were totally exhausted: they had dominated three quarters of the game and had rushed for over three hundred yards on the ground. They were hanging on by a thread, and as Parker sat

*From the Outhouse to the Penthouse and Somewhere in Between*

on the bench, he just prayed that with a minute and a half to go in the game, that the Gunslingers' defense would come through. Houston would have to go all the way down the field to score. Parker hoped that the defense would keep everything up front of them, not get beat deep, and make them use up the clock. Maybe they would get lucky. Parker knew, to the man, that the Gunslinger offensive line had given everything they had, and then some. Parker Thomas just sat on the bench, closed his eyes, and prayed.

Parker could tell by the crowd noises whether San Antonio would be successful or not. As the entire stadium was on their feet, Houston came out in their two-minute offesnse and frighteningly moved the ball down the field with a series of passes that took them immediately into San Antonio territory. As Kelly dropped back to pass, he threw the ball right into Dr. Doom's hands for an apparent interception. But then Doomie dropped the ball. Parker had immediately leapt to his feet, having finally opened his eyes to watch a few plays, but just with the passing of that split second, he felt his heart drop.

"Come on. Lord, what are you doing to us?" Parker prayed. Parker got a sick feeling in his stomach as he felt that Houston was going to score. The Gunslingers had been so close to winning that game just a second ago. Houston surely wasn't going to give San Antonio a second chance. And sure enough, on the next play, as Kelly dropped back, he threw a strike to one of his streaking wide receivers for the go-ahead touchdown. Houston kicked the extra point to go up 28 to 26.

As San Antonio watched the kick-off return man run the ball back to Houston's twenty-three yard line, the Gunslingers went out on the field with thirty seconds on the clock. Houston apparently had the game in the bag. They dropped into a prevent defense and forced San Antonio to throw the football, something that was an obvious weakness on the Gunslingers' team. Parker wished management had spent some money on at least one big play back and one wide receiver, because those were the only bullets the Gunslingers lacked in their gun. But the old bottom line of business reared its ugly head. Right then and there, Parker realized it was a total team effort. The team had to do it on the field, and so did management.

As the Gunslingers came out in their shotgun, the first pass fell incomplete. Now there were twenty-five seconds to go. As Newell called the play and came up to the line of scrimmage, Parker felt himself cramp up as he leaned over to snap the ball for the shotgun. As Parker snapped the ball back, Rick Newell scrambled, and at the last second before he ran out of bounds, ripped the frozen rope downfiield for a twenty yard completion. The clock showed thirteen seconds left. Parker had fallen on the ground as both his calves started cramping on him. The pain was so intense that Parker was just rolling on the ground as San Antonio called its last time-out. There was no way

Parker Thomas was going to go out of that game. The trainers came in, masssaged his calf muscles, and got him on his feet.

"You all right, Parker?" asked the trainer.

"I'll be all right. Just give me some of that water." Parker said as he took as big a shot of water as time would permit. Parker started getting flashbacks to the Dallas game when he was with the Giants. Here he was, laying his ass on the line again without being taken out. This time, however, he hoped the result would be different. If Newell could get the ball another ten to fifteen yards, San Antonio might get lucky and kick a field goal and win the game.

As Parker got into the huddle, he watched the left tackle, Lonnie Elton, get carried off the field. It looked like he had blown a knee. A back-up who hadn't played a snap came in at left tackle. He had been a scout team player with limited skills, and again, if management had only spent the money, the Gunslingers would have had a quality back-up. As Newell called the play and the team came up to the line of scrimmage, before the ball was snapped for the shotgun, penalty flags flew into the air. The rookie, being put into a pressure situation, made a false start as a Houston defensive end took advantage of his lack of experience. The end had just flashed, like he was going to take off, and he had faked the rookie out of his stance. Parker felt that management was preventing him and his team mates from hitting their objective.

Parker had everything riding on this game, and there was management, slapping him back. Parker felt that Mike Meyer, the San Antonio field goal kicker, would hit it, but now, with time going down, the Gunslingers would be damned lucky if they even got the chance. Nobody said anything to the rookie as he came back into the huddle: the players were too damned exhausted to say anything. It was now first and fifteen, and the Gunslingers were down to their last chance.

As Parker snapped the ball to the shotgun, barely hearing the quarterback bark the signals above the roars of the crowd, Newell heaved a sixty yard pass down the field to the streaking San Antonio receiver that hit him right in the hands. He dropped the pass. Parker walked back to the huddle now as if he had palsy, his legs were cramping so badly. The clock was down to three seconds, and Parker battled to stay on the field. Parker had wondered why Newell hadn't tried to go for the short pass instead of the bomb. But Houston had taken the short pass away from him, and had dared San Antonio to throw the ball deep. Even though Newell had delivered a perfect pass, it just wasn't the Gunslingers' day.

With the feeling of helplessness and the noose firmly around the team's neck just waiting for the trap door to open, Newell dropped back and threw a long Hail Mary that fell incomplete as the game ended and the trap door opened.

The Gunslingers had lost, and their team was completely exhausted. The Houston fans came streaming out onto the field as Parker and his team mates made their way to the locker room. The Gunslinger players were solemn, and not one of them said a word. All the San Antonio team knew was that they had lost their chance to make the play-offs. Michigan had won their game and had clinched the last remaining play-off spot. All San Antonio had to do was beat Houston, and they would have been in. But with the loss, Michigan clinched.

As Parker Thomas showered and drank as much water as he could, he collapsed with leg cramps onto the tile floor and passed out. He woke up a few minutes later with an I.V. in his arm and a nurse over his head.

"Whoa, big fella, you'll be all right. You got dehydrated out there." As Parker Thomas lay there on the stretcher feeling the fluid go back into his body, he looked over and saw Ralph Waterson, the right tackle, hooked up with an I.V. also. He watched both bags of fluid be drained down in a matter of minutes, as if somebody was guzzling the water. The nurse hooked up another bag of fluid to both players.

"You guys have lost too much fluid. You have to go back to San Antonio in the ambulance. We've gotta keep an eye on you."

As the ambulance door opened, Parker and Ralph were loaded in. Two women pounded on the door just as it was closing..

"We're riding with you!" they both insisted in unison. The two women hopped into the ambulance. Katie and Ralph's wife, Vanessa, joined the players in the back of the vehicle.

As the ambulance headed back to San Antonio, both players, one black, one white, and their women holding their hands and at their sides, made the long trip home.

# FROM THE OUTHOUSE TO THE PENTHOUSE AND SOMEWHERE IN-BETWEEN

Parker Thonmas sat in the lazy boy recliner and watched the Houston game on video that night at Katie's house. He had checked out of his hotel a few weeks earlier and had been spending all his time with her at the ranch. The season had ended, and most of the players had already gone their separate ways. Parker had replayed that game tape at least twenty times. He had been pumped up when Paul McGuire, the announcer, said, after Parker had fallen with cramps: "Well, Parker Thomas is down. They can't afford to lose that player. They can't win without him in the line-up. He's made all the difference. That team's come a long way since they got Parker Thomas!" Parker just watched and listened to that segment, and felt bitter-sweet when he viewed it. The announcement from the courthouse would be coming in a matter of minutes, and Parker had another television set up and tuned to to the channel that was showing a reporter outside the courthouse on the steps.

Katie had fixed Parker a sandwich and a tall glass of iced tea before going out to ride her horses. Parker Thomas was all alone in the house.

The volume rose on the other television. The reporter appeared to be more animated.

"We are live at the Federal Courthouse in Washington, D.C., where the USFL-NFL anti-trust case verdict has just been handed down. We should have that verdict for you in the next two minutes. Please stay tuned." Parker, once again in his football playing life, had his fate in the hands of somebody else. This time it was the jurors who would decide his fate.

The television station cut away from the court case coverage for a commercial. In an effort to kill the time and ease his tension, Parker Thomas started going through the stack of mail that had arrived earlier that day. His mother had forwarded it from Florida. Parker had written to all the NFL teams and had received instant replies. He glanced across the room at the desk where a stack of envelopes with team emblems on them lay. Every one was a rejection. Parker opened a letter that was hand addressed to him first. It was an invitation to a memorial service with a newspaper clipping attached to it. "Jacksonville Bulls Player Dies of Liver Complications."

Parker started to cry and went into a state of shock. He stared out at the television set that was now announcing the court case decision.

"What's the verdict?" asked the reporter.

"We found the NFL guilty of anti-trust." said one of the jurors coming down the steps. Parker felt yet another shock go through his system. The additional emotional blow was overwhelming to him. He could feel his hands go cold as he shook uncontrollably.

"With the NFL having been gound guilty, what's the monetary award?" the reporter asked.

"We have awarded a judgement of one dollar." said the straight-faced juror.

"One Dollar?" uttered Parker as he dropped his jaw in disbelief.

"The award was potentially so large, we felt that it would be best if the judge came up with a dollar amount for the NFL to pay."

"Didn't you realize that only a jury could award damages?" urged the reporter.

"Well, yes. No, I mean no. Ask someone else on the jury." said the flustered woman on camera.

The other five jurors came down the courthouse steps. The same questions were asked of each of them. Some jurors said yes, others said no, and the scene became one of confususion for all involved. The reporter recapped the scene: "Well, there you have it, ladies and gentlemen, the NFL has indeed been found guilty in the anti-trust case file against them. And it appears at this time that the damages settlement is one dollar."

Parker immediately flipped the channel to ESPN to see if they had a better analysis of the scenario he had just witnesses on the other channel. He watched as the ESPN Sports Center staff recapped the verdict and brought their legal expert on camera for clarification. Again, the scene was on the Federal Courthouse steps.

"Doug, what does all this mean? Can you break it down? Whre does the USFL go from here?"

"I've already been informed by USFL lawyers that they don't know whether or not they're going to appeal. But chances are the league won't because they've already spent millions on the trial and an appeal could take at least eighteen months. Some marquee players' agents have told me that the marquee players want to be released from their contracts so that they can go back to the NFL. They don't want to wait eighteen months for a decision. Some USFL franchises have already announced that they have suspended operations. They're releasing players as we speak. It doesn't look good for the

*From the Outhouse to the Penthouse
and Somewhere in Between*

USFL, and my personal view of the whole situation is that the USFL will fold. I'm sure the younger players that were high round draft choices and the younger NFL players who had jumped ship to the USFL will get another opportunity to re-sign with the NFL."

"What does that mean for the rest of the players in the USFL, particularly the older players?"

"It looks extremely bleak for them. They are caught somewhere in-between, and I guess they'll have to try out, if they even get a chance. But I don't think the NFL will bite for a variety of reasons."

Parker Thomas slumped down in his chair and in every corner of his soul knew that the analysis he had just heard would indeed be the case. He could look over at the pile of rejection letters that lay on the desk if he needed any affirmation.

Parker Thomas looked down at the table on the side of his chair and reached for the black gun that lay next to the stack of mail. He picked up the gun and put the barrel against the side of his head. Out of the corner of his eye, he caught the word 'urgent' hand written on one of the letters. Parker reached for the letter with his other hand and read it:

"Dear Parker.

Your twenty thousand shares of Microtek that you bought at three dollars per share on margin before you left for camp is now worth sixtly-seven dollars per share. Your total investment of $35,000 is now worth well over $1.3 million! I suggest you call the office and sell immediately. Congratulations on a good job!

Stan Levine<br>RLS Securities

Parker Thomas put down the letter. He steadied his hand on the gun and pulled the trigger. A stream of water shot across the room and onto the stack of rejection letters on the desk.

"Touchdown!" yelled Parker Thomas, "Touchdown!"

# ABOUT THE AUTHOR

Bill Winters graduated from Princeton University. He was a free-agent lineman with the Redskins and Giants. He later played in the C.F.L and now-disbanded U.S.F.L. He is a registered securities rep and insurance broker who resides on the West Coast of Florida. He is also pursuing an acting and modeling career.

JoAnne V. McGrath has a B.A. magna cum laude in English and M.S.T. in English. She has taught literature and composition on the high school and junior college levels for almost two decades. Currently a resident of Florida's West Coast, she has had articles, short stories and poetry published in *Woman for Woman, NEA Magazine. Modern Maturity* and *Readers' Digest.*

Made in the USA
Coppell, TX
07 June 2020